D0312462

# SILENCE

Book One of The Queen of the Dead

## MICHELLE SAGARA

# DAW BOOKS, INC.

## DONALD A. WOLLHEIM, FOUNDER

375 Hudson Street, New York, NY 10014

### ELIZABETH R. WOLLHEIM
### SHEILA E. GILBERT
### PUBLISHERS

http://www.dawbooks.com

First Printing May 2012
1   2   3   4   5   6   7   8   9

This is for the girls:

Callie
Katie
Caroline
Molly
Alexandra
Rada

With thanks, with gratitude, although admittedly they
might not understand why.

# ACKNOWLEDGMENTS

This book was a bit of a departure for me, and with departures, I generally pester my friends, because I'm less certain of myself. Chris Szego, who manages the bookstore at which I still work part-time (because it's about the *books*), was hugely encouraging. And nagging. In about that order. So were Karina Sumner-Smith and Tanya Huff.

And, of course, Thomas and Terry had to read the book a chapter a time, because that's what alpha readers are for.

# EMMA

EVERYTHING HAPPENS AT NIGHT.

The world changes, the shadows grow, there's secrecy and privacy in dark places. First kiss, at night, by the monkey bars and the old swings that the children and their parents have vacated; second, longer, kiss, by the bike stands, swirl of dust around feet in the dry summer air. Awkward words, like secrets just waiting to be broken, the struggle to find the right ones, the heady fear of exposure—what if, what if—the joy when the words are returned. Love, in the parkette, while the moon waxes and the clouds pass.

Promises, at night. Not first promises—those are so old they can't be remembered—but new promises, sharp and biting; they almost hurt to say, but it's a good hurt. Dreams, at night, before sleep, and dreams during sleep.

Everything, always, happens at night.

Emma unfolds at night. The moment the door closes at her back, she relaxes into the cool breeze, shakes her hair loose, seems to grow three inches. It's not that she hates the day, but it doesn't feel real; there are too many people and too many rules and too many questions. Too many teachers, too many concerns. It's an act, getting through the day;

Emery Collegiate is a stage. She pins up her hair, wears her uniform—on Fridays, on formal days, she wears the stupid plaid skirt and the jacket—goes to her classes. She waves at her friends, listens to them talk, forgets almost instantly what they talk *about*. Sometimes it's band, sometimes it's class, sometimes it's the other friends, but most often it's boys.

She's been there, done all that. It doesn't mean anything anymore.

At night? Just Petal and Emma. At night, you can just be yourself.

Petal barks, his voice segueing into a whine. Emma pulls a Milk-Bone out of her jacket pocket and feeds him. He's overweight, and he doesn't need it—but he wants it, and she wants to give it to him. He's nine, now, and Emma suspects he's half-deaf. He used to run from the steps to the edge of the curb, half-dragging her on the leash—her father used to get so mad at the dog when he did.

*He's a rottweiler, not a lapdog, Em.*

*He's just a puppy.*

*Not at that size, he isn't. He'll scare people just by standing still; he needs to learn to heel, and he needs to learn that he can hurt you if he drags you along.*

He doesn't run now. Doesn't drag her along. True, she's much bigger than she used to be, but it's also true that he's much older. She misses the old days. But at least he's still here. She waits while he sniffs at the green bins. It's his little ritual. She walks him along the curb, while he starts and stops, tail wagging. Emma's not in a hurry now. She'll get there eventually.

Petal knows. He's walked these streets with Emma for all of his life. He'll follow the curb to the end of the street, watch traffic pass as if he'd like to go fetch a moving car, and then cross the street more or less at Emma's heel. He talks. For a rottweiler, he's always been yappy.

But he doesn't expect more of an answer than a Milk-Bone, which makes him different from anyone else. She lets him yap as the street goes by. He quiets when they approach the gates.

The cemetery gates are closed at night. This keeps cars out, but there's no gate to keep out people. There's even a footpath leading to the cement sidewalk that surrounds the cemetery and a small gate without a padlock that opens inward. She pushes it, hears the familiar creak. It doesn't swing in either direction, and she leaves it open for Petal. He brushes against her leg as he slides by.

It's dark here. It's always dark when she comes. She's only seen the cemetery in the day twice, and she never wants to see it in daylight again. It's funny how night can change a place. But night does change this one. There are no other people here. There are flowers in vases and wreaths on stands; there are sometimes letters, written and pinned flat by rocks beneath headstones. Once she found a teddy bear. She didn't take it, and she didn't touch it, but she did stop to read the name on the headstone: *Lauryn Bernstein.* She read the dates and did the math. Eight years old.

She half-expected to see the mother or father or grandmother or sister come back at night, the way she does. But if they do, they come by a different route, or they wait until no one—not even Emma—is watching. Fair enough. She'd do the same.

But she wonders if they come together—mother, father, grandmother, sister—or if they each come alone, without speaking a word to anyone else. She wonders how much of Lauryn's life was private, how much of it was built on moments of two: mother and daughter, alone; father and daughter, alone. She wonders about Lauryn's friends, because her friends' names aren't carved here in stone.

She knows about that. Others will come to see Lauryn's grave, and no matter how important they were to Lauryn, they won't see any evidence of themselves there: no names, no dates, nothing permanent. They'll be outsiders, looking in, and nothing about their memories will matter to passing strangers a hundred years from now.

Emma walks into the heart of the cemetery and comes, at last, to a headstone. There are white flowers here, because Nathan's mother has visited during the day. The lilies are bound by wire into a wreath, a fragrant, thick circle that perches on an almost invisible frame.

Emma brings nothing to the grave and takes nothing away. If she did, she's certain Nathan's mother would remove it when she comes to clean. Even here, even though he's dead, she's still cleaning up after him.

She leaves the flowers alone and finds a place to sit. The graveyard is awfully crowded, and the headstones butt against each other, but only one of them really matters to Emma. She listens to the breeze and the rustle of leaves; there are willows and oaks in the cemetery, so it's never exactly quiet. The sound of passing traffic can be heard, especially the horns of pissed-off drivers, but their lights can't be seen. In the city this is as close to isolated as you get.

She doesn't talk. She doesn't tell Nathan about her day. She doesn't ask him questions. She doesn't swear undying love. She's *done all that*, and it made no difference; he's there, and she's here. Petal sits down beside her. After a few minutes, he rolls over and drops his head in her lap; she scratches behind his big, floppy ears, and sits, and breathes, and stretches.

One of the best things about Nathan was that she could just sit, in silence, without being alone. Sometimes she'd read, and sometimes he'd read; sometimes he'd play video games, and sometimes he'd build things; sometimes they'd just walk aimlessly all over the city, as if footsteps were a kind of writing. It wasn't that she wasn't supposed to talk; when she wanted to talk, she did. But if she didn't, it wasn't awkward. He was like a quiet, private place.

And that's the only thing that's left of him, really.

A quiet, private place.

A T 9:30 P.M., CELL TIME, the phone rang. Emma slid it out of her pocket, rearranging Petal's head in the process, flipped it open, saw that it was Allison. Had it been anyone else, she wouldn't have answered.

"Hey."

"Emma?"

*No, it's Amy*, she almost snapped. Honestly, if you rang her number, who did you *expect* to pick it up? But she didn't, because it was Allison, and she'd only feel guilty about one second after the words left her mouth. "Yeah, it's me," she said instead.

Petal rolled his head back onto her lap and then whined while she tried to pull a Milk-Bone out of her very crumpled jacket pocket. Nine years hadn't made him more patient.

"Where are you?"

"Just walking Petal. Mom's prepping a headache, so I thought I'd get us both out of the house before she killed us." Time to go. She shifted her head slightly, caught the cell phone between her chin and collarbone, and shoved Petal gently off her lap. Then she stood, shaking the wrinkles out of her jacket.

"Did you get the e-mail Amy sent?"

"What e-mail?"

"That would be no. How long have you been walking?"

Emma shrugged. Which Allison couldn't see. "Not long. What time is it?"

"9:30," Allison replied, in a tone of voice that clearly said she didn't believe Emma didn't know. That was the problem with perceptive friends.

"I'll look at it the minute I get home—is there anything you want to warn me about before I do?"

"No."

"Should I just delete it and blame it on the spam filter? No, no, that's a joke. I'll look at it when I get home and call you—Petal, come back!" Emma whistled. As whistles went, it was high and piercing, and she could practically hear Allison cringe on the other end of the phone. "Damn it—I have to go, Ally." She flipped the lid down, shoved the phone into her pocket, and squinted into the darkness. She could just make out the red plastic handle of the retracting leash as it fishtailed along in the grass.

So much for quiet. "*Petal!*"

Running in the graveyard at night was never smart. Oh, there were strategic lamps here and there, where people had the money and the desire to spend it, but mostly there was moonlight, and a lot of flat stones; not all the headstones were standing. There were also trees that were so old Emma wondered whether the roots had eaten through coffins, if they even used coffins in those days. The roots often came to the surface, and if you were unlucky, you could trip on them and land face first in tree bark—in broad daylight. At night, you didn't need to be unlucky.

No, you just needed to try to catch your half-deaf rottweiler before he scared the crap out of some stranger in the cemetery. The cemetery that should have bloody well been deserted. She got back on her feet.

"*Petal, goddammit!*" She stopped to listen. She couldn't see Petal, but he was a black rottweiler and it was dark. She could, on the other hand, hear the leash as it struck stone and standing wreaths, and she headed in that direction, walking as quickly as she could. She stubbed her toes half a dozen times because there was no clear path through the headstones and the markers, and even when she could see them—and the moon was bright enough—she couldn't see enough of them in time. She never brought a flashlight with her because she didn't need one normally; she could walk to Nathan's grave and back blindfolded. Walking to a black dog who was constantly in motion between totally unfamiliar markers, on the other hand, not so much.

She wondered what had caught his attention. The only person he ran toward like this was Emma, and usually only when she was coming up the walk from school or coming into the house. He would bark when Allison or Michael approached the door, and he would growl like a pit bull when salesmen, meter men, or the occasional Mormon or Jehovah's Witness showed up—but he wasn't much of a runner. Not these days.

The sounds of the leash hitting things stopped.

Up ahead, which had none of the usual compass directions, Emma could see light. Not streetlight, but a dim, orange glow that flickered too much. She could also, however, see the stubby, wagging tail of what was sometimes the world's stupidest dog. Relief was momentary. Petal was standing in front of two people, one of whom seemed to be holding the light. And Emma didn't come to the graveyard to meet people.

She pursed her lips to whistle, but her mouth was too dry, and anyway, Petal probably wouldn't hear her. Defeated, she shoved her hands into her jacket pockets and made her way over to Petal. The first thing she did was pick up his leash; the plastic was cool and slightly damp to the touch, and what had, moments before, been smooth was now scratched and rough. Hopefully, her mother wouldn't notice.

"Emma?"

When you don't expect to meet anyone, meeting someone you know is always a bit of a shock. She saw his face, the height of his cheekbones, and his eyes, which in the dim light looked entirely black. His hair, cut back over his ears and shorn close to forehead, was the same inky color. He was familiar, but it took her a moment to remember why and to find a name.

"Eric?" Even saying the name, her voice was tentative. She looked as the shape in the darkness resolved itself into an Eric she vaguely knew, standing beside someone who appeared a lot older and a lot less distinct.

"Mrs. Bruehl's my mentor," he said, helpfully. "Eleventh grade?"

She frowned for a moment, and then the frown cleared. "You're the new guy."

"New," he said with a shrug. "Same old, same old, really. Don't take this the wrong way," he added, "but what are you doing here at this time of night?"

"I could ask you the same question."

"You could."

"Great. What are *you* doing here at this time of night?"

He shrugged again, sliding his hands into the pockets of his jeans. "Just walking. It's a good night for it. You?"

"I'm mostly chasing my *very annoying* dog."

Eric looked down at Petal, whose stub of a tail had shown no signs whatsoever of slowing down. "Doesn't seem all that annoying."

"Yeah? Bend over and let him breathe in your face."

Eric laughed, bent over, and lowered his palms toward Petal's big, wet nose. Petal sniffed said hands and then barked. And whined. Sometimes, Emma thought, pulling the last Milk-Bone out of her jacket pocket, that dog was so embarrassing.

"Petal, come here." Petal looked over his shoulder, saw the Milk-Bone, and whined. Just . . . whined. Then he looked up again, and this time, Emma squared her shoulders and fixed a firm smile on lips that wanted to shift in entirely the opposite direction. "And who's your friend?"

And Eric, one hand just above Petal's head, seemed to freeze, half-bent. "What friend, Emma?"

But his friend turned slowly to face Emma. As she did, Emma could finally see the source of the flickering, almost orange, light. A lantern. A paper lantern, like the ones you saw in the windows of variety stores in Chinatown. It was an odd lamp, and the paper, over both wire and flame, was a pale blue. Which made no sense, because the light it cast wasn't blue at all. There were words on the shell of the lamp that Emma couldn't read, although she could see them clearly enough. They were composed of black brushstrokes that trailed into squiggles, and the squiggles, in the leap of lamp fire, seemed to grow and move with a life of their own.

She blinked and looked up, past the lamp and the hand that held it.

An old woman was watching her. An *old* woman. Emma was accustomed to thinking of half of her teachers as "old," and probably a handful as "ancient" or "mummified." Not a single one of them wore age the way this woman did. In fact, given the wreath of sagging wrinkles that was her skin, Emma wasn't certain that she *was* a woman. Her cheeks were sunken, and her eyes were set so deep they might as well have just been sockets; her hair, what there was of it, was white tufts, too stringy to suggest down. She had no teeth, or seemed to have no teeth; hell, she didn't have lips, either.

Emma couldn't stop herself from taking a step back.

The old woman took a step forward.

She wore rags. Emma had heard that description before. She had even seen it in a movie or two. Neither experience prepared her for this. There wasn't a single piece of cloth that was bigger than a napkin, although the assembly hung together in the vague shape of a dress. Or a bag. The orange light that the blue lantern emitted caught the edges of different colors, but they were muted, dead things. Like fallen leaves. Like corpses.

"Emma?"

Emma took another step back. "Eric, tell her to stop." She tried to keep her voice even. She tried to keep it polite. It was hard. If the stranger's slightly open, sunken mouth had uttered words, she would have been less terrifying. But, in silence, the old woman teetered across graves as if she'd just risen from one and counted it as nothing.

Emma backed up. The old woman kept coming. Everything moved slowly, everything—except for Emma's breathing—was quiet. The quiet of a graveyard. Emma tried to speak, tried to ask the old woman what she wanted, but her throat was too dry, and all that came out was an alto squeak. She took another step and ran into a headstone; she felt the back of it, cold, against her thighs. Standing against a short, narrow wall, Emma threw her hands out in front of her.

The old woman pressed the lantern into those hands. Emma felt the sides of it collapse slightly as her hands gripped them, changing the shape of the brushstrokes and squiggles. It was *cold* against her palms. Cold like ice, cold like winter days when you inhaled and the air froze your nostrils.

She cried out in shock and opened her hands, but the lantern clung to her palms, and no amount of shaking would free them. She tried hard, but she couldn't watch what she was doing because old, wrinkled claws shot out like cobras, sudden, skeletal, and gripped Emma's cheeks and jaw, the way Emma's hands now gripped the lantern.

Emma felt her face being pulled down, down toward the old woman's, and she tried to pull back, tried to straighten her neck. But she couldn't. All the old stories she'd heard in camp, or in her father's lap, came to her then, and even though this woman clearly had no teeth, Emma thought of vampires.

But it wasn't Emma's neck that the old woman wanted. She pulled Emma's whole face toward her, and then Emma felt—and smelled—unpleasant, endless breath, dry as dust but somehow rank as dead and rotting flesh, as the old woman opened her mouth. Emma shut her eyes as the face, its nested lines of wrinkles so like a fractal, drew closer and closer.

She felt lips, what might have been lips, press themselves against the thin membranes of her eyelids, and she whimpered. It wasn't the sound she wanted to make; it was just the only sound she *could*. And then even that was gone as those same lips, with that same breath, pressed firmly and completely against Emma's mouth.

Like a night kiss.

She tried to open her eyes, but the night was all black, and there was no moon, and it was *so damn cold*. And as she felt that cold overwhelm her, she thought it unfair that this would be her *last* kiss, this unwanted horror; that the memory of Nathan's hands and Nathan's lips were not the ones she would carry to the grave.

# CHAPTER
# TWO

THE ROTTWEILER WAS WHINING in panic and confusion. His big, messy tongue was running all over Emma's face as if it could, by sheer force, pull her to her feet. Eric watched him in silence for a long minute before turning to his left. There, sprigs of lilac moved against the breeze.

He had been waiting in the graveyard since sunset. He'd waited in graveyards before, and often in much worse weather; at least tonight there was no driving rain, no blizzard, and no spring thaw to turn the ground to mud.

But he would have preferred them to this.

He felt the darkness watching. He knew what lived inside of it.

"It can't be her," he said.

*She saw me.*

"It's a graveyard. People see things in a graveyard." He said it without conviction.

*I could touch her.*

He had no answer for that. His fingers found the side of Emma's neck, got wet as dog-tongue traveled across them, and stayed put until he felt a pulse. Alive.

"It can't be her," he said again, voice flat. "I've been doing this for years. I *know* what I'm looking for."

Silence. He glanced at his left pocket, half-expecting the phone to ring. If the rottweiler couldn't wake her, nothing would, at this point. She was beyond pain, beyond fear. If he was going to do anything—anything at all—this was the time; it was almost a gift.

But it was a barbed, ugly gift. Funny, how seldom he thought that.

"No," he said, although there was no spoken question. "I won't do it. Not now. It's got to be a mistake." He glanced up at the moon's position in the sky. Grimacing, he began to rifle through her pockets. "We can wait it out until dawn."

But the dog was whining, and Emma wasn't standing up. He flipped her cell open and glanced at the moon again. He knew he should leave things be; he couldn't afford to leave the graveyard. Not tonight. Not the night after.

But he had no idea how hard she'd hit the tombstone when she'd toppled, and had no idea whether or not she'd wake without intervention.

Emma opened her eyes, blinked, shook her head, and opened them again. They still felt closed, but she could see; she just couldn't see well. On the other hand, she didn't need to see well to notice that her mother was sitting beside her, a wet towel in her hands.

"Em?"

She had to blink again, because the light was harsh and bright in the room. Even harsh and brightly lit, Emma recognized the room: it was hers. She was under her duvet, with its faded flannel covers, and Petal was lying across her feet, his head on his paws. That dog could sleep through anything.

"Mom?"

"Open your eyes and let me look at them." Her mother picked up, of all things, a flashlight. The on switch appeared to do nothing. Her mother frowned, shook the flashlight up and down, and tried again.

Emma reached out and touched her mother's arm. "I'm fine, Mom." The words came naturally to her, even if they weren't accurate, she'd used them so often.

"You have a goose egg the size of my fist on the back of your head," her mother replied, shaking the flashlight again.

Emma began a silent count to ten; she reached eight before her mother stood. "I'm just going to get batteries," she told her daughter. She set the towel—which was wet—on the duvet and headed for the door.

Mercy Hall was not, in her daughter's opinion, a very organized person. It would take her mother at least ten minutes to find batteries—if there were any in the house. Batteries, like most hardware, had been her father's job.

If her mother were truly panicky, the kitchen—where all the odds and ends a house mystically acquired had been stowed—would be a first-class disaster. It wouldn't be dirty, because Mercy disliked dirt, but it would be messy, which Mercy barely seemed to notice. Emma looked at her clock. At six minutes she sat up, and at six minutes and ten seconds, she lay back, more heavily. Petal shifted. And snored.

She was still dressed, although her jacket hung off the back of her computer chair. Her fingers, hesitantly probing the back of her head, told her that her mother was, in fact, right. Huge bump. It didn't hurt much. But her eyes ached, and her lips felt swollen.

She gagged and sat bolt upright, and this time Petal woke. "Petal," she whispered, as the rottweiler walked across the duvet. His paws slid off her legs and her stomach, and she shoved him, mostly gently, to one side. He rewarded her by licking her face, and she buried that face in his neck, only partly to avoid his breath.

It was fifteen minutes before her mother came back, looking harassed.

"No batteries?"

"Not a damn one."

"I'll stop by the hardware store after school."

"I'm not sure you're going to school. No, don't argue with me." She came and sat down on the chair. "Em—"

"I'm *fine*, Mom."

"What happened?"

Her mother didn't ask her what she'd been doing in the cemetery. She never did. She didn't like the fact that Emma went there, but she knew why. Emma wanted to keep it that way.

"Allison phoned, I dropped Petal's leash, and he ran off." Petal perked up at the sound of his name, which made Emma feel slightly guilty. Which was stupid because it was mostly the truth.

"And you ran after him? In the *dark*?"

"I wasn't carrying scissors."

"Emma, this is not funny. If your friend hadn't been with you, you could have been there all night!"

"Friend?"

"Eric."

"What, he brought me home?"

"No, *he* was smart. He called me from your phone. I brought you home." She hesitated and then added, "He helped me carry you to the car, and he helped me carry you to your room."

"He's still here?"

"He said he was late and his mother would worry."

"What, at 9:30 at night?"

"10:30, and it's a school night." But her mother seemed to relax; she slumped into the chair. "You sound all right."

"I told you—"

"You're fine, I know." Her mother's expression was odd; she looked slightly past her daughter's shoulder, out the window. "You're always fine."

"Mom—"

Her mother smiled that bright, fake smile that Emma so disliked.

"I'll help you get changed. Sleep. If you're feeling 'fine' in the morning, you can go to school."

"If I'm not?"

"I'll call in sick."

There was no way that Emma was not going to school. "Deal," she said.

The only thing in the room that shed light was the computer screen; the only words were voiceless, silent, appearing, letter by letter, as Emma's fingers tapped the keyboard.

*Dear Dad,*

*It's been a while. School started last month, and it did not miraculously become interesting over the summer. Mr. Marshall, on the other hand, still has a sense of humor, which is good, because he now has me.*

*Marti moved when her dad got a job transfer. Sophie moved when her parents got divorced (why she couldn't just live with her dad, I do not know; she asked). Allison and I are still here, holding it down, because Allison's parents are still married. Takes all kinds.*

*Michael is doing better this year. He had a bit of a rough time because he's always so blunt when anyone asks him anything, and he doesn't remember to be polite until someone is threatening to break his nose. Oh, and Petal's going deaf, I swear.*

*I wish you were here. I must have tripped in the cemetery; Mom's freaking because she thinks I have a concussion. I think I had the world's worst dream before I woke up, and I'd be sleeping now, but, frankly, if it's a choice between sleep and that dream? I'm never sleeping again.*

*And we have no batteries.*

She stopped typing for a moment. Petal snored. He had sprawled across the entire bed the minute Emma had slid out of it, but he always did. Every night was a battle for bed space because technically Petal wasn't allowed to sleep in her bed. He'd start out at the foot of the bed. And then he'd roll over, and then he'd kind of flatten out. Half of the time, Emma would end up sleeping on her side on six inches of bed with her butt hanging just off to one side of the mattress.

She rolled her eyes, winced, and went back to the keyboard.

> *But I'm fine, Mom's fine. She doesn't say it, but I think she misses you.*
>
> *I'll write something more exciting later—maybe about drugs, sex, and petty felonies. I don't want to bore you.*
>
> — *Em*

She hit the send button. After a few minutes, she stood and made her way back to the bed, nearly tripping over the cord of the desk lamp that was probably going to be hulking on the footboard of her bed for the next six weeks. Her mother didn't really use it; she did most of her work on a small corner of the dining room table.

She hadn't lied, though; she really, really did not want to sleep.

In the morning, she was fine. She was fine at breakfast. She was fine watering and feeding her dog. She was fine clearing the table and loading the dishwasher. She was even fine pointing out that the dishwasher was still leaking, and the ivory and green linoleum beneath it was stained yellow and brown.

Mercy Hall looked less than fine, but Emma's mother had never, ever been a morning person. She looked at her daughter with a vaguely suspicious air, but she said nothing out of the ordinary. She watched her daughter eat, criticized her lack of appetite—but she always did that—

and asked her if it was entirely necessary to leave the house with her midriff showing.

Since it wasn't cold, and since Emma was in fact wearing a blazer, sleeves rolled up to her elbow, Emma ignored this, filing it under "old."

But she hugged her mother tightly as they both stood up from the table, and she whispered a brief *thanks* to take the edge off her mother's mood. She put her laptop into her school bag, made sure she had her phone in her jacket pocket, and looked at the clock.

At 8:10, at precisely 8:10, the doorbell rang.

"That'll be Michael," her mother said.

You could set clocks by Michael. In the Hall household, they did; if Michael rang the doorbell and the clock didn't say 8:10, someone changed it quickly, and only partly because Michael always looked at clocks and began his quiet fidget if they didn't show the time he expected them to show.

Emma opened the door, and Petal pushed his way past her, nudging Michael's hand. Michael's hand, of course, held a Milk-Bone. No wonder they had the world's fattest dog. He fed Petal, and Petal sat, slobbering and chewing, just to one side of the doorframe. "Be right there," Emma told Michael. "Petal, don't slobber."

Michael looked at Emma. He had *that* look on his face. "What?" she asked him. "What's wrong?"

"Is it Friday?"

"No. It's Wednesday."

He seemed to relax, but he still looked hesitant. Michael and hesitant in combination was not a good thing. "Why are you asking?"

"Your eyelids," he replied promptly.

She lifted a hand to her eyelids. "What about them?"

"You're wearing eye shadow."

She started to tell him that she was wearing no such thing but stopped the words before they fell out of her mouth. Michael was many things—most of them strange—but he was almost never wrong. "Give me a sec."

She stepped back into the house and walked over to the hall mirror.

In the morning light her reflection looked back at her, and she automatically reached up to rearrange her hair. But she stopped and looked at her eyes instead. At her eyelids. Michael was right— they were blue, the blue that looks almost like bruising. Her lips were . . . dark. Reaching up with her thumb, she tried to smear whatever it was on her eyes.

Nothing happened.

She grimaced. Okay, it looked like she was wearing makeup. It did not, however, look like *bad* makeup, and she didn't have time to deal with it now; Michael had a mortal terror of being late. She picked up her backpack again and headed out the door.

They picked up Allison on the way to Emery. Allison was waiting because Allison, like Emma, had known Michael for almost all of her school life. Ally could be late for almost anything else, but she was out the door and on time in the morning. Mrs. Simner stood in the doorway and beamed at the sight of Michael. Most parents found him off-putting, or worrying. Mrs. Simner never had, and Emma loved her for it.

There was something about Mrs. Simner that screamed *mother*. It was a primal scream. She was short, sort of dumpy, often seen in polyester, and she *always* thought that anyone who walked anywhere near her house must be, you know, starving to death. She could listen sympathetically for hours on end, and she could also offer advice for hours on end—but somehow she knew when to listen and when to talk.

She never tried to be your friend. She never tried to be one of the guys. But in her own way, she was, and it was to the Simner house that Emma had gone in the months following Nathan's death.

Allison was sort of like her mother. Except for the polyester and Allison's glasses. When you were with Allison, you were, in some way, in the Simner household. It wasn't the only reason they were friends, but it helped. She carried the same blue pack that Emma did, with a slightly different model of laptop (for which official permission had been required). They fell into step behind Michael, who often forgot that he was tall enough to outpace them.

"Did you get a chance to read Amy's e-mail?"

Damn. Emma grimaced. "Guilty," she said quietly. "I'm sorry I didn't call you back last night—I kind of fell asleep."

"I guessed. She's having a party next Friday."

"Why?"

"I think her parents are going out of town."

"The last time she tried that—"

"To New York City. Without her."

"Oh. Well, that would do it." Amy was famed for her love of shopping. She was in particular famed for her love of shopping in NYC, because almost everything she was willing to admit she owned—where admit meant something only a little less overt than a P.A. announcement between every class—came from NYC. "How big a party?"

"She invited me," Allison replied.

Emma glanced at Allison's profile. She thought about saying a bunch of pleasant and pointless things but settled for, "It's not the only time she's invited you."

"No. She invited me to the last big party as well." Allison shrugged. "I don't mind, Em."

Emma shrugged, because sometimes Emma minded. And she knew she shouldn't. Allison and Amy had nothing in common except a vowel and a gender; Amy was the golden girl: the star athlete, the student council representative, and the second highest overall GPA in the grade. She was also stunningly beautiful, and if she knew it, the knowledge could be overlooked. When people are tripping over their own feet at the sight of you, you can only *not* notice it by being disingenuous.

Amy also never suffered from false modesty. In Amy's case, *any* modesty was going to be false. "Are you going to go?"

"Are you?"

Emma, unlike Allison, had managed to find a place for herself in Amy's inner circle of friends. Emma could, with relative ease, hit a volleyball, hit a softball, or run a fast fifty-yard dash. She had decent grades, as well, but it wasn't about grades. It had never been about grades. If people didn't cause car accidents when they saw Emma in the street, they still noticed her. She had no trouble talking to boys, and no trouble not talking when it was convenient; she had no trouble shopping for clothes, and when she did, she bought things that matched and that looked good.

Allison, not so much.

Allison was plain. In and of itself, that wasn't a complete disaster; Deb was plain as well. But Deb could do all the other things; she knew how to work a crowd. She had the sharpest tongue in the school. Allison didn't. Allison also hated to shop for anything that wasn't a book, so after-school mall excursions weren't social time for Allison; she would simply vanish from the tail end of the pack when the pack passed a bookstore en route to something more interesting, and frequently fail to emerge.

But Allison, like Nathan, was a quiet space. She didn't natter and she didn't gossip. She could be beside you for half an afternoon without saying two words, but if you needed to talk, she could listen. She could also ask questions that proved that she was, in fact, listening—not that Emma ever tested her. They'd been friends since the first grade. Emma knew there was a time when they hadn't been, but she couldn't honestly remember it.

Emma didn't always understand what Allison saw in her, because Emma was none of those things, even when she tried. "Do you want me to go?"

"Not if you don't want." Which wasn't a no.

"I'll go. Friday when?"

"I don't think it matters."

Emma laughed.

\*    \*    \*

There was a substitute teacher alert, which passed by Emma while she was pulling textbooks from her locker. Why they had to have textbooks, instead of e-texts, Emma didn't know.

She dropped one an inch to the left of her foot but managed to catch the messenger, Philipa, by the shoulder. "Substitute teacher? Which class?"

"Twelve math."

"Ugh. Did you tell Michael?"

"I couldn't find him. You want to check on him on the way to English?"

Emma nodded. "Who's the teacher, did you catch the name?"

"Ms. Hampton, I think. Or Hampstead. Something like that." Philipa cringed at the look on Emma's face. "Sorry, I tried, but it wasn't clearer."

"Never mind; good enough." It wasn't, but it would have to do. Emma scooped up the offending book and headed down the hall and to the left, where the lockers disappeared from walls in favor of the usual corkboards and glass cabinets. She narrowly avoided dropping the books again when she ran into another student.

Eric.

"Hey," he said, as she stepped to one side of him and started to walk again.

"Can't talk now," she replied, without looking back. Had she had the time, she would have admitted that she didn't particularly *want* to talk to him, because he reminded her of the graveyard, and she didn't want to think about that right now. Or ever.

He fell in beside her. "Where are you headed?"

"Mr. Burke's math class."

"That's a twelve, isn't it?"

She nodded. "But Michael's in that one. I need to reach him before the teacher does, or at least as soon as possible."

"Why?"

"Because," she said, cursing silently, "Mr. Burke is not actually teaching the class today."

"Who is?"

"A substitute teacher. Ms. Hampton or Ms. Hampstead." She reached the math twelve door and peered through the glass. Michael was standing beside a desk that already contained another student. It was, unfortunately, the desk that Michael always sat at, and Emma could tell the student—Nick something-or-other—knew this and had no intention of moving. Grinding her teeth, Emma pushed the door open.

Michael was not—yet—upset.

Emma reached his side, handed him her pack, and then dropped a book on Nick's head.

"What the fuck—"

"Get your butt out of the chair or I'll upend the desk on you," Emma said tersely. She would have asked politely if she'd had more time. Or if she felt like it, and honestly? At this moment she *so* did not feel polite.

He opened his mouth to say something and then stopped. Eric had joined Emma. He hadn't said a word, and from a brief glance at his face, he didn't look particularly threatening, but Nick shoved the chair back from the desk and rose. He added a few single and double syllable words as he did.

"Michael," Emma said, ignoring Nick as she pushed the chair back in a bit, "Mr. Burke's not here today. He's ill. Ms. Hampton or Ms. Hampstead—I didn't hear her name clearly, but it's only one person— will be teaching the class today. I don't know if she has Mr. Burke's notes, so she might not be covering the same material."

"What type of illness?"

"I'm sorry, I didn't ask."

Michael nodded. Emma was very afraid that he was going to ask her what Ms. Hampton or Ms. Hampstead actually looked like. "You shouldn't have dropped the book on Nick's head," he said instead.

Emma said, "If it were up to me, I wouldn't have." She did not add, *I would have slugged him across his big, smug face,* because when Michael gave a lecture, it generally lasted a while, and it was hard to interrupt him. "I was in a hurry, and the book slipped. I've dropped it once today already."

Michael nodded, because he could parse the words and they made sense. As a general rule, Emma did not go around the school dropping books on people's heads.

"I'll see you at lunch?"

He nodded, and she said, "The substitute teacher probably doesn't understand everything about you."

"No one understands everything about anyone, Emma."

"No, but she probably understands much less than Mr. Burke. If she does the wrong things, remember that. She doesn't know any better. She hasn't had time to learn."

He nodded again and sat down, putting his own textbook on the table and arranging his laptop with care so it was in the exact center of the desk. She left him to it, because it could take him ten minutes.

Eric followed her out. He hadn't said a word.

"What was all that about?"

"Michael's a high-functioning autistic," she replied. She had slowed down slightly, and while she didn't have the time to have this conversation unless she wanted to add to her late-slip collection, she felt that she owed it to him. "I've known him since kindergarten. He does really, really well here," she added, half defensively, "and he hasn't needed a permanent Ed. Aide since junior high. But he's very particular about his routine, and he doesn't react well to unexpected changes."

"And the person you dropped the book on?"

"He's an asshole."

"You go around dropping books on every asshole in the school, you're not going to make many classes."

In spite of herself, Emma smiled. "Michael always sits at the same desk in any class he's taking. Everyone who's in his classes knows this. All the teachers too," she added. "But substitute teachers might not know. If Nick had stayed in that chair, Michael would have probably blown a fuse before the teacher showed up, and a strange teacher on top of that interruption—" she shook her head. "It would have been bad. And Nick knew it."

"And you really would have upended the desk on him?"

"I would have tried. Which, to be fair, would probably have upset Michael just as much. He's not a big fan of violence." She added, "Thanks."

"For what?"

"For coming in. I'm not sure Nick would have moved if you hadn't been there."

It was Eric's turn to shrug. "I didn't do anything."

"No. You didn't have to." She smiled ruefully. "I'm not always this . . . aggressive. Michael doesn't sit in on all of the normal classes. He has trouble with the less academic subjects, but he also hates English."

"Hates?"

"There's too much that's based on opinion, and he has to make too many choices. Nothing is concrete enough, and choice always causes him stress. You should have seen him in art classes. On the other hand," she added, as she stopped in front of a door, "*I'm* expected to attend all the regular classes."

"So am I," he told her, and he opened the door to the English class.

"Emma, are you okay?"

Emma blinked. Half of English had just passed her by. Normally, anything that made English go by faster was a good thing. But she'd missed the good thing—whatever it was—and was left looking at a clock that was twenty minutes ahead of where it was supposed to be.

"Emma?"

She turned to look at Allison, who was watching her with those slightly narrowed brown eyes, which her glasses made look enormous. "I'm fine."

Allison glanced at the computer on Emma's desk. The screen on which notes were in theory being typed was a lovely, blank white. "I'll e-mail you what you missed."

"Don't worry about it. I can read up on it." She put her fingers on the home row of her keyboard and listened to Ms. Evan's voice. It was, as always, strong, but some of the syllables and some of the words seemed to be running together in a blur of noise that was not entirely unlike buzzing. This, Emma thought, was why the word droning had been invented.

She tried to concentrate on the words, to separate them, to make enough sense of them that she could type something.

"Em?" Allison went from expressing minor concern to the depths of worry by losing a single syllable—but that was Allison; she never wasted words in a pinch.

Emma looked at her friend and saw that Allison was not, in fact, looking at her. She was looking at Emma's laptop screen. Drawn there by Ally's gaze, Emma looked at it as well. She lifted her hands off the keyboard as if it had burned her.

She had typed: **Oh my god Drew help me help me Drew fire god no**

Reaching out, she pushed the laptop screen down. "E-mail me your notes."

"Emma?" Allison was worried enough that she almost walked into the edge of a bank of lockers in the crowded between-classes hall.

Emma shook her head. "I'm—I'm fine." Nothing had happened in art, and nothing had happened in math; her computer hadn't suddenly sprouted new words that had nothing to do with either her class or her. But she felt cold.

"Emma?" Great. Stereo. She glanced up as Eric approached. "You okay?"

Closing her eyes, she took a deep breath, made sure she had her laptop, and made double sure it was closed. "Yeah. Allison," Emma said, "this is Eric. He helped me out when Nick was being a jerk in Michael's math class this morning. Eric, my best friend, Allison."

Allison smiled at Eric, but she would—he was new, and he'd helped Michael. Which, Emma had to admit, was part of the reason she found him less scary. She started to walk more quickly. "We've got to hurry," she told him. "We meet Michael for lunch."

The cafeteria, with its noise and its constant press of people, wasn't Michael's favorite room. It was also not a room in which a table could easily be marked out as his. The first day he'd come to Emery, Emma had found him loitering near the doors. He hadn't been waiting for her. He'd been walking in tight little circles.

Shouting in his ear when he was like that did nothing. Touching him, on the other hand, always got his attention; she'd put a hand very firmly on his shoulder, and when he said, "Oh, hi, Emma," she had steered him into the cafeteria. Philipa and Allison had pulled up the rear, and Amy had gone on ahead, clearing a path by simply, well, telling everyone to get out of the way. They had found a table with enough space, deposited Michael at one end, and had taken turns braving the lunch line.

The big advantage to having Amy as the unofficial spokesperson on that first day? It made clear that she, too, was watching out for Michael, and anyone who chose to pick on his strangeness was going to have social difficulties that lasted pretty much until they died, which would probably not be that far in the future. And it worked reasonably well, at least where the grade nines had been concerned.

It was harder to control the other grades, though, and they had made Michael's life a little less smooth.

After the first day, Allison and Emma explained that if Michael found a space at a table and sat there, they would get lunch and join him. He did that, although he always chose the empty table closest to the door.

Michael brought a bagged lunch from home. Given the food in the cafeteria, this was probably for the best. He would sometimes eat other food if it was offered to him, but he was—no surprise—enormously picky. He would also join in a conversation if the topic interested him. Given that it was the cafeteria that was seldom. But he had made a few more friends since ninth grade, and one of the things that fascinated him was *Dungeons and Dragons*. He also liked computers, computer games, and web comics, and by tenth grade, Oliver and Connell frequently took up spots beside or facing Michael.

This had continued into the eleventh grade, and a long and tortuous discussion—to those who were not interested in *D&D*—was well under way by the time Emma reached their table. She frowned because there was someone sitting beside Michael, and she didn't recognize the student. He wasn't in their year, but she knew most of the grade twelves on sight. Maybe he was new?

But he was sitting beside *Michael*, he was a total stranger, and Michael didn't even seem to be concerned. One glance at the table made clear he hadn't braved the cafeteria lines for what passed for food, either.

"Emma?" Allison asked. Emma stood holding her tray, and Allison shrugged and sat down.

She sat down on top of the stranger—and passed right through him.

For a moment the strange student and her best friend were superimposed over each other. Emma blinked rapidly as the lines of the stranger's face blended with Allison's, the cafeteria tray listing forward in her hands. Eric caught it before she lost her grip completely.

"Emma?"

She shook her head as the stranger stood. Allison's expression slowly untangled from his as he moved. His eyes widened as he met Emma's, and then he smiled and waved. She opened her mouth; he shook his head, and as she watched, he faded from sight.

ERIC SET EMMA'S RESCUED TRAY down across from Allison's and took a seat himself.

Emma stared at her food. There was no way she was now up to eating any of it.

"Em?"

She smiled across the table at Allison; it was a forced smile, and it obviously didn't make Ally feel any better. "I'm fine. Honest, I'm fine— I have a headache, that's all."

Michael turned to her. "You have a headache?"

This was not exactly what Emma needed. She could lie to Allison in a pinch. She could lie to Eric, because she didn't know him and didn't need a near stranger's obvious concern. Lying to Michael, however, was different. She could tell Eric—or Allison—that she had headaches all the time, and they'd pretend to believe her; Michael would call her on it, and if she argued, it would upset him because what he knew and what she was claiming was true weren't the same.

"I tripped when I was walking Petal last night. I hit my head on something."

Allison's brows rose, but she said nothing.

Michael, *Dungeons and Dragons* forgotten, frowned. To no one's surprise except Eric's, he began to question her about possible symptoms. Emma interrupted to ask what, exactly, these might be symptoms *of,* and he very seriously replied, "Concussion. I think you should go to the doctor, Emma."

Emma didn't particularly like visiting the doctor. Neither, if it came down to it, did Michael—but Michael persisted in being logical. And if you wanted him to persist in being calm, you had to toe the same logic line.

Rescue came from an unexpected quarter. "Hey, don't waste your time on Emma," said the clear and annoyingly perky voice of Deb McAllister, who, accompanied by Amy and Nan, had paused in her walk to the exit.

"Oh?" Eric asked, turning on the bench.

"She's not looking for anyone."

Eric glanced at Emma, who shrugged and nodded. "It's true. I'm not."

Eric returned the shrug. "Neither am I." He smiled politely at Deb and Nan, smiled in an entirely different way at Amy, and turned back to what was left of his lunch. He was not, unlike most of the guys, a fast eater.

"Too bad." Deb's voice was friendly. In fact, given Deb, she was probably trying to be helpful. In her own special way.

Nan smiled shyly and introduced herself to Eric, who—as if he were someone's grandfather and not their classmate—actually *got up* from the table to *shake her hand*. This caused a little ripple of silence, but it was a pleased silence. Nan was not, in the classical sense of the word, beautiful, but she had long, thick, straight black hair that was the envy of every girl in the school who wasn't Amy, and her eyes were a perfect brown in equally perfect skin. She could speak Mandarin, but she hated doing it unless she was with her cousins, five of whom attended Emery.

Emma had asked her why once, and Nan had said, "I'm not someone's exotic pet seal. I don't want to bark on command."

And Amy?

"Eric, what are you doing Friday night?"

"Why?"

"I have a big—I mean *big*—open house planned at my place. Pretty much everyone in our year should be there, if you want to meet them all. I would have invited you by e-mail," she added, "but you're new enough here that I don't have yours yet.

"Are you coming, Emma?"

"Yeah."

"Good. Can you tell Eric where and when, and send me his e-mail address if he has one? I have to go to the yearbook committee meeting—I'm running late."

"Sure." She watched Amy head out the cafeteria doors and then said, "Pull your tongue back in. You're drooling."

Eric laughed. "That obvious?"

"Well, you're male. And at least you didn't try to eat and miss your mouth."

He laughed again.

"Don't laugh," she told him with a grimace. "I've seen it happen at least once every semester."

When history was over, school was done for the day. Emma went to her locker, deposited her textbooks, and then stood leaning against the narrow orange door.

"Emma?"

She looked up. Eric, pack hanging loosely from his left shoulder, was watching her.

"Are you feeling all right?"

"Yeah, I'm fine." She pulled herself off the locker door and grimaced. "I have a bit of a headache."

"Should you be walking?"

Emma shrugged. She slung her backpack over her right shoulder and started to head down the hall. "I'll be fine," she told him, when it became clear he was following her. "Allison will walk me home."

"Did your mother take you to a doctor?"

"I did not, and do not, have a concussion. I have a headache."

"Migraine?"

"Eric, look, you are not my mother, for which I'm grateful because I can barely handle the *one* I have now." She gritted her teeth and lifted a hand, palm out. "No, look, I'm sorry, I know that was unfair. I have a headache. I will walk home. I will sleep it off."

Eric lifted both his hands in surrender. If her waspish comment had bothered him at all, it didn't show, and if her head had not, in fact, been pounding at the temples, and if the light in the halls had not begun to actually hurt, she would have smiled.

"Tell you what. You can follow me at a discreet distance, and if I collapse, you can call my mother again. She might take a little longer to show up, though, because she's at work."

Allison was waiting for her on the wide, shallow steps from which less adventurous skateboarders leaped. The one thing Emma missed about winter was the lack of skateboards.

Allison bypassed the usual quiet and concerned questions she liked to open with and went straight to the single syllable. "Em?" She held out a hand, and Emma took it. Clearly, from the way Allison's expression changed, she had gripped it a little too hard.

"Sorry," Emma managed to say. "The light is killing my eyes, Ally. And the noise—it's making me dizzy. I feel like someone is stabbing the top of my spine with—with hot stabbing things. I think I'm going to throw up."

"Let me call your mom."

"Are you *kidding*? I'll throw up in the car, and you *know* who's going to have to clean it up later." Not that her mother wouldn't try. "Just help me get home." She paused and then managed to say, "Where's Michael?"

"He's talking to Oliver."

Going home from school had never been as stressful for Michael as getting there. Which made sense—going to a very strange place from a safe one was always worse. "Ask him if he needs us to wait for him?"

Allison nodded and then said, very softly, "You need to let go of my hand. Sit down on the steps so you don't fall over." She helped Emma lower herself to the steps and then hovered there for a minute.

Emma heard steps behind her. Actually, she heard steps in all directions, but the ones behind her were louder. Allison hadn't really moved, so they couldn't be hers.

"Emma," Eric said, speaking very, very quietly. "Let me take you home."

"I'm fine."

"No, you are not. I have a car," he added.

"You drive?"

"Depends on who you ask. I have a license, if that helps."

"No, look, I—"

"And if you throw up in the car, I can clean it up. Go ask Mike if she needs to wait," he added. Emma couldn't see Eric; at this point her eyes were closed, and her hands were covering them. But she could guess who he was talking to, and she did hear Allison's retreat.

"Don't call him that," she said.

"What?"

"Don't call him Mike. It's not his name, and he doesn't recognize it as his name." She wanted to weep with pain. She stopped talking.

"I'm driving you home," he said, in the same quiet voice.

She didn't have the energy to say no again. She did, apparently, have the energy to throw up.

\*     \*     \*

The car was agony. Curled up in a fetal ball, Emma almost cried. Almost. She did throw up again, but Allison was in the backseat beside her, and she was holding something in front of Emma's face. Eric was either the world's worst driver, or *any* motion caused waves of nausea.

She tried to say Michael's name, but it really did not come out well. Mostly, it was whimpering, and Emma decided not to talk.

"Michael's here," Allison said quietly. "He's in the front seat with Eric." Allison's hand was cool when it touched Emma's forehead. She wanted to lean into it.

"Make it stop," she whispered, to no one. Or to everyone. "Please, make it stop."

And she heard Eric's voice, cool and quiet, drop into the noise that was so loud it should have been making her ears bleed. "It will, Emma. I'm sorry."

Eric had lied. He didn't drive her home.

Emma survived the painful and endless stops and starts that were Eric's driving, and she must have arrived in one piece, because she felt the agonizing crack of a car door opening, felt the change of light as she left the car, her eyes clamped shut. Eric lifted her; it must have been Eric. Allison and Michael wouldn't have been able to carry her that far between the two of them.

But he didn't take her up the familiar walk to her home; he didn't take her to where Petal would be barking or whining. Instead, he carried her up a different stretch of road into a familiar building: the hospital and its emergency waiting room.

She could hear the short, harsh stabs of conversation that passed between Allison and the person at admitting. She couldn't see the person, but the voice registered as female, crashing in, as it did, on all the other unfamiliar voices that were screaming—literally—for attention.

She wanted to pass out because, if she did, she would be beyond them. But she didn't, because that would have been a mercy. Instead, she heard Michael's clear voice answering questions. She couldn't hear the questions nearly as clearly, but it didn't matter; Michael had come for a reason, and he would make himself heard. Even if, in fact, the questioner had no desire to hear any more. You had to love that about Michael, because if you didn't, you'd strangle him.

She shifted, attempted to sit up, and ended up curled forward in a chair, trying desperately not to throw up for a third time. At some point, she felt familiar arms around her shoulders and back, and she knew that her mother had been called and had somehow arrived.

She tried to apologize to her mother, failed, and also gave up on not throwing up. Because her mother was there. There was something about being sick that made it so easy to turn your whole life over to your mother. Even when her father had been there, it was her mother who had spent hours by the sickbed, and her mother who had cleaned her up, made sure she drank, and monitored her temperature.

It was her mother who was here now, losing work hours and work time. Emma tried to sit up again, tried to open her eyes, tried to tell her mother she was, as always, fine. Even if it was a lie. Some lies, you could *make* true, if you said them enough.

But she couldn't say them, now.

She tried. She tried to make them loud enough to drown out all the other sounds, all the other words. She felt a hand in hers and couldn't tell whose it was. She wanted to grip it tightly, but even that movement made her wrist ache, made the skin of her arm shriek in protest.

She wanted it to stop. She didn't care if she died; it would be better than this. Better. Than. This.

It wasn't the first time in her life that she'd wanted something to stop this badly. But that time? The pain had been different. She wanted to weep. But it was as if old pain and new pain combined by some strange alchemy to allow her to remember, to allow the images a lucidity and clarity that the pain denied everything else.

Nathan's funeral. Nathan's death.

She could remember standing and watching by the side of an open grave. She had thought to help, to dig at the earth with a shovel, to roll up her sleeves—or not—to stand in the dirt as it yielded, inch by inch, becoming at last a resting place, a final stop. But there were no shovels. When she'd arrived there, no shovels. Umbrellas, yes, because the sky was cloudy and overcast, but the umbrellas had yet to be wielded; they were bound tightly, unopened, waiting for rain. Instead, there was a hole, beside which a tall mound of dirt had been heaped over a large tarpaulin. And beside that, in a bag—a *bag*—a small container, a nondescript wooden one.

Her mother had said she didn't have to go to see the ashes interred. As if. Nathan's mother, eyes red and swollen with weeping, voice raw, had turned to her, hugged her, hanging on for a second to the only other female in the cemetery who had loved Nathan so much. That was why she'd come. That. To stand, to be hugged, to acknowledge a loss that was different from, and almost as great, as her own.

Emma did not weep. Emma did not wail or speak; she had been invited to say something at the funeral service, and she had stared, mute, at the phone while Nathan's father waited for a reply that would never come. Emma had never been a drama queen. Why? Because she had cared what other people thought. Of her. That caring, it was like a fragile, little shield against the world; things broke through it all the time. Things hurt.

But not like this. The shield was gone; shattered or discarded, it didn't matter.

Watching. Distant. Seeing the truth of headstones. No name of hers engraved in rock. Dates, yes. Birth. Death. Nothing at all of the in-between. Nothing about love. Nothing about quiet spaces. Nothing about who he was, who he'd been. Because it didn't matter. None of it mattered anymore to anyone but Emma. Emma and Nathan's mother.

She had wanted to die. She had wanted to *die*. Because then it would be over. All the loss, all the grief, all the pain, the emptiness—over. And she had said nothing, then. Nothing. Nor had she crawled into her room and swallowed her mother's pills, or crawled into her bath and opened up her own wrists. As if death were somehow personal, as if death were somehow an enemy that could be faced and stared down, she would not give it the satisfaction of seeing how badly it had hurt her. Again.

She wanted to scream. She opened her mouth.

She felt the movement, felt the stabbing pain of it, felt the press of sound against her skull, as if her fontanels had never closed, and her head could be crushed by carelessness, not malice.

And then, suddenly, all the sound and all the pain seemed to condense into one point, one bright point, just outside of her body. She felt, for a moment, that she was falling, that the only thing holding her up had been sensation. A cool—a cold—breeze touched her forehead, like soft, steady fingers gently pushing hair out of her eyes.

*Sprout, Sprout, you shouldn't be here.*

She felt the pain condense, all sound becoming a single point that fled the whole of her, and she was suddenly sitting up, her body light with the lack of pain.

"Dad?"

*Em*, he said.

She opened her eyes. The room wasn't dark; it was fluorescent with light and half full of people in various states of health. She could see Michael sitting beside Allison, could see Allison beside her mother. She could see other people, strangers, sometimes sitting beside people and sometimes entirely alone. And, in the light of the emergency admitting room, she could also see her father.

She stood, freeing her hands.

"Dad."

He turned to face her. *Em*, he said again, and then his gaze drifted away from her face and fell, slowly, to her mother's. Her mother's worried face, her mother's pained expression. Emma started to say something and then stopped. Her mother was trying not to cry.

"She can't see you, can she?"

*No.*

"Dad . . ."

Her father's eyes were faintly luminescent; they *were* his eyes, but they were subtly wrong. He watched his wife. Emma turned again to look at her mother. To see that her mother's hands were *holding her daughter's,* even though Emma was now standing five feet away from the chair into which she'd curled. She tried to look at herself, at the her that her mother was still holding onto so tightly. She couldn't. She could see a vague, blurry outline that might, or not might not, be Emma-shaped.

It was very, very unsettling.

"She can't see me right now either, can she?"

*No, Em.* He looked back to his daughter, his expression grave. *You shouldn't be here, Sprout.*

"No. I shouldn't. Does this mean I'm . . . dead?"

His smile was quiet, weary; he had some of Mercy Hall's worry embedded in his expression. *No.*

"Does this mean I'm going to *be* dead soon?"

*No.*

"Dad—what's happening to me?"

Her father turned to look at Eric, who was standing very quietly in the center of the room.

Eric, arms folded across his chest, looked at Brendan Hall. At him, not through him. Emma glanced at her other friends. They were still sitting beside her mother, or each other; none of them had noticed the standing-Emma.

But Eric, clearly, did. He was, Emma realized with a bit of surprise, taller than her father, and he had lost the friendly, easygoing smile she associated with his face. His hair looked darker, the brown of his eyes almost the same color as his pupils.

*Tell her.*

"Tell me what? Eric?"

Eric met her gaze, held it a moment, and then looked away.

"Eric, I don't mean to be a bitch, but you know, if I wind up being one, I think I'm entitled. What the hell is going on?"

He said nothing, and she walked toward him, trying not to ball her hands into fists. When she was three feet away from him, she stopped. "Eric," she said, her voice lower. "Please. Tell me what's happening to me because I cannot spend every day from now until I die doing this."

He closed his eyes, but when he spoke, it wasn't to Emma. It was to her father.

"You're the one who shouldn't be here," he said quietly.

Her father said nothing.

"It's not too late," Eric continued, his voice lower than Emma's had been, the words quietly intense. "She's standing on the edge. She doesn't have to fall over it."

*She can't continue like this*, her father said at last. *Do me the favor of allowing me to know my own daughter.*

"I do. I am."

Emma thought her father would say nothing; he had that expression. She'd seen it often enough to know it, because he used to wear it when he argued with her. And when he argued with her mother. But he surprised her. *I couldn't stand back and do nothing. She can't survive hearing all of the—*

"She can," Eric said. "She only has to do it for three days. Maybe you don't understand what her life will be like," he added. "Maybe you're as shortsighted as she is and you can only see the now. But you're doing her no kindness. You shouldn't be here."

Her father nodded, slowly. He took a step back, and Emma shouted, wordless, and ran past Eric.

Eric called her name, and she felt it like a blow; it slowed her, and it hurt her, but neither of these was enough. Her father was there, and somehow, somehow he understood what she was going through and had tried to spare her some of the pain.

And she wanted that.

She wasn't willing to let him go. And he was going to leave; she saw that too. *No. No.* She'd done that. She'd done that once. She saw her father's eyes widen as she ran toward him, and she saw him lift his hands, palms out, telling her, wordlessly, to stop. She slowed, but again, not enough.

"Dad—"

*Emma, don't—*

She reached out and grabbed the hands he had put up to fend her off. His hands were cold. His eyes widened, rounding; the light that burned so strangely in them dimmed.

And she heard, from right beside her, and at the exact same second, from behind her, her mother's single shocked word.

"Brendan!"

# CHAPTER
## FOUR

EVERYTHING HAPPENED SLOWLY, and everything happened at once; it was as if Emma were two people, or two halves of one person. The one, sitting beside her mother, holding her mother's hands, heard her mother's sudden shift in breath: the sharpness of it, the strange fear and hope.

The other half, holding her father's cold hands, turned to look at her mother and realized that her mother could suddenly see her father. Could see Brendan Hall. She could see the color ebb from her mother's face, because fear had always done that to her.

She could see Allison stand, could see her mouth the words, "Mr. Hall?" although no sound came out. And she could see Michael. Michael's gaze, on her father's face, was unreadable. It always was when he was processing information that he hadn't expected and wasn't certain how to deal with.

He lived in a rational universe. He had to. All the irrational, unpredictable things made no sense to him, and, worse, they were threatening *because* they made no sense. Things that could be explained, in however much exhaustive detail he demanded—and he could demand quite a lot—were not things he had to fear.

But things like . . . Emma's dead father . . . How could she explain something like that to Michael? When she didn't understand it herself?

She said, felt herself say, "Michael, he's still my father. He's the same person he was. He's not dangerous."

But Michael didn't appear to hear her. He probably had; it had taken him years to learn to look at people when they talked. She remembered—and what a stupid thing to remember now, of all times—telling him that he had to look at people when they spoke so they knew he was listening. And she remembered the way he had looked at her, his expression serious, and what he'd said.

"Emma, I don't hear with my eyes."

"Well, no. No one does."

"Then why do I have to look at people so they'll know I'm listening?"

She wasn't always very patient, and it had taken her three days to come up with a better phrasing. "So that they'll know you're paying attention." She'd been so proud of herself for that one, because it had worked.

"Brendan?" her mother whispered.

Her father—the expression on his face one that Emma would never forget, said, "Mercy." Just that.

She wanted to let go of her mother's hands. She couldn't.

Instead, watching Michael, she let go of her father's.

The room collapsed; the lights went out. Emma felt a sudden, sharp tug, as if she'd been floating and gravity had finally deigned to notice her. She fell, screaming in silence, to earth—but earth, in this case, was a lot like cheap vinyl, and it didn't hurt when she hit it. Much.

She opened her eyes, blinking in the harsh fluorescent lights of the emergency waiting room. Lack of feet caused a moment's panic before she realized they were curled beneath her. She looked to her side and saw her mother's profile, her slightly open jaw, her wide eyes circled by dark lack of sleep.

"Mom," she croaked. "My hands." Her fingers were tingling in that pins-and-needles way, and they looked gray. Or blue.

Her mother shook her head; Emma's voice had pulled her back. "Oh, Em, I'm sorry," she said. It was pretty clear she had to work to free her hands, or to free her daughter's. Their hands shook, but Emma curled hers in her lap; her mother lifted hers to her face, and very slowly let her head drop into them.

"Mom—"

Mercy Hall shook her head. "I'm sorry, Em—I'm—I've had a long day."

Emma looked away from her mother. "Michael?" she said, slowly and distinctly. Michael didn't appear to hear her. He was staring straight ahead. "Allison?"

Allison, on the other hand, turned to meet Emma's gaze.

Emma gestured in Michael's direction, and after a second, Allison took a deep breath and nodded. She turned and walked over to Michael, calling his name. Michael was still staring. When Allison stepped in front of him, he didn't stop; what he was seeing, Emma could only guess.

Allison knelt in front of Michael and picked up his hands, one in each of hers. "Michael," she said again, voice softer.

He blinked, and his gaze slowly shifted in place, until he could see Allison. He was rigid. But he was quiet. Emma wished it didn't resemble the quiet of a rabbit caught in headlights quite so much. He blinked.

Emma slowly pulled her feet out from under her. They were tingling as well, and she grimaced as she flattened them against the floor. But she tried to stand, and as she did, Eric moved. She had almost forgotten him, which was stupid.

He crossed the room and offered her his hand; she stared at his palm until he withdrew it. He was silent. She was silent as well, but her look said, *We're going to talk about this later.*

His said nothing, loudly.

She walked over to Allison and Michael, and stood beside Allison; she would have crouched beside her, but she didn't trust her knees or her feet yet. "Michael?"

He looked up. He was still seated, and that was probably for the best. "Emma," he said. She smiled, and not because she was happy. It was meant to reassure.

"I'm here," she told him, while Allison continued to hold his hands.

"Emma, that was your dad." It wasn't a question.

Had he been anyone else, she would have lied, and it would have come cleanly and naturally. Lies were something you told other people to make things easier, somehow—hopefully, for them, but often more selfishly for yourself. Lies, Emma realized, as her glance flicked briefly to her mother and back, were things you told yourself when your entire world was turned on its end for just a moment, and you needed to put it right side up again.

But Michael? Michael hadn't even understood what a lie was supposed to do until he'd been nine years old. He hadn't understood that what he knew and what other people knew were not, in fact, the exact same thing. Emma didn't remember a time when she didn't understand that. And she wasn't certain why, at nine, Michael began to learn. But he had; he just didn't bother lying because he could see the advantage of honesty and of being known for it.

Not lying, however, and not being lied to were different. Emma could have lied, but that—that would have pushed him over the edge he was clearly teetering on. Because he knew what he'd seen, and nothing she could say was going to change that.

She took a breath, steadied herself. "Yes," she told him quietly, just as Eric said, "No."

Allison turned to stare at Eric. She rose, still holding Michael's hands. She passed them to Emma, who could now feel her feet properly. Michael looked at Eric and at Emma, and Emma said, quickly, "Eric doesn't know, Michael. Remember, he never met my father. He's new here."

Eric opened his mouth to say something, and Allison stepped, very firmly, on his foot. She didn't kick him, which Emma would have done. Allison hated to hurt anyone.

Michael, however, was nodding. It went on too long. Emma freed one of her hands and very gently stroked the back of Michael's hand until he stopped.

"He's dead, Emma."

"Yes."

"He used to fix my bike."

"Yes."

"Why was he here?"

She started to say *I don't know,* because it was true. But she stopped herself from doing that as well. Things were always more complicated when Michael was around. But they were cleaner, too. "He was trying to help me," she said, instead.

"How?"

"I think he knows what's causing the—the headaches."

"It's not a concussion?"

"No."

"Oh." Pause. "Where did he go?"

"I don't know."

"Will he come back?"

"I don't know, Michael. But I hope so."

"Why?"

"Because I miss him," she said softly.

Michael nodded again, but this time, it was a normal nod. "I miss him, too. Was he a ghost?"

"I don't think ghosts exist."

"But I saw him."

She nodded. "I saw him, too. But I don't know what he was."

"He looked the same," Michael told her. "And you said he was the same."

She had said that. She remembered. "I think ghosts are supposed to be scary," she offered. "I think that's why I don't think he's a ghost. Was he scary?"

"No. Well, yes. A little."

Emma could accept that.

"He doesn't want to take you away?" Michael continued. "You aren't going to die, are you?"

"Everyone dies," she told him.

"But not now."

"No, Michael," she managed to say. "He doesn't want to take me away. And even if he did, I'm not leaving." She knew, suddenly, where this would go, and she *did not* want to go there.

Michael closed his eyes. Emma braced herself as Michael opened them again and asked, "Will Nathan come back, too?"

And, after a moment, Emma managed to say, "I don't know."

Emma knew her mother was upset. But upset or not, Mercy Hall insisted on waiting for a CAT scan. Emma told Allison she should go home with Eric and Michael, but that fell flat as well. They huddled together in silence. Emma's mother said almost nothing to anyone who wasn't a doctor, and Michael sat quietly, thinking Michael thoughts. Allison was worried, but she didn't say much, either; it was hard to find a place to put words in all the different silences in that waiting room.

The CAT scan was a four-hour wait. The results, they were told, would be sent to the Hall family doctor, which meant, as far as Emma was concerned, that they hadn't found anything that constituted an emergency. To confirm this, the doctor filled out discharge papers, or whatever they were called, gave Emma's mother a prescription for Tylenol, but stronger, and also gave her advice on headaches. Emma was tired, and her body still felt strangely light, as if part of her had gone missing. But she was no longer in any pain.

Not physical pain.

Eric said nothing. He waited. When Emma's tests were done, he offered Allison and Michael a ride home. Emma would have preferred to have their company, but it was clear that her mother wouldn't. Michael and Allison went home with Eric.

Emma went home with her mother in a car that was as silent as the grave. It was worse than awkward. It was painful. Mercy kept her eyes on the road, her hands on the steering wheel, and her words behind her lips, which were closed. Her expression was remote; the usual frantic worry about work and her daughter's school were completely invisible.

Emma, who often found her mother's prying questions difficult, would have welcomed them tonight, and because the universe was perverse, she didn't get them. She got, instead, a woman who had seen her dead husband, and had no way of speaking about what it meant. Possibly no desire to know what it meant; it was hard to tell.

When they got home, it was 8:36.

Petal greeted them at the door with his happy-but-reproachful barking whine.

"Sorry, Petal," Emma said, grabbing his neck and crouching to hug him. She knew this would get her a face full of dog-breath, but didn't, at the moment, care.

Emma's mother went to the kitchen, and Emma, dropping her school backpack by the front door, followed, Petal in tow. They briefly, and silently, held council over the contents of the fridge, which had enough food to feed two people if you wanted to eat condiments and slightly moldy cheese. There were milk and eggs, which Emma looked at doubtfully; her mother often stopped by the grocery store on the way home from work.

Today, she had stopped by the hospital instead.

"Pizza?" Emma asked.

Her mother lifted the receiver off the cradle and handed it to her daughter. "Pizza," she said, and headed out of the kitchen. It was a damn quiet kitchen in her absence, but Emma dialed and hit the button that meant "same order as previous order." Then she hung up and stared at her dog. Her dog, the gray hairs on his muzzle clearer in the kitchen light than they were in the light cast by streetlamps, stared at her, his stub wagging.

She apologized again, which he probably thought meant "I'll feed you now." On the other hand, she did empty a can of moist food into his food dish, and she did fill his water bowl. She also took him out to the yard for a bit; she hadn't walked him at all today, but she knew that tonight was *so* not the night to do it. From the backyard, she could see the light in her mother's bedroom window; she could also see her mother's silhouette against the curtains. Mercy was standing, just standing, in the room.

Emma wondered, briefly, if she was watching her or if she was watching Petal. She kind of doubted either.

When Emma was stressed, she often tidied, and god knew the kitchen could use it. She busied herself putting away the dishes whose second home was the drying rack on the counter. She had homework, but most of it was reading, and like procrastinators everywhere, she knew that tidying still counted as work, so she could both fail to do homework and feel that she'd accomplished something.

But when the doorbell rang, Mercy came down the stairs to answer, and she paid for the pizza and carried it into the kitchen. She looked tired but slightly determined, and she had that smile on her face. "I'm sorry, Em," she said. "I'm not sure what got into me there. Things are stressful at work."

Emma accepted this. She usually asked what was causing the stress, but she didn't actually enjoy listening to her mother lie, so she kept the question to herself and nodded instead. She also got plates, napkins and cups, because her mother didn't like drinking out of cans.

They took these to the living room, while Petal walked between them. The pizza box was suspended in the air above him, of course. He was too well trained to try to eat from the box when they put it down on the table in the den. He was not, however, too well trained to sit in front of it and beg, and he had the usual moist puppy eyes, even at the age of nine.

Emma fed him her crusts.

He jumped up on the couch beside her and wedged himself between the armrest and her arm, which meant, really, between the armrest and half her lap; she had to eat over his head.

Her mother didn't like to eat while the television was on, but even she could take only so much awkward silence before she surrendered and picked up the remote. They channel surfed their way through dinner.

Eric stood in the graveyard, beneath the same dark willow that he'd leaned against for half of the previous night. He carried no obvious weapons, and he hadn't bothered to wear any of the less obvious protections because he didn't expect to need them. He wanted to need them. He wanted to need them right now, in this place, but what he wanted didn't matter; almost never had.

The graveyard was silent. The distant sound of cars didn't change that; they blurred into the background. His night vision was good; it had always been good. But he stared at nothing for long stretches. Once or twice he turned and punched the tree to bleed off his growing frustration.

*Not Emma*, he thought bitterly.

*Emma.*

He tensed.

*I have never been mistaken before. I am not mistaken now.* She approached, emerging from a forest of headstones.

*She is powerful, Eric.*

"You've got to be wrong," he told her, grim and quiet. He expected an argument, was surprised when it failed to come.

*I will . . . leave it up to you*, she said at last. *I will not call the others yet.*

"Why?"

*Because she* is *different, to my eyes, and I have reasons to doubt that feeling. You know why.*

Eric swallowed and turned his attention back to a graveyard that remained empty for the rest of the night.

# CHAPTER
# FIVE

EMMA WOKE UP ON FRIDAY MORNING, which had the advantage of being formal day at school. This meant, among other things, that she didn't really have to work out what she was going to wear; she was going to wear a plaid skirt, a blazer, and a white shirt. Ties were optional if you weren't male, although most of the girls wore the non-stupid thin leather ones. They often wore makeup on Fridays as well, because, face it, there weren't too many other things you could wear to set yourself apart.

Emma, for instance, didn't wear earrings. Watching a toddler grab a dangling hoop and rip through the earlobe—literally—of a friend in grade seven had cured her of the growing desire to ever have her ears pierced. Admittedly, this was viewed as a bit strange, but they were her ears, and she wanted to keep them attached to the rest of her face.

She did spend more time in the bathroom on Fridays, which was worked into what passed for an early morning schedule in the Hall household, partly because her mother did everything she could to stay in bed until the last minute.

Emma finished dressing and went downstairs. She expected the kitchen to be quiet, and it was; Petal was hyper but not yappy. Her mother was not yet in the kitchen. Emma glanced at the clock and winced. She put the coffee on, because if her mother was still not here, she was going to need it, and she took milk, blueberries and cereal to the table, which she also set.

She stopped on the way to get napkins and hollered up the steps, waited for five seconds to hear something like a reply, failed to hear the wrong words—of which there were several—and continued on her way. When her mother came thundering down the stairs in a rush, she handed her mother the coffee and ushered her to a chair. This would have been awkward had Mercy actually been awake.

Then again, given the last few days? Being awake was highly overrated. They ate in relative silence, because Petal had emptied the dry food dish and was trying to mooch. He didn't actually like any of the food his two keepers were eating this morning, but that never stopped him.

Emma, who had marshaled her arguments, waited, with fading patience, for her mother to tell her that she was not going to school today. When it was dangerously close to 8:00, she gave up on that, and instead said, "Don't forget, I'm going to Amy's party tonight."

"Amy's? Oh, that's right. You mentioned it yesterday. You're going straight from school?"

"What, dressed like this?"

Mercy seemed to focus for a minute. "You look fine to me," she said, but it was noise; Emma would have bet money that she hadn't actually noticed what her daughter was wearing. "Are you going to be home for dinner?"

"Why, are you working late?"

Mercy nodded slowly.

"I'll grab a sandwich or something if you're not here." Emma pushed her chair back from the table and gathered up her empty dishes. "I won't be too late," she added.

"When is not too late?"

Emma shrugged. "Midnightish. Maybe 1:00." She waited for any questions, any comments. "Mom?"

Her mother looked up.

"Are you feeling all right?"

"I'm fine," her mother replied. Emma thought dying people probably sounded more convincing. They certainly did on television.

"You're sure?"

Mercy looked at her daughter and shook her head. "Of course I'm sure. I'm always fine the morning after I've seen my dead husband in a hospital."

The silence that followed was profoundly awkward. It was worse than first-kiss awkward. "Mom—"

Her mother lifted a hand. It should have been a familiar gesture; Emma used it all the time. But coming from her mom, it looked wrong. "You can mother Michael," Mercy Hall said firmly, and with a trace of annoyance, "and any of the rest of your friends. I already have a mother, three bosses, and any number of other helpful advice-givers in the of-fice. I don't need mothering."

Emma, stung, managed to stop herself from saying something she'd probably only feel guilty about later. Guilt, in the Hall household, was like the second child of the family. The secret one that you tried to lock in the attic when respectable people were visiting.

Instead, she turned and walked into the hall, where she gave herself the once over in the mirror, frowned at both her eyes and her lips, which were slowly returning to normal, and then picked up her backpack to wait.

Michael rescued her at 8:10.

The walk to school would have been the same type of awkward that breakfast had been, but it was made easier by Michael, because Michael didn't worry that someone would think he was crazy. Michael, by dint of understanding his own condition, also understood that he saw the world in entirely different ways than the rest of the students in his grade did; he was used to this. Because he was, he didn't really question what he saw, and he didn't second-guess himself; he second-guessed (and third, fourth, and fifth for good measure) everyone else.

So he asked Allison if she'd seen Mr. Hall, as they all still called Emma's dad, and when Allison reluctantly admitted that she had, he was silent for a half a block.

When Michael was silent, it didn't mean anything in particular. It didn't mean that he was trying desperately to think of something to say, and it didn't mean that he was worrying about what you might say behind his back, because for the most part, he didn't worry about that kind of thing. It didn't mean he was really thinking about the last thing he'd asked about either, because he could slide into a segue so quickly you had to wonder if you'd heard the first part of what he said correctly.

But for the first time in years, Emma privately wished that she didn't have the responsibility of walking him to school, because she didn't want him to pick up the conversation from where it had left off last night. Guilt came and bit her on the backside; clearly, she hadn't left it in the attic this morning.

"Do you think Eric saw him?"

Since this was so much better than the question she'd been dreading, Emma pounced on it. "I'm sure Eric saw him."

"Oh. Why?"

"Everyone else did. Probably," she added, "everyone in the waiting room. Most of them wouldn't notice or care."

"Until he disappeared?"

"Until then, yes." She shrugged and added, "but they probably wouldn't really notice that either unless they were staring right at him. People in emergency rooms are usually thinking about other things."

Michael nodded. "But Eric?"

"Eric saw him."

"He's worried about you, Emma," Michael told her.

Allison winced.

"Oh. Why? Did he say something in the car last night?"

"Yes."

"What?"

"That he was worried about you."

Of course. This was Michael. "Did you ask why?"

"No." He stared at her for a minute and then added, "Your father is dead. And he came to the hospital. I think most people would be worried about that."

"I'll talk to Eric," she said, with feeling. She turned to Allison and added, "Did he say anything else?"

"Not very much," Allison offered. "It was a pretty quiet car ride."

Emma skipped English that morning. Eric also skipped English that morning. It wasn't a coincidence; she collared Eric before he entered the class. The way she said "Can I talk to you for a minute?" would have made teachers throughout her history proud.

Eric, to give him credit, didn't even try to avoid her. He met her eyes, nodded without hesitation, and took his hand off the doorknob. "Here, or off-site someplace?"

Off-site sounded better, but it made the chance that they'd be attending any of the rest of the morning classes a lot slimmer. Given everything, Emma reconciled herself to absence slips and parental questions and said, "Let's go somewhere where we won't be interrupted." She grimaced and added, "And if I collapse again, just drive me home."

They went to a very quiet cafe around the corner. Where around the corner meant about ten blocks away. Emma chose it out of habit, but at this time of day, almost nothing was crowded.

She took a seat by the window; a booth was at her back. Eric sat opposite her. They waited until someone came to take their order; Emma ordered a cafe au lait and a blueberry scone; Eric ordered black coffee and nothing. He glanced out the window, or perhaps at Emma's reflection; it was hard to tell. His normal, friendly expression was completely absent. It made his face look more angular, somehow, and also older. His eyes were clear enough that she couldn't quite say what color they were, although she had thought them brown until now.

When their order had come and the waitress had disappeared, Emma cupped her bowl in both hands and looked across the table. She took a deep breath. "Eric," she said softly.

He was watching her. His hands were on the table, on either side of his coffee cup, and she noticed for the first time how callused they were, and how dark compared to the rest of his skin. He wore a ring, a simple gold band that she hadn't really seen before. It looked . . . like a wedding ring.

"What happened last night?" she asked when it became clear that he was waiting for her. Waiting, she thought, and judging. She didn't much care for the latter.

"What do you think happened last night?"

*If I knew, I wouldn't be asking.* She forced the words to stay put, but it was hard. Instead, taking a deep breath, she said, "Something happened the other night in the graveyard. You were there."

He said nothing.

"I don't know if you saw—saw what I saw." She hesitated, because it still made her queasy. "I thought you couldn't have. Now I think you must have and that you understood it."

"Go on."

"But I don't. I know that I saw my father last night." She took another, deeper breath. "And there were two of me. You saw both. No one else in that room did. But when I touched my father, everyone saw him." She added, "And he was cold." She wasn't sure why she'd said it, but she couldn't claw the words back. "The headache has nothing to do with my falling."

"You're sure?"

"No. But you are."

He picked up the coffee cup as if it were a shield. And then, over the steam rising from it, he met her eyes. "Yeah," he said, not drinking. "I am." He turned just his head, and looked outside. Emma watched his face in the window. "Why were you in the graveyard, Emma?"

It was her turn to look out the window, although it wasn't much protection; their gazes met in reflections, both of them transparent against the cars parked on the curb outside. "It's quiet there," she said at last.

"Don't ask me questions," he replied, "until you're ready to answer them."

"I'm ready to answer them," she said, more forcefully. "I'm not willing to share the answers because they are none of your goddamn—" She bit her lip.

He shrugged. "No, they're not. They're not my business."

"But this is my business."

"No, Emma. It's not. I'm trying to spare you—"

"Oh, please."

His jaws snapped shut, and his eyes—if she hadn't been so angry, so surprisingly, unexpectedly angry, she would have looked away. But really? She had been so many things since Nathan had died. Self-absorbed. Even self-pitying. Desolate. Lonely. But furious? No. And right this second, she wanted to reach across the table and slap him. Emma had never slapped anyone in her life.

She swallowed. She picked up her bowl. Held it, to steady her hands, to keep them from forming fists. He sat there and watched.

"I was at the graveyard," she said, words clipped so sharply they had edges, "to visit Nathan's grave."

"A friend?"

She laughed. It was an eruption of sound, and it was all the wrong sound. "Yeah," she said bitterly. "A friend."

He put his own cup down and laid his hands flat against the table. "This . . . is not going well. Can we start again from the beginning?"

She shrugged. She could carry any conversation; it was a skill, like math, that she had learned over the years. Sometimes she tried to teach Michael. But it was gone. Whatever it was that had made her carry pointless conversation, underpinning it with a smile and an attentive expression, had deserted her.

She tried to make herself smile. She could manage to make herself talk. "We can try."

"I'm sorry. I didn't mean—"

"It doesn't matter. If I talk about it, if I don't. If I cry or I don't. It doesn't change anything." She shook her head, bit her lower lip. Tried to make the anger return to wherever it had unexpectedly come from. It fought back. "I go there," she added, "because it doesn't change anything. I don't expect him to answer me if I talk. I don't expect to turn around in the dark of night and see him. I don't expect him to—" She looked across at Eric, really looked at him.

Something about his expression was so unexpected, she said, "You lost someone too?"

It was his turn to laugh, and his laughter? As wrong as hers had been. Worse, if that was possible. He turned his hands palms up on the table and stared at them for a long time.

*Begin again*, Emma thought. There was no anger left. What she felt, she couldn't easily describe. But she wondered, watching him in his silence, if this was what people saw when they watched her. Because she wanted to say something to ease his pain, and nothing was there. It made her feel useless. Or helpless.

"You're right," he said softly. "It's none of my business. I don't even know why I asked." He took a breath and then picked up his coffee. This time, he even drank some of it, although his expression made her wonder why he bothered. Which was a whole lot safer than wondering anything else at the moment.

"Can you see them?" Emma asked, trying to shoulder her part of the conversation.

"The dead?"

She nodded.

"Yeah. I can see the dead."

"Does it help?"

He gave her the oddest look, and then his smile once again spread across his face. It made him look younger. She wanted to say it made him look more like himself, but what did she really know about him?

"No. It doesn't help anything. It doesn't help at all." He paused and then said, "Did it help you?"

She nodded. Lifted her hands, palms up. "He's my dad," she said. "It was almost worth it—the pain. To see him again."

He grimaced. "Don't go there," he said, but his voice and tone were different. Quieter. "You're not dead. He is. Emma—" he hesitated, and she could almost see him choosing the right words. Or choosing any words—what did right mean, now? "I know the pain is bad. But you can get past it. It stops. If you can ignore it for two more days, you'll never be troubled by the dead again."

Thinking of Nathan's grave, she was silent.

"Why can I see them? Is it because of—"

"Yes." He didn't even let her finish the question. "It's because of that. You can see them," he said, "and you can talk with them." He hesitated, as if about to say more. The more, however, didn't escape.

"And it's only that?"

He looked out the window again. After a long pause, he said, "No."

Emma hesitated. "I can touch them," she said, a slight rise at the end of the sentence turning it into a tentative question.

He nodded.

"My dad—people could see him because I touched him."

"Yes. Only because of that. If you hadn't, he would have stayed invisible and safely dead."

She wanted to argue with the use of the words "safely" and "dead" side by side, but she could see his point. "Can you?"

"Can I?"

"You can talk to them. You can see them. Can you touch them?"

"No."

"Oh. Why not?"

He didn't answer.

"Eric, why is it important to you that I—that I stop seeing the dead?"

"Because," he replied slowly, "then I won't have to kill you."

# CHAPTER
# SIX

EMMA BLINKED. "Can you say that again?"

"I think you heard it the first time."

"I want to make sure I heard it the first time. Sort of."

He merely watched her. She watched him right back. It was almost as if they were playing tennis and the ball had somehow gotten suspended in time just above the net; she wasn't sure which way it would fly when it was released.

"Why were you at the graveyard?" she finally asked.

"I can see the dead," he replied. "And oddly enough, there are very few dead in the graveyards of the world. It's not where they lived," he added, "and it's not where they died. They're not all that concerned about their corpses. I like graveyards because they're quiet."

"But—but you were with someone."

"Yes. Not intentionally," he added, "but yes. I expected some difficulty. I did *not* expect you." He picked up his coffee again. Set it down. Picked it up.

"Eric, it's not a yo-yo."

And he actually smiled, although it never reached his eyes.

"What did you expect?"

"Trouble," he finally said. "Not Emma Hall and her dog. Which she calls Petal for some reason, even though he's a rottweiler."

She winced. "My dad called me Sprout. Petal was a puppy when my father brought him home, and it seemed like a good idea at the time. Because of his ears. And my nickname." She looked at Eric and said, "You were expecting me."

"Emma—"

"You didn't know *who*, but you had some idea of *what*."

He shrugged.

"Why did you phone my mother? Why did you help me home? Eric, what were you planning to do in the graveyard?"

He continued to say nothing. But at length, he replied. "I watched you, in school. All of you. Amy, with her ridiculous entourage, her obvious money."

"And her fabulous body?"

"That too. But not just Amy. Philipa. Deb. Nan. Allison. Connell and Oliver. Michael. You all have your problems, your little fights—but you also have your generous moments, your responsibilities. This may come as a surprise to you, but your thoughtless kindnesses made being in a new school a lot more pleasant."

"Thoughtless kindness?"

"Pretty much. You do it without thinking. There's not a lot of calculation, and I can't see how most of it directly benefits any of you." He paused again and then added, "I did *not* expect to see any one of you in that graveyard. Even when I saw you, I didn't expect what happened."

"If it hadn't been me, or any of us, what would you have done?"

He looked at her for a moment and then shook his head, and something about his expression was painful to look at: not frightening, not threatening, but almost heartbreaking.

"What I should have done, I didn't do. What I should be doing, I haven't done. Instead, I'm sitting here in a cafe in the middle of a school day drinking coffee that isn't very good with a confused, teenage girl."

"Teenage girl?"

"And talking too damn much," he added. He drained the coffee cup.

"Eric, you're not exactly ancient, yourself."

He laughed. It was not a good laugh. "Come on," he said, as if the bitterness of the dregs of the coffee had transferred itself to his voice. "You shouldn't have touched your father." He grimaced. "Emma, understand that what I know about—about what you can do was learned only so that I could prevent most of it. I can't tell you what you can do; I don't want you to know. I want you to turn your back on it and walk away."

"So you won't have to kill me."

"I told you you heard me."

She managed to shrug.

"I don't want to draw your mother into this; I don't want to draw your friends into it, either. Usually that's not much of a problem; most of the people who are affected by this are loners."

"Like you?"

"Like me. You're not. You're tied to your life, and you take it seriously." He looked out the window again. "I shouldn't be talking to you, and you shouldn't be skipping school. Let me pay for this, and I'll drive you back."

"Are you coming to Amy's party tonight?"

He looked at her as if she were almost insane, and she had to admit that as a non sequitur, it was pretty damn ridiculous. "I'm probably driving you home, where you'll sit in the dark until all this has passed. But yes, I intend to go to Amy's." He stood.

She stood as well. He waved the waitress over, and they had a small argument about who was paying, which Eric won by saying, "You can get the next one."

As they were heading to his car, he asked, "Will you try?"

She didn't pretend to misunderstand him. "Yes."

He nodded, as if that were the most he could expect.

Allison caught up with Emma in the lunch line-up, looking slightly anxious. "You missed English. Is anything wrong?"

Emma grimaced. "My mother has given up pretending she didn't see my father in the hospital, if that's any indication."

Allison winced. "Is she okay?"

"She's the Hall version of okay, which is to say, she's *fine*."

"What's she going to do?"

"If I'm lucky it won't involve joint trips to the nearest psychiatrist." Emma paused and pointed at the macaroni and cheese, which was one of the hot meal choices. "You know what my luck is like."

"And English?"

"I was talking to Eric," Emma replied. She hesitated and then added, "And I'll tell you all about it tonight. If I'm not curled up in the dark someplace whimpering." She reached out and caught Allison's hand; it was a gesture she'd learned to use with Michael over the years, and it meant, more or less, *I'm serious, pay attention*. Allison, who had also learned the same gesture, understood. "I'll tell you everything, but you have to promise that you will do your absolute best not to worry at me."

Allison nodded. "I'll try."

"I'm going to try to go to Amy's tonight because I *like* having a social life, and I already told her I'd be there."

"Michael's going to go."

Even the horrendous background noise that was the cafeteria didn't disguise the utter silence that followed this statement. Michael was always invited to the larger gatherings, he just never went. Ever.

"Oliver's going," Allison told Emma, nudging her to get her moving. "And I think Connell might go as well."

"How's Michael getting there?"

"I'm not sure. We can figure it out when we get back to the table."

Eric seemed to have decided that their table—that being whichever table Michael sat at—was also his table. Even given his concerns, most of which she still didn't understand and most of which she was now certain she didn't *want* to understand, he was pleasant and low-key company. He listened to Michael without eye rolling, which was pretty much the only requirement in a lunch companion at this table.

Not, Emma thought, if she was being fair, that she didn't sometimes engage in eye rolling, but she felt she'd earned that, and Michael understood what it meant when she did it. Michael didn't ask her about her father, for which she was grateful. It was a normal day, and Emma wanted to hold on to the normal for as long as she could.

But as they were filing out of the cafeteria, Emma noticed that Allison was hanging back, and she was doing it in front of Eric. She started to say something and thought better of it, following Michael out of the cafeteria instead.

Allison was clearly nervous. Determined, but nervous.

Eric, leaning on the warped wood of the stair railing on portable D, watched her, waiting. He didn't look bored, and he didn't look angry; he didn't seem confused. He just . . . waited. When it became clear that waiting was going to be rewarded with a lot of awkward silence, he cleared his throat. "You wanted to talk to me?"

She nodded. And then said "Yes," just in case.

He waited for a bit longer. "Allison—"

"I'm sorry," she said, and looked at her feet. "It's about Emma." She looked up in time to see the way his expression changed. It closed up, like a trap.

"Ah. I'm not interested in Emma in that way," he said carefully.

"She's really not looking for anyone," Allison said, at the same time. The words collided. It was all so awkward.

"Why don't you start at the beginning?"

"Beginning?"

"You want to tell me why she's not looking for anyone. Or anyone special." When Allison nodded, he took his arm off the railing and shoved his hands into his front pockets. And waited. Then, when it became clear the awkwardness wasn't going away anytime soon, he very quietly took the threads of the conversation into his own, figurative, hands.

"You've known her for a long time?"

"Since we were six. Well, I was five."

"You've been friends since then?"

Allison nodded.

"You're not really like her, though."

"No."

"And you're not really interested in the same things."

"Some of the same things, but . . . no." Allison hesitated. "You've met Amy."

"It's impossible to be a student at Emery and *not* meet Amy."

"Do you like her?"

Eric shrugged. "She's a girl."

"I hated her, in junior high."

Eric's brow lifted slightly, as if in surprise.

"I hated that age," Allison added softly. "I thought she was so full of herself, and so cruel. But Emma liked her," she added.

"Emma liked you."

"Out of habit. But it was Emma who told me that Amy's not cruel on purpose. She doesn't enjoy being mean—she's just thoughtless; she's caught up in her own life and in her own problems. Just as I was then. To Emma, Amy was important. Amy's friendship was important. You've seen Em," Allison added. "Emma fits in with them. She always has."

"She doesn't seem to spend much time with them, now."

"No. She worked hard," Allison said, staring out into the field, or into a memory. She lost the nervous look, and her hands fell to her sides. "She worked hard to belong. She did what they did, went where they went. I was so afraid of losing her. I was jealous. Of them."

"Ah."

"But . . . we survived. It was even harder, for me, when Emma started seeing Nathan."

"Nathan?"

"Her boyfriend. He died this summer, in a car accident. They were always together. Things she'd do with me—things that she couldn't do with Amy and her friends—she started doing with Nathan instead. She spent all her time with him. Even Amy was getting annoyed. Nathan was quiet, though. He was never mean, and he was never showy. I liked him," she added, "and I hated him. I never told her about the hate part."

"I won't," he said softly.

"But when he died . . . It was bad. I don't even remember who told me, but it wasn't Emma. She came to school and she did her work and she hung out with Amy, but . . . she'd stopped caring. She always seems so self-confident to people who meet her now. It's not that, though—she just doesn't care anymore. She says what she's thinking because she doesn't care what other people think about her. None of it matters.

"And I felt guilty for a long time, because I sometimes wanted Nathan to *go away*. I wish he hadn't," she added, her voice still soft. "Because Emma is always "fine" now. Even at the burial, she was fine." She took a deep breath. "And Amy, who I always thought of as selfish? After Nathan died, she gathered all of us together, and she tried to arrange a different schedule for Michael, so that Emma would have time to grieve and pull herself together."

"She offered that to Emma?"

"No. But she was thinking of Emma, of what Emma had lost. They treat her a little differently now than they used to. They understand, and they try to give her space. All the stupid social games they used to play? They don't play them with Emma anymore." She frowned. "They still play them with each other, though."

"So if Amy arranged for someone else to meet Michael, why is he coming to school with the two of you?"

"I told them no."

He stared at her, his expression odd. "Why?"

"Because Michael hadn't changed. He still needed Em. And I think Emma needed the responsibility of watching him, the way she'd always done. Besides," she added, with a grimace, "Michael would have taken three months to readjust to a new routine, and Michael needed to know that Nathan, not Emma, was gone. Nathan understood Michael. It was why Emma started to like him in the first place."

"You're worried about her."

Allison nodded. "Emma has always gotten along with Michael because Emma *sees* Michael. She doesn't see what she wants him to be; she doesn't see what he lacks. She just sees what he is, and she understands it. She sees me the same way. She doesn't think about "normal." She just sees what we are. Mostly only the good parts," she added. "But they're still true.

"When Nathan died, Emma's mother always tried to offer comfort, and Emma didn't want it. She spent a lot of time at my house, because my mother didn't. My mom didn't need Emma to cry or scream or be angry or grieve. She let Emma be. And that's what Emma needed. It's hard," Allison added. "Sometimes it's hard. But I try to do the same."

"And you're telling me that's what I have to do?"

Allison nodded.

History was the last class of the day, and Emma approached it warily, watching for any signs of the odd dislocation that could be mistaken for concussion symptoms. Allison was watching her as well. They made their way to their seats.

Emma blinked.

"Em?"

She heard the word from a long way off; it was a tinny sound, something small and so stretched she could tell it was Allison talking only because Allison used that single syllable so effectively. She could hear the droning of Ms. Kagayama, but that, too, could barely be resolved into a familiar voice; there were no words.

No, that wasn't true. There were no familiar words, and the words that she *could* hear were spoken in so many voices, all overlapping, they almost made her dizzy. But the voices were clearer, and if it seemed as if there were thousands of them, they were distinct. This time, instead of fading into painful noise, they stayed at the edge of a shout, a chorus of shouts.

She blinked again, and she realized why.

She had thought that light hurt her eyes. Yesterday and the day before, she would have sworn it. But she realized now that it wasn't the light, it was the images that swirled around her vision, sharpest at the periphery. They formed an aurora of scintillating colors—but they had shapes now, textures that she recognized.

Clothing. Hair. Faces.

None of them stayed in one place long enough for her to really *look*. But she had the sense that she was standing still and they were streaming past, shouting, screaming, or crying as they did.

"Em?"

She lifted a hand. She couldn't speak and look at the same time. And she wanted to look. She had told Eric she would try, but she *wanted* to see her father. Or hear him. She wouldn't touch him again, she promised herself that much. But it was *hard*. Her head began to pound with the effort it took to keep looking, to *listen*, to break out one voice from the multitude.

But she managed, somehow.

And realized, as she did, that it was not her father's voice that she had reached for and not, therefore, her father that she could see.

Instead, she saw *fire*, and she shouted, bringing her hands up to cover her face. She would have let go, then. She would have let go and slid into oblivion and nausea and darkness. But she could see, wreathed in fire, the face of a small child, and she could hear, in the distance, the screams.

No, the scream. One voice. One voice shouting words that were familiar because Emma had typed them, in a half-trance, on the day of the first headache.

**Oh my god Drew help me help me Drew fire god no**

She stood—she managed to stand.

Allison was standing as well; she felt Allison's hand on her arm. And then she felt a familiar arm encircle her shoulder. It was tight, meant to brace her and hold her up. She swallowed, closed her eyes, and forced them open again.

She heard Eric's voice, and his voice was blessedly clear. "Strength, Emma." It was a whisper of sound, a tickle in her ear. But she could hear it. She nodded and managed to say, "Take me home."

She felt herself being lifted.

"Strength," Eric said again.

She nodded.

She threw up in the parking lot. Eric seemed to expect this, and although he set her down, he hovered. "Where's Allison?" she asked, as she pushed herself to her feet.

"I told her to stay. There's not much she can do."

"And she listened?"

He chuckled. "Very reluctantly. I'm not sure she trusts me."

"She's smarter than I am," Emma said. She caught his arm. Her knees felt like rubber, but they held. "I think I can walk," she told him, as he put an arm around her shoulder.

**Drew**

She closed her eyes. "How can you live like this?" she whispered.

"I don't see what you see now."

"Oh. Did you ever?"

"Never. I am not what I fear you are, Emma."

**DREW**

One voice in the maelstrom. She opened her eyes to fire; fire and black, thick smoke. She could almost taste it, and fell to her knees against the asphalt. Eric picked her up. He had never looked particularly large to Emma, but he carried her as easily as Brendan Hall had when she had been a small girl.

"Eric."

His arms tightened, but he continued to walk. "Em," he whispered. "Don't do this. Please."

She opened her eyes; she could see his profile, because her head was resting against his shoulder. His eyes were faintly luminescent in her vision, although they were also dark brown; his jaw was tensed, as if with effort. She said, "Eric, there's a child—"

He almost missed a step, but he caught himself—and Emma— before they both fell.

"There's a child, in the fire."

"What fire, Emma?" He asked it as if she were a fevered child. It should have irritated her, but it didn't. She wasn't sure why.

"I don't know. There's a fire and a child standing in it. There's smoke, it's thick and heavy. And I can hear *one* voice, over all the other voices."

He had reached his car, and now set her down close to the front passenger seat. He unlocked the door manually, and then put an arm around her waist as she slid into the car. She felt the vinyl against her legs; it was warm.

"But, Eric," she continued, as he closed the door gently and walked around the front of the car to the driver's side. She waited while he slid behind the steering wheel. "Eric?"

"I'm here. Take this," he added, and handed her a small bucket. "I thought you might need it."

"The voice I hear sounds different. It's not—it's not like the other voices."

"How is it different?" He spoke patiently and slowly.

"I don't know for certain—I can't shut the other voices out, not completely, so it's hard to listen." She grimaced, and added, "and I can see the child."

"Now?"

"Yes." She'd already nodded a couple of times, but this time remembered that speaking was less painful.

**Drew oh my god oh god**

He started the car.

"He's not very old. I think he's four. Maybe a bit older, maybe a bit younger, it's hard to tell." And she was concentrating now. Her vision was a strange collage of things she expected to see and things it should have been impossible to see.

The phone rang. She blinked. The fire wavered, its roar diminishing to a crackle. She automatically reached into her pocket before she realized that the ringtone was wrong; it wasn't her phone.

It rang again. "Eric, I think that's your phone."

He said nothing, and Emma listened to it ring three more times before it fell silent. When it did, the roar of the fire returned.

The child's eyes were wide, and she could see black tears trace the delicate lines of his cheeks. He was staring *at* her, his lips slightly open.

"Yes," Emma said, although she couldn't say why. "Yes, I'm coming." She turned to Eric. "Go left here."

The car rolled to a halt. He opened his mouth, and shut it when the phone rang again.

"Are you going to answer that?"

"No. I know who it is."

"Without looking?"

"Not many people have my number. What do you mean, turn left here?"

"We have to drive that way," she replied, lifting a shaking arm.

"Why, Emma?"

"Because we—we just have to drive that way."

Eric lifted a hand to his face. "All right. All right, we'll play it your way for now."

Eric followed Emma's ad hoc directions. Emma concentrated on staying upright. She gave right, left, and straight calls, and he followed them, paying attention to the lights. But she must have given him the wrong direction, because he turned instead of going straight, and Emma screamed as the car drove up a curb, over an unwatered lawn, and *into* a large shed.

"Eric!"

His knuckles whitened on the wheel, and she watched as the shed and the car converged. The car passed right through it, leaving no wood, boards, or broken glass in its wake. She turned to look over her shoulder; there was nothing at all behind them but a two lane residential street.

He glanced at her once, but said nothing.

"I'll just stick with directions," she said, shakily. "Sorry for screaming."

One-way streets made the drive more difficult. Eric attempted to follow her directions, but told her curtly that he found having a driver's license convenient when he was forced, by street signs, to ignore Emma. "It would help," he added, as his phone began to ring again, "if you knew any of the street names."

She did. She just didn't know *these* streets. "Eric, can you answer the damn phone?"

"No."

"Then give the damn thing to me, and I'll answer it."

"No."

She rubbed her temples. It didn't help, but it gave her something to do with her hands other than try to strangle Eric. Given that Emma didn't have her license, strangling the only driver in an increasingly unfamiliar part of town seemed like a bad idea. As if to argue with that, the phone started ringing again immediately after it had stopped.

Eric ignored it. Emma gritted her teeth and tried to do the same. "Has it ever occurred to you that it could be an emergency?" she asked, through those gritted teeth.

"Just keep your mind on the road."

She did. She found it easier as the driving continued. It wasn't that the light, and the quality of its shifting images, lessened; the opposite happened. But as those phantasms grew more concrete and she could hold the images in the center of her vision as if they were just another part of the landscape, the pain decreased.

And the voices dimmed as well, until there was only one voice, screaming to be heard against the cracking of timber and the roar of fire.

Emma said, "Here, Eric."

But the car had already rolled to a stop.

The phone rang.


It was pretty difficult, in the city of Toronto, to find any patch of land that did not have a building on it. This one was a partial exception; it had what looked like the remnants of several buildings, with partly blackened walls, a total lack of glass in window frames, and boards over where the doors would have been.

Emma experienced, for a second time, the sudden cessation of noise and light. This time, though, she could feel the movement of all of these things as they left her in a rush, condensing, at last, to a single point that existed outside of her head. She shook her head, partly to clear it, and partly because sitting this close to a row of burned out townhouses wasn't something she did every day.

Eric turned the engine off and glanced at her.

"Here," she said quietly. She started to tell him that she no longer had the headache and then gave up; his expression made clear that he knew. And that, unlike Emma, he wasn't happy about it.

She opened the car door and slid out of the car. "Do you want to wait here?"

"Wouldn't dream of it," Eric replied. He opened his door, and his phone rang. Again.

"Look, if you don't want to answer it, and you don't want me to answer it, why don't you just throw it away or step on it or something?"

He looked as if he was considering it, and then shrugged. "I'll turn it off."

Emma's phone had only ever been off when she'd forgotten to recharge the batteries. She grimaced. "Or that," she said.

She made her way off the road, over the dead patch of lawn that was usually bracketed by sidewalk and curb, and onto the sidewalk itself, and then she began to walk toward the second house from the end.

"Where are you going?" Eric asked, following her.

She pointed to the house. "Do you know what street we're on?"

"Rowan Avenue."

Emma took her phone out of her pocket, and made a note to herself.

"It's two words," Eric said, raising a brow. "You're not going to remember two words?"

"Probably not." She slid the phone back into her pocket and headed up the walk. "Do you think this is safe at all?"

Eric said nothing. It was a lot of nothing. And to be fair, the obvious answer was No. "Emma, what are you going to do?"

"I don't know," she said quietly. "But I think—I think the child's in that building."

"He's dead."

"Very funny."

"Only by accident," he replied.

"Stay here."

"Emma—"

"Just let me check the floor." She moved very slowly up the walk, and then detoured to the lawn, to get closer to the ruined building. It was at least two stories in height; a third floor might still exist, small rooms cramped beneath the peak that was suggested by the buildings, farther down, that seemed in better repair. The fire must have occurred recently; the building was still standing. There was no evidence of bulldozers; no evidence of people's handiwork beyond the haphazard boarding that had been put up. As she approached what had once been windows—the facade was damaged enough that the frames on this floor looked a lot like big, black holes—she felt heat and saw, for a moment, fire.

They weren't ghostly flames; they were hot, and high, and adorned by billowing smoke as air moved from the outside of the house toward them.

She heard, again, the screams. But she heard them at a distance, and she turned to where Eric was standing, expecting to get a glimpse of the woman—for it was a woman's voice—that had once been capable of uttering them. The street, except for Eric and a couple of cars, was quiet.

"Eric?" She waved him over.

He shoved his hands into his pockets and walked slowly toward her.

"Pretend that you won't have to kill me if you answer my questions."

"Emma, do you understand how serious this is?"

She looked up, to the second story. "Yes. I need to know something about the dead."

He waited, and after a minute of silence, she said, "I saw a student in the cafeteria the other day. He *looked* alive to me. I realized something was really wrong when Allison sat *through* him."

"Go on."

"But he seemed to notice *me*. He smiled at me," she added, "just before he disappeared. I can see the fire," she added softly. "I can feel its heat."

"You're right. It has to be recent."

"What I need to know is if the child—"

"The dead child?"

"The dead child. Will he be able to see me and react to me?"

The silence was longer and more marked, but Eric eventually said, "Yes."

"Will he be able to see you?"

"Yes."

"Anyone else?"

"Not unless you touch him."

"Why?"

"I'd rather not say."

"Is he stuck there?"

"He's dead."

"*Eric.*"

"Emma, it may come as a surprise to you, but I'm not dead." He took his hands out of his pockets; they were fists. He relaxed them slowly, but it looked like it took effort. "But yes, there's a good chance that *he* feels he can't come out."

"Can we make him come out?"

"Why?" The word was sharper, and harsher.

"Because he's stuck in a *burning house*, and he's *four years old*."

The phone rang.

Emma's eyes widened. "I thought you said you shut it off?"

Eric shrugged. "I did. Welcome to my life." He slid his hand into his jacket pocket—school jacket, for formal day—and took the phone out. "I can't talk right now," he said, as he lifted the phone to his ear. "No. I left early. Someplace downtown." He rolled his eyes. "Rowan Avenue. No, I'm with another student. Yes. No." He glanced at Emma, and then said, "It might not be a problem. Look up Rowan Avenue. No. Because I'm not near a computer. Look, I can't talk right now. I'll call you as soon as I can."

He hung up and slid the phone back into his pocket.

It started to ring again. Eric raised a brow in her direction and she grimaced and threw up her hands. "You win," she told him. "Ignore it."

"Why, thank you."

She walked up to what was left of the house and raised her arms to shield her face as the flames leaped out of the windows, driving her back and into Eric. He put his hands on her arms to steady her. "Fire?"

"You can't feel it?"

"No."

"See it?"

"No. You may need to wait this out," he added softly. It was loud anyway; his lips were beside her ear.

"If you can't see it," she told him, gritting her teeth, "it's not *real*." She shook herself free of his hands, and approached the building again. She forced herself to approach the fire. It singed her hair, and she jumped back again.

"Emma—"

"I don't understand," she whispered.

"The fire *is* real, in some way, for you. It's not real for me." He exhaled sharply and then said, "In twenty years, you'll see it, but it won't sustain the ability to burn you. Or it shouldn't."

"Twenty *years?*"

"More or less. Come on, let me drive you home."

"You mean that child is going to be trapped in a burning building for *twenty years?*" She turned to face him, and grabbed one arm to prevent him from walking away. "Eric, if the fire isn't real *to you*, you can enter the building."

"If the building has any structural integrity, yes."

"If you can make it in without feeling the fire, I might be able to go with you. And if I collapse because of smoke inhalation, you can drag me out."

She heard the screaming again and turned. Street and cars. Nothing else. Frowning, she said, "I don't think the voice I can hear is a dead person's voice."

Eric said nothing, which was starting to get old.

"I think—I think it might be his mother's voice."

"Emma, let it go. Please. If it's strong enough that you can hear her voice, he is *too* strong for you."

"He's four."

"A living four-year-old and a dead four-year-old are not the same. Trust me."

"I can't."

Silence. Then, "No, I don't suppose you can." He looked away, toward the house. "Even if I get you into the house, I probably won't be able to get you up the stairs. I don't think enough of them are left standing to support my weight."

"But enough is left standing to support mine?" The quality of his silence was as good as an answer. "Because it was standing, or almost standing, when he was trapped there. I'm where he is, when I approach the house. Some part of me is walking to where he is."

"Yes. And no. You're here," he added softly. "This isn't like the hospital."

"No. In the hospital there were two of me." Her eyes widened slightly. "The one part sees the dead," she said softly, as if testing the words. "And the other part sees the living. Why aren't there two of me now?"

"You only get that dislocation at the beginning," was the quiet reply.

She looked at the burning house carefully and then said, "All right. We need a ladder. A big, solid ladder." And she turned and walked back to the car.

"Why is he trapped in the house?"

"He's not."

"Why is he *staying* in the house?"

"Better question. I honestly don't have the answer."

"Why are any of the dead here *at all*?"

Eric glanced at her in the mirror, but otherwise kept his eyes on the road. He had to, since Emma had no idea at all of how to get home. "Where should they be?" he asked at length.

He was testing her somehow, and she knew it. She had always been good at tests, but this test was decidedly unfair; she didn't even know what the subject was. "I don't know. Heaven? Hell?"

"I'm not dead. I don't know either."

"And you don't care."

"No. I care. But there's nothing I can do about it."

"There must be something *I* can do about it."

His silence was long, and she watched the way his jaw tightened into it. "If this is your idea of trying to stay out of things," he told her, "you fail."

"Full of fail. That happens when a four-year-old is going to be trapped forever in a burning house, reliving the moment of his death."

The phone rang, but it had been doing that on and off since they'd gotten back into the car. "You could change the ringtone," Emma suggested.

"This is the shortest ring I could find."

# CHAPTER
## SEVEN

ERIC DROVE EMMA HOME and parked on the street. Emma opened the car door and then turned to Eric. "If you need to go home before Amy's party, I can send you the directions to get there."

He blinked. "Amy's party?"

"Remember? We spoke about it before we left school?"

He shook his head. "You're crazy."

"If you think she looks good in school, you've never seen her when she's actually trying."

He didn't smile. "And what are you going to do?"

"I'm going to go hit the computer and then call Allison."

"And?"

"Get ladders," she replied quietly. "And go back to Rowan Avenue. If we're lucky, we can figure out what needs to be done before Amy's party."

"And if you're not?"

"If I'm not," she said starkly, the half smile deserting her face, "I don't think we're going to have to worry about it."

"Emma you can't go in there blind. You have no idea what you're doing!"

"No, I don't. I'm going to try to find out more before I head out there." She turned toward the door and then turned back again. "I don't understand what you're afraid of, Eric. I don't understand what's going on with you. What I understand, at the moment, is that that child is somehow stuck in that house. And I want to get him out."

"To what end?"

She stared at him. And then she got out of the car without looking back, and shut the door.

The phone rang. Eric listened to it, his hands still gripping the steering wheel, knuckles white. Prying his fingers free, he picked up the phone and stared at the screen while the ring died into silence. He looked up to see Emma and got a brief glimpse of her ridiculously named rottweiler before her front door closed.

When the phone rang again, he answered.

"Yeah."

"Eric—"

"Rowan Avenue?"

"Ten days ago."

Eric whistled.

"Eric?"

"Ten days. I would have guessed three, tops."

The silence was cold. "And why would you have guessed that?"

Eric shrugged. He realized that this wasn't likely to convey itself over the phone and decided he didn't care enough to put the gesture into words.

"Eric, what is happening there?"

"Not much. I'm going to Amy's party tonight," he added, just for the momentary amusement of silent outrage on the other end of the line. It came and was followed by brief spluttering, an added bonus.

"Eric, *did you find the Necromancer*?"

Eric counted four uses of his name in six sentences, which was about as far as he could push it without things getting ugly. "Yes."

"Good. Dead?"

"No."

"No?"

"No."

"You arrived too late." It wasn't a question.

Eric was not one of nature's natural liars. He said nothing, which was neutral. It was also not enough.

"Eric, did you arrive too late?"

"No."

The silence that followed his monosyllabic confession was long. " . . . No. And the Necromancer is not dead."

"No."

"You need backup."

"Not really."

"And I'm sending it."

"If you send Chase, I won't guarantee he'll survive."

"If he doesn't, I'll come myself."

Fuck.

Emma had to work not to put her fingers through the keyboard. It was almost not worth the trouble. Yes, Eric was a stranger. Yes, they had no history. Yes, he knew something about her that she *did not know herself,* and he wasn't about to share. And yes, if it came down to it, she *knew* somewhere in the back of her hindbrain that if she did something wrong, somehow, he would kill her.

She also didn't doubt that he could, and that was strange, because it wasn't something she usually worried about. What she usually worried about was saying the wrong thing, alienating her friends, or pissing off her mother or her teachers. And it was beside the damn point. He knew that there was a child trapped in that house, and he didn't *care.*

Google was not slow to load answers to her query, and she looked at them, opening the first five in tabs. She began to read, and as she did, anger at Eric dimmed. She didn't like to hold on to anger, and she let it go.

Only one person had died in the fire—Andrew Copis, four years of age. Cause of fire: under investigation. From the sounds of it, though, the fire hadn't started in Andrew's home; it had started one house down. The walls were not cinderblock, and the fire had spread. Maria Copis, Andrew's mother, was twenty-eight years of age. She was a divorced single parent; her ex-husband was not in residence. She had—oh.

Three children. Andrew was the oldest; she had an eighteen-month-old girl and a two-month-old boy. She had picked them up, and carried them both out of the house. The little girl had suffered smoke inhalation.

She had not been able to carry Andrew at the same time, and she had screamed at him to follow her. And he had screamed at her to *carry him*. A brief moment of outrage at all news reporters came and went. How could you *ask* a mother something like that?

Emma closed her eyes. She knew, now, why Andrew stayed in the house.

It was a few moments before she could read again, but she did. Andrew had died of smoke inhalation; the screaming, the deep breaths required *to* scream, hadn't helped. He had suffered burns as well by the time the firefighters reached him, but it wasn't direct fire that had killed him.

The firefighters had gone into the building; the building at that time had supported their weight. They were all heavier than Emma, especially with the gear they wore. They'd gone in through the second story windows. Check.

She sat back in her chair and rubbed her eyes with the heels of her hands. How was she going to talk a terrified, hysterical four-year-old out of a burning building if she was trapped in the same burning building?

She pulled her phone out of her pocket and called Allison.

\*     \*     \*

She told Allison everything.

Everything except the part about Eric not having to kill her—which of course implied that he *might* have to kill her— because there was no way to say that without causing panic. Then she waited while the silence on the other end of the phone stretched out.

She finally said, "I know it sounds crazy."

Allison replied, "Em, I *saw* your father. We all did. I don't think *you're* crazy. But it does sound kind of crazy."

Emma reminded herself, as her shoulders eased down her back and she relaxed, that there were reasons she loved Allison. "What are you doing?"

"Googling. I've got your article on the fire," she added. "Oh."

"Three kids. Two of them had no hope of walking out of that place on their own," Emma said softly.

"Did you write down where Andrew's buried?"

"I don't think I know," Emma replied. "I think there was a service that was open to the public, but I don't think it mentioned the burial site. Why?"

"Because," Allison replied, "I don't think you're going to be able to get Andrew to leave that house without his mother."

A *lot* of reasons why she loved Allison. "You don't think so, either?"

"No. We can try," she added. "With what we've got here, we can try. But . . ."

"I know." Emma got out of her chair and walked toward the window. "We could probably find her in the phonebook. She's a divorced single parent, now. How many Copises could there be?"

"There could be an unlisted one." Allison hesitated—her breath was different when she was trying to figure out which words to say. "But I have no idea how we're going to approach her."

Emma had avoided thinking about that as well. Pacing in her room, her phone against her ear, she thought about it now. And grimaced. "Me either. But even if we look like a couple of lunatics, wouldn't it be worth listening?"

"We're not going to look like lunatics. We're going to look worse. We're going to look like the meanest, most vicious, malicious people *ever*."

Emma tried to imagine Allison in this context and failed utterly. "We have to try," she said quietly.

"I know. But we have to find her first, and we're probably not going to manage that tonight. If we knew where the grave was, that might be the best way to meet her in person."

"It'd be the *worst* place to approach her, though." She glanced out the window again and saw that Eric's car was still parked in the street in front of her house. She turned, and ran into Petal, who had decided that it was time to be taken for a walk. "Not now, Petal," she told him, scratching behind his ears.

But dogs can be particularly dense when it comes to understanding English. He padded out of the room and appeared again two minutes later, dragging his leash across the carpet and wagging his stub. "I have to take Petal for a walk," Emma said, surrendering.

"Call me when you get back?"

"I will. Maybe I'll have thought of something useful by then. Maybe we could pretend to work for the insurance company or something. I mean, we only have to *get* her there."

"Single mother of two."

"Ugh. Later," she added, hanging up. She picked up the leash that was attached to her dog in the wrong way—mostly by his mouth—and changed that.

Eric's car was still in the street, and he was still behind the wheel, when Emma left the house and locked up behind herself. Most of her anger had evaporated, but a small core of it remained, and she hesitated while Petal tried to drag her down the walk.

Then, squaring her shoulders, she dragged her dog down to the street and rapped on the front passenger window. Eric turned his head to look at her, and then he nodded and got out of the car. "You're walk-ing your dog?"

"I'm about to be walked by my dog. Subtle difference."

He smiled at that, and it was the comfortable and genuine smile that she liked on his face. She surrendered the rest of her anger, then.

"You want company?" Eric asked.

She shrugged. "If you're going to just sit here in the car, you might as well join us."

She didn't realize where she was walking. Petal was doing his usual intense inspection of anything that might be a garbage can. Given that it wasn't a collection day and he wasn't always the brightest dog, that took him a little too close to the actual houses.

Eric laughed, and Petal was thankfully old enough not to find this flattering. He did find it slightly encouraging, but that was probably a Hall fault; if people were laughing, they were a lot less likely to order you to heel.

"No ladders?" he asked, as Petal decided that forward was better than sideways and actually let them gain half a block of sidewalk before he started barking at a squirrel.

"No . . ."

"No?" When she looked at him, he shoved his hands in his pockets and continued the slow, meandering stroll that was walking her nine-year-old dog.

"We'll need them later," Emma told him.

"I didn't think you'd given up, if that's any consolation."

"Not really."

He shrugged. "Later?"

"Allison doesn't think that Andrew will leave the house if his moth-er's not there."

"You *told Allison?*"

"She's my best friend. There's not a lot about my life that she doesn't know."

"And she didn't think you were insane." It wasn't really a question, but the last few words did tail off in a slight rise.

"She's my best friend," Emma said again. "Look, Eric, she sees the world in a way I don't. She picks up things I might miss. I do the same for her when she asks." And even when she didn't, sometimes, but Emma had gotten better since junior high. "And she wasn't saying anything I hadn't thought, she was just more certain."

Eric shook his head again. "Emma," he said, raising his face to the bower of old maples that lined the street. "I give up. I just . . . give up."

Petal tugged at the lead, and they picked up their pace a little, coming to rest at the side of a busy street. Petal turned left, and Emma turned with him. "Is that a good thing?"

"What?"

"Giving up."

"Depends on you who you ask, but I can guarantee that some people aren't going to like it." He looked at her. "How are you going to contact the child's mother?"

"His name is Andrew. Drew for short."

"You didn't get that from him."

"Google is your friend," she said. "But the nickname? His mother is screaming it. Or was. He can hear her, and I'm almost positive that's what *I'm* hearing."

"He's strong," Eric said quietly.

"He's dead. What difference does strength make to the dead?"

"Well," he said, sliding his hands out of his pockets as Petal ran back. "There are always ghost stories. You've heard them. I've heard them."

"Yes, but when *I* heard them, I didn't think they were *true.*"

His smile was both faint and genuine. "The sightings are often false," he told her, "if that makes any difference."

"Not much at this particular moment. And besides, I don't want to hear about the false ones."

"All right. The real ones, then. Ghosts don't tend to haunt things. Your father doesn't, for instance, but he's here."

She spun on her heel. There was no sign of her father.

"Sorry. By 'here' I mean he's dead, and of the dead, but he's not throwing furniture at people's heads in a fury."

"Got it. Can he just show up whenever he wants?"

"You mean can he visit you?"

She nodded.

"I'm not entirely sure it's that easy. He's not without power," Eric added as the lights changed and they crossed the street, "but what he has is nothing like what Andrew has."

"Andrew's age doesn't matter?"

"No. And before you ask? I have no idea why some of the dead have more power than others. There used to be theories that said the manner of death defined the amount of power the dead would have, but that's been debunked." He looked moodily into the distance, and his eyes narrowed.

*By whom?* Emma wondered. But Eric was talking, and she didn't know how long that would last; she didn't want to interrupt him, and judging by his expression, she wasn't certain she wanted the answer.

He shook himself. "But there are some ghosts who are powerful. Powerful enough to affect the living world."

"Andrew's not."

"No. He's a step down. The ones that are, though? Those are your ghost stories, your poltergeists. They're dangerous," he added softly. "But Andrew is powerful enough. He is, however, still four years old. What he creates out of what he remembers is something you'll have to walk through to get to him—at all. To get him to *listen* to you, or anything you have to say, is going to be very, very difficult."

"Probably impossible," Emma said quietly. "I think our best chance is his mother. If she could go in there—with me—and I could touch her son, she'd be able to see him and hear him. I think he would follow her out."

"Which brings us back to the original question: How are you going to contact her?"

"Cold calls," Emma said. "We'll think of something because we *have* to think of something. I know he's already dead," she added softly, "but it seems so wrong to leave him there for god knows how long, just burning."

"Emma," he said gently, "even if you do manage to get him out of the house, he's still dead."

"So?"

"What do you think you're going to do with him once he's outside?"

She stopped walking. "Do with him?"

"He's dead, and he's lost," Eric replied, looking at Petal's back. It seemed deliberate to Emma. "If you can talk him out of the house, he'll still be both dead—and lost." He looked at her then; she was standing still, although Petal was causing a bit of a tilt.

"What do you mean, lost?"

"I mean lost. There's nowhere for him to go."

"But—that can't be right."

"Ask your father sometime. *No*, not now."

"Wait."

"Petal is going to pull your arm off."

"He'll try. Can the dead see the other dead?"

"Not always, not clearly, and not at first."

"So he couldn't see my dad?"

Eric looked at her oddly. "Not in his current state, from everything you've said. Why?"

She lowered her eyes because they suddenly stung her. "My dad," she said softly, "is good with lost kids."

He rolled his eyes, but he also smiled.

"I really don't understand you," Emma said, dredging up a smile from somewhere and surprising herself because it was genuine.

"Lucky you."

She didn't realize where Petal was headed because she was engrossed in conversation and thought. But when he led her to the fence that bordered the cemetery, she knew. She stopped walking for a moment, compressing her lips in a thin line.

"Not here," she told Petal. Petal came back to her, his tongue hanging out of his mouth. He cocked his head to one side, and after a moment she fished a Milk-Bone out of her pocket and offered it to him.

"I wasn't lying," Eric said quietly. "Graveyards really are one of the quietest places on earth."

She shook her head. "I can't," she told him.

"Why?"

"I don't want to—" She grimaced. "They're not quiet *enough*." Squaring her shoulders, she looked straight at Eric. "What did you see the night you met me here?"

"Not what you saw," he replied. It was evasive, but he didn't look away. "I saw the ghost," he continued, when she didn't speak. "She spoke to you."

"She did *way worse* than speak to me."

"What did she do?"

"I don't want to talk about it."

He laughed. The laughter grew louder as she glared at him. It was hard to glare at Eric when he was laughing.

"I didn't bring it up," he said, when he could finally stop. "But I didn't see anything other than that. She talked to you, you backed up, tripped, and banged your head."

"She handed me something," Emma said quietly. This much, she wasn't too embarrassed to say.

Eric could get so still when he was already mostly standing there. "What did she hand you?"

"A lantern. I think it was made of . . . ice."

Eric looked at her for a long moment, and then he shook his head. "Emma," he said softly, "if you ever meet any of my friends, fail to mention that."

"I haven't mentioned it to anyone but you." She paused, "And Allison."

They walked down the path into the cemetery. At this time of day, the gates weren't shut, and cars could drive in as well. Petal loved it.

"She was so old, Eric. *So* old."

He said nothing for a long moment.

"Is that how you saw her?"

"No," he said quietly.

"She looked like a bag lady out of nightmare. Why did you see her differently?"

"Some of the dead can choose their form."

"You mean they don't look the way they did when they died?"

"I mean they don't have to. Andrew, in a few decades, will probably be able to appear older, if he thinks about it."

"Why would he bother? Why would any of them bother?"

Eric shrugged. "I'm not dead," he told her. "Remember?"

"That could be arranged."

Eric laughed. Petal decided that this was his cue to get lots of attention, where attention at his age meant another Milk-Bone.

"Who was she?" Emma asked, when Petal once again decided to test the tensile strength of his leash.

He looked at her, and then looked away. "The mother of a friend," he said, in the wrong tone of voice.

She thought of the ring on his finger and said nothing. And this nothing? It was comfortable. She knew how to give him this space because in some ways, it was the space she herself needed.

Still, she hesitated as Petal began to crawl, sniff, and occasionally piss his way across the cemetery. She had never come to visit Nathan with any company but Petal before. *Nathan*, she thought. For just a moment, she wanted to see him, and she wanted it so badly she forgot to breathe.

But she remembered to breathe after a few seconds, and she remembered to keep her mouth shut. It didn't happen often, but it did happen. She covered her eyes with her hand for a few seconds, and then, when she dropped that hand, she was fine.

Eric was watching her.

"Don't," she said softly.

"Nathan?"

"I said don't."

He lifted both hands and took a step back. "I surrender. *And* I'm unarmed."

"And that," an unfamiliar voice said, "is really strange. On both counts."

Emma frowned and looked past Eric's shoulder. A boy was leaning, with one hand, against the hem of an angel's long, flowing robes. Admittedly the angel was on a pedestal on top of a tombstone that would have been at home over a dozen graves.

The stranger was taller than Eric, and his hair was an orange-red that would have been at home on Anne of Green Gables. He had green eyes, and his skin was the same pale that redheads often have, but it was dusted with freckles and rather puckish dimples.

He wore a jacket, the type of navy blue that said School, but in a cut that said Money; it had no crest. Beneath that? Collared shirt and a thin wool pullover. He also wore gray pants, with perfect pleats.

Eric grimaced and turned, slowly, to face the stranger. "Chase," he said.

"Eric." Chase grinned broadly. "I came to lend a hand; the old man said you wanted some help. Who's your friend?"

"A classmate," Eric replied tersely. "And the old man was wrong. Why don't you go play in traffic?"

"Not much traffic to play in around here, frankly. And I am bored out of my mind."

"You're always bored. Did no one ever tell you that bored people are generally also boring?"

"You have. About a thousand times." He straightened up, his hand leaving the angel's hem and falling into his pocket. His jacket pocket. "But I'm rarely bored when you're around," he added, with a grin. "So, come on, introduce us."

"I'd rather not."

Chase clucked. "Well, then, unless you're going to kill me here and now—"

"Seriously considering it, Chase."

"—I'll just introduce myself, shall I?"

Eric said, to Emma, "You don't have to be friendly. I try to offend him frequently, but he's so dense none of it sticks."

She laughed. "Are you brothers?"

They both snorted with obvious derision and then glanced at each other.

"I'll take that as a yes."

"It's a definite no," Chase said. "If he were related to me, I wouldn't let him out in public dressed that way. He's often rude, frequently sullen, and generally unfriendly."

"And Chase," Eric added, "is often rude, frequently whiny, and never shuts up. Emma, this is Chase Loern. Chase, this is Emma Hall."

"Pleased to meet you," Emma said. "I think."

Chase laughed. "You *have* been hanging around our Eric, haven't you?"

She shrugged. "He's never been rude, he's never been sullen, and he is unfailingly helpful and friendly."

"Which is another way of saying boring."

"Only to teenage boys with too much time on their hands."

Chase's red brows arched up into his hairline. "On the other hand," he said, "maybe you're meant for each other."

The silence that followed these words was both awkward and telling.

"If you'll excuse me for a moment," Eric said to Emma, recovering first. He grabbed Chase by the arm and began to drag him away, "I'm going to kill someone."

It was almost true. Eric pulled Chase around the trunk of a messy weeping willow. Chase allowed this with apparent good humor until his back was against the tree. Chase and humor were funny things, if you liked black humor liberally laced with violence. Eric often referred to him as Loki.

"What the hell are you doing?" Eric pushed him, and when Chase brought both of his hands up, let go and stepped back, finding his feet.

"You need backup," Chase replied. "I'm here."

"I don't need backup. And I don't need to babysit."

Chase's pale skin darkened. "You found the Necromancer. The Necromancer is not dead. Ergo, backup."

"I found the Necromancer; the Necromancer is not dead. I'm not dead either, and as you can see, not close. Backup doesn't equal cleanup. I don't want to have to clean up after you again."

"Is it Emma?" Chase asked. He waited for a half-beat and then said, "Don't be stupid, Eric."

Eric said nothing.

"You've historically had a weakness for the girls." A brief grin animated Chase's mouth.

Eric didn't try to break his jaw, but that took effort.

"Well?"

"Don't make me kill you."

Chase laughed. He would. But he could laugh just before he killed, and he could laugh a good deal after, as well. "I think that's a yes." His amused expression vanished, as if it had just run for its life. "What's your game, here?"

Eric really did not want to kill Chase. "She's not what—or who—I expected."

Red eyebrows disappeared into hairline. Chase was genuinely shocked. Eric could tell, because Chase didn't have anything to say for almost two minutes.

"You need to take a vacation," was all he could manage.

"After this."

"Now. Are you *out of your mind*? She's *not what you expected*?"

"Keep it down," Eric said quietly, nodding in the direction of Emma, which also happened to be in the direction of the willow.

"Pardon me for being outraged. If they find her—and you know damn well they will—you *know* what she'll become. What she *is* now doesn't make a goddamn difference. She's a fucking *Necromancer*, Eric!"

"The rest of her life is about what she is," Eric replied quietly. This usually didn't work with Chase; Chase generally spoke as if conversational volume had to be a constant.

Chase was still shocked. He reached into his pocket and pulled out his phone. Eric pivoted and kicked it out of his hand; it flew, like an ungainly silver bird, in an arc past the tree.

"How many times have I saved your life?"

"About as many," Chase said, still staring in the direction of the phone, "as I've saved yours."

Eric snorted. "Good to see you're still incapable of counting." He lowered his hands. "Give me a week."

"A week to do *what*? She's not going to get *less* dangerous in a week!"

"Give me a week, Chase."

"Fuck that." Chase started to move, and Eric blocked him.

"Give me a goddamn week, or we can finish what we started the first time we met."

The silence was profound. They had so much history, these two. They argued like the brothers they technically weren't, but beneath those arguments they had always shared a single, common goal.

"I'm not going back to the old man," Chase finally said.

"No. You're not."

"Eric, he'll know. We're the two best agents he's got. If we don't call in, if we don't tell him the Necromancer is dead, he'll come himself."

"I'll deal with that if it happens."

"*When* it happens. What the hell is so special about that girl, anyway?"

"Nothing that would make any difference to you."

"And what's going to happen in a week?"

Eric tensed and stepped back slightly, adjusting his stance. Chase saw, and he noted it, drawing himself in as well. "She's going to try to talk a four-year-old ghost out of the burned-out wreck of his home."

"What?"

"You heard me."

Chase laughed. "Are you *kidding* me?"

"No."

"Does she even know what you are?"

"No. She doesn't care, either. I can stay away," he added, "or I can be there; she's going to try anyway."

"And you intend to help her."

"How? I've got nothing to help with. She's already singed her hair," he added, "and she's determined to keep going."

"So you get out of killing her when she dies."

"Pretty much."

Chase put his hands down. "You're taking too many risks."

It was true. Eric didn't deny it because he couldn't. He also didn't relax his own stance, because he was dealing with Chase.

"I understand why you're pissed off," Eric said. "And I understand why she's a threat. But I would rather she died that way than—"

"Than by your hand."

"Pretty much. I don't want to kill her, Chase. I can't think of the last time that happened."

"Because, clearly, you were *still sane* before. Look, buddy, don't weaken here." Chase stretched. "I'll give you the week." And he held up his pinky.

Eric grimaced. He *hated* this part.

"Shake on it, pinky shake, or we don't have a deal."

"You're an asshole," Eric told him.

"Pretty much." He waited until Eric did, in fact, lock pinkies with him.

"But you know," Chase added, "You owe me a phone if that one's broken."

"I'll buy you another phone."

"And there better be someone around here to kill. I don't like to get dressed up for nothing."

# CHAPTER
# EIGHT

EMMA, WHO COULD RECOGNIZE an argument-in-the-making when she saw it, had retreated, skirting the stone angel with its ostentatious pedestal and heading toward more familiar markers. Daylight transformed them, as it often did, but Petal didn't seem to notice. He paused in front of standing wreaths, sniffed his way across the mostly shorn grass, and headed more or less straight to Nathan's grave.

Emma approached the headstone quietly. It looked so new, compared to many of the others; light glinted over the sheen of perfect, polished stone.

Eric could see the dead. Eric said that the dead didn't gather in graveyards.

She knelt, slowly, in front of the headstone. Usually she sat farther back, but today she chose to sit within touching distance. She could see her reflection across its surface, broken only by the engraved grooves of letters and numbers.

Her reflection. His name, yes. But she was alone.

Petal padded over and sniffed at her pockets, and she pulled a broken Milk-Bone out and held it in her open palm. He ate it, of course, and then dropped his head into her lap. She smiled and glanced up again. She was alone except for her big, old, stupid dog. On impulse, she wrapped her arms around his neck and hugged him.

Nathan wasn't here.

But then again, she hadn't come here for his sake. And it *was* quiet, in the graveyard. She'd missed that the past few days. She certainly wasn't going to experience any of it tonight.

Petal's head rose and reminded her that on some days, quiet was a lost cause. On the other hand, he was a good early-warning system. She stood, straightening her jacket and rearranging the pleats of her skirt, and then turned to see who he was barking at.

She felt both guilty and relieved when it wasn't Nathan's mother. Eric, standing about twenty feet away, slid his hands into his pockets, and waited for her to leave the space she'd created for herself here. She did, walking carefully between the headstones.

"Do you think Amy would mind if Chase tagged along tonight?"

"Probably less than you will," she offered.

Chase laughed.

"If she called the police on him, I'd be grateful." Eric was smiling.

"If he does anything that would make a police visit worthwhile, there probably won't be enough of him left to take into custody."

Chase lifted a hand. "Bored with being talked about in the third person now."

"Sorry," Emma said, cheerfully.

"That's sorry? Try harder."

"I'll work on it," she promised. "I have to get home and get changed. Do you want to meet me back at my place, or do you want me to text you Amy's address?"

"We'll meet you at your place," Chase said cheerfully.

Eric hesitated, then shrugged.

\*     \*     \*

"You gave me a week."

Chase, sharpening his knife, shrugged. "We can't afford to lose you, too."

Eric stiffened. "What happened?"

"The old man sent Else and Brand out hunting. Brand didn't make it back."

Else and Brand worked on a different continent. "They found the Necromancer?"

"Yeah. He wasn't alone." Metal scraped against stone in a way that was both soothing and dissonant. "Eric—"

Eric started to clean the kitchen.

"Don't wash anything," Chase said, putting the knife down.

Eric ignored him.

"You don't put the cutlery in the water *first*. Glasses. Glasses first." He elbowed Eric to the side. "This is your idea of hot water?"

"Chase—"

"You had to choose the only house in the neighborhood without a dishwasher?"

"It was the only one in range for sale."

Chase ignored this and turned on the hot water. "The old man's worried," he said to the rising steam. "I think he's done with solo hunting assignments for a while."

"You haven't talked to him?"

"I gave you a week. And I'm not going to be the one to tell him the Necromancer's still not dead, and we're going to a *party*."

"Amy's party," Eric said, giving up on the washing.

"Where are you going?"

"To get our jackets." He wasn't really looking forward to Chase's reaction when he saw them.

Emma fed and watered Petal before she went foraging in the fridge for something that resembled dinner. Although Emma could cook, and sometimes even enjoyed it, she seldom bothered when it was only herself she was feeding. It was too much like work. And it wasn't as if there wasn't going to be food at Amy's. It was almost 7:00 by the time she headed up the stairs to get changed.

She phoned Allison first. "Hey, Ally, how is Michael getting to Amy's?"

"Philipa's picking him up."

"Isn't that a little far for her to walk?"

"She's driving."

Philipa was not, perhaps, the worst driver known to man. She was, however, in the running. "We needed new lampposts anyway. Are his parents coming to get him, or are we supposed to get him home?"

"I told his mother we'd get him home. When are you leaving?"

"I'm not sure. Eric's meeting me here, and we'll leave when he shows up. Did you want us to pick you up on the way?"

"Philipa's also picking me up."

Emma laughed. "I hope Michael appreciates this."

"It's Michael," Allison replied.

There was a long pause.

"Emma? Em, are you there?"

"Yes," Emma said softly, "but I have to go. My—my dad's here."

Brendan Hall was standing in front of the computer, his arms folded. He didn't move, but the computer screen blinked on, and the screen began to flicker as windows opened. Emma watched in silence for a moment, the hair on the back of her neck beginning to rise.

"Dad?"

He nodded without turning, and Emma knew what he would be looking at: the Letter Graveyard. The place where anonymous people—or people who used handles like **imsocrazy** and **deathhead666** at any rate—sent letters that would never be read.

Except that these *were*.

"Sprout," he said quietly, reading—of course—the letters she had sent him over the years. She tried to remember if anything in them was horribly embarrassing, but she couldn't.

"I missed you," she said softly, answering the comment he didn't—and hopefully wouldn't—make. "Sometimes it helped. To write. Even if you couldn't read it."

"Your mother knew about this?"

"Of course not. She'd just worry. I mean, worry *more*." Emma paused and then asked, "Were you always watching?"

"No. Not for the first year. Not really for the second."

She hesitated. She wanted to touch him. To hug him. But she remembered the cold of his hands, so much like the lantern, and instead curled her fingers into fists and kept them at her sides. "Dad, can I ask you something?"

He sat in her chair, and she turned it so that he was facing her. His eyes were still oddly colored, and they suggested a light that burned beneath the surface of what looked, to Emma, to be perfectly normal skin. There was no translucency to him, nothing to mark him as a ghost, although if she were being truthful, she didn't *want* to see him that way. "Ask," he said, in that quiet father's voice of his that meant he was serious and paying attention.

"Is it true that after you died, you had nowhere to go?"

The silence was lengthy. In Hall parlance, this usually meant yes.

"Em," he finally said, "I'm dead. You're not. You should concern yourself with the living."

"I concern myself," she replied tightly, "with the things that concern me. Is it true?"

"What did Eric tell you?"

"Pardon?"

"What did Eric say about this?"

"He told me to ask you, if you want the truth."

Her father nodded as if this made sense. "Yes."

She almost laughed, but it would have been a strained laugh; she kept it behind her lips. "So . . . you've been stuck here for almost six years, with nowhere to go?"

"Yes."

"And what about the others?"

"The others?"

"The other dead people. The other ghosts."

"There are people," he told her quietly, "that have been trapped here far longer than I have. I have you," he added. "I have your mother. I can watch you, sometimes, and see how you've grown. How both of you have grown. I've never been able to speak with you before, but—your presence here attracts me. It binds me," he added.

"Binds you?"

"It keeps me here."

Emma was silent for a few minutes. At length she said, her voice thicker, "What about the others?"

"When the people they knew in life die, there's nothing to keep them where their lives once were."

"And they move on?"

He was silent. It was not a good silence.

"Dad, where do they *go*?"

He rose, as if the chair were confining, but he didn't turn to face his daughter; instead, he walked to the window. Shaking his head, he let his hands drop. "Emma, can you understand that I don't want you involved in this if it's at all possible?"

"No. I'm not eight years old anymore," she added, feeling slightly defensive. "And I *am* involved. I can see you. I can talk to you." She took a deep breath. "I don't want you to leave," she said starkly. "I'm selfish enough to be happy that I can still talk with you. It's been so long.

"But if you're trapped here, if you're trapped in this—this half-life, I don't want that. I want you to be here because you want to be. I don't want you to be here because you have no place else to go." She hesitated, then said, "There's a four-year-old boy who's trapped in a burning house."

He did turn his head to look at her then.

"I don't want him to stay trapped there. He—Eric says his memories are strong enough that he stays in the burning building and strong enough that when I approach the house, it burns *me*. But he's four. And I want him to come out of that house. I don't want him to stay there forever.

"And I'm going to *get him out*. Don't even think of trying to talk me out of it."

His smile was rueful, but she saw the pride in it, and it was brighter, for a moment, than the odd luminescence. "I wouldn't dream of it, Sprout."

"But Eric says . . . if I manage to get him out somehow, he's still lost. He has nowhere to go. Dad," she added, her voice dropping to a whisper, "he's *four*. I don't want him to be stuck wandering the streets alone until his mother finally dies. Is that going to happen to him?"

"If he's lucky," her father replied. He shoved his hands into his pockets. But he looked at the curtains, and after a moment, Emma crossed the room to open them herself. To let the light in.

"It's not that we're not drawn," he told her. "It's not that we don't know *where* to go when we die. There *is* a place for us. We can't *get there*, but we're always aware of it."

"Can't get there?"

He nodded. "It's like looking through glass. But it's not glass; we can't shatter it. We can't pass through it."

Emma folded her arms tightly across her chest. "Where is it?"

"It's not a geographical location, Em. I can't pull up Google Maps and point it out."

"But you could find it?"

"I could find it now. I could find it now without moving." He rose and made his way to the window that Emma had revealed. "But it's painful. To see it, to see what I can only describe as light, and to be shut out forever. The dead, especially the newly dead, will often gather there, wailing."

She didn't ask her father if that's what he'd done because she didn't want to know. Her father had been the pillar of the world with his patience, his quirky humor, his ability to override anger. "If you free your four-year-old, that will be where he's drawn, if he's lucky. He won't see the others," her father added. "Not immediately. But he'll linger, for a year or two."

"It's got to be better than burning," she whispered.

"It's better," he agreed. But his tone said *it's the same.*

"What's on the other side of the glass?"

"Home," he replied softly. "Peace. Warmth. I would say love, but I don't think any one of us can say for certain because we can't reach it. We're like moths, Em," he added.

"And this is *lucky*?"

He glanced at her, then, and she knew he had come to the end of the words he was willing to share. But she'd lived with him for years. "Dad?"

"Yes?"

"When I touched you in the hospital, Mom could see you."

He closed his eyes.

"Why?"

"I won't answer that either, Em. Don't ask."

"Why?"

"Because Eric, if I'm not mistaken, is already having some difficulty with you, and I would like very much that it not get harder for him."

"For *him*. Why?"

"Because," her father said, "he'll have to kill you, or try, and while I want to see you, I want you to have a life. You've only just started," he added softly.

"But *why* will he have to kill me?"

"Because he'll see only what he fears in you. He won't see what he admires." Her father lifted one hand. "I can't judge him," he added softly. "I can hate him, but I can't judge him. Don't touch me. Don't touch *any* of the dead."

"If I don't touch the child, his mother won't be able to see him."

His father looked at her, his expression darkening. But he knew her, knew her far better than Eric did; he said nothing. Instead, he began to fade.

Conversation over.

When Eric came to the door, Petal was already there, barking his lungs out. The Hall household didn't need an alarm system; they had Petal. On the other hand, alarm systems didn't require feeding, watering, walking, and endless cleanup.

Emma opened the door and let herself out, locking the door while Petal's barking deteriorated into a steady, guilt-inducing whine.

"Michael?" Eric asked, and she smiled. He was wearing a gray collared shirt and dark jeans but otherwise looked entirely like himself.

"Allison's got that taken care of."

Chase, on the other hand, had decided to go insane. His red hair was a mass of gel, he wore incredibly angular sunglasses, and he wore a tank under a black leather jacket that looked more like studs than coat.

"You," she told him, "don't get to tell Eric how to dress."

He lowered the rim of said glasses. "Thank you. You don't clean up badly yourself. Are we ready to go?"

"One of us was ready half an hour ago," Eric told him.

"Two of us," Emma said helpfully. They headed down the walk to Eric's car. She stood by the back passenger door, and when the locks clicked, she got in. Chase took the front passenger seat, and Eric got behind the wheel of the car.

"I should warn you," Eric told Emma, "that I will kill Chase if he divulges any personal information of an embarrassing nature. So if you like him at all, don't ask."

Emma laughed.

"Easy for you," Chase muttered, "since he's not going to kill *you* for asking."

It had been such a long week. It felt as though Tuesday night had happened months ago. Emma stared out the window as the streets moved past, thinking about her father. Thinking, as well, about Nathan, and where Nathan might be. It was hard. She worked *not* to think about him, but she wasn't used to it; there had been no reason not to think of him before.

A year, her father had said. Maybe two. Two years, and then he'd drift back, either to his home or to hers.

"Emma?"

"Hmmm?" She looked up. "Oh, sorry. I forgot." She started to give him the directions he needed to get them to Amy's.

If there had been any question about which house the party was at, it was answered definitively the minute the car doors were opened: You could hear the music from the street. Emma listened for a few tense minutes and then relaxed.

"DJ?"

"Yeah. Last time she did this, she hired a band."

Eric laughed.

"I'm not kidding. The band was louder," she added, "and they kind of had to be escorted out of the house when one of them got dead drunk and started hitting on anything that moved. And I mean *anything*."

"Escorted how?"

"Oh, the usual. Someone called the police before things got really ugly." She shrugged and added, "Not that it wasn't ugly afterward. Mr. Drunk and Amorous really didn't appreciate the shabby treatment and he broke a few things to make his point."

"She does this often?"

"Not too often. Depends on what her parents have been doing—or not doing, in this case."

"Not doing?"

"Not taking her to New York City, for a start."

Eric glanced at Chase, and Chase shrugged. "What's so great about New York City?" he asked.

"Everything, basically. Look, if you can avoid saying that anywhere where Amy can actually hear you, things will go a lot smoother."

"What?" Chase shouted, as they approached the front door.

"Good point," Emma grinned, shouting back.

Amy's house was huge. If palaces had been built in a modern style, they would probably have been only slightly larger; Emma's whole house, from top to bottom, would fill only two of the rooms. The grounds—and really, only Amy's house had grounds, everyone else being stuck with simple lawns—extended back into a forested ravine, and the front was only disturbed by a circular road that was too wide to be called a driveway. There was, of course, a sidewalk beside the road.

Chase whistled.

"Amy's family is pretty well off," Emma admitted.

Chase knocked on the door, and Emma hit the doorbell instead. Had Allison been standing beside her, they would now be betting on how many times she would have to hit the doorbell before someone actually heard it. But Eric and Chase were not Allison.

And the answer was five.

Amy's brother answered the door, which surprised Emma enough that her smile froze on her face.

"Hey," he shouted.

"Skip?" This was not actually his name, but for some reason, it was what all of Amy's friends called him. Emma suspected that this was a leftover artifact from elementary school excursions through the mansion that was Amy's house, but she couldn't remember for certain. "Aren't you on the east coast?"

"Something came up," he replied. "I had to come home for a few days. Good damn thing I did," he added, although she saw the beer in his hand. "Someone needs to keep an eye out. If the neighbors call the police again, Amy'll be homeless. These friends of yours?"

She nodded. "Eric's in our year, but he's new to the school. Chase is his cousin."

"Chase? What kind of a name is that?"

"Skip?"

He laughed. "Good point. *Amy!* The last member of the Emery mafia is here!"

Eric looked at Emma, who reddened slightly.

"Mafia?"

"Don't ask. Skip has no sense of humor. Unfortunately, he still tries."

Eric laughed, and they entered the house as Skip left the door and wandered away. Emma caught up with him before he got too far. "Skip, do you know where Allison is?"

"Who?"

"Never mind."

Amy's house was huge. It had five bathrooms, not including the pow-der room in the main foyer—a powder room that even without shower or bath was still bigger than the main bathroom in the Hall household. The foyer itself was larger than the living room and dining room in the Hall house combined, but at the moment, the rows upon rows of shoes and fall boots that lined the walls near the door made it look slightly less palatial.

"I'm *not* taking my boots off," Chase said loudly.

"Why? Someone's going to steal them?"

He bent down and picked up a pair of running shoes. "They're better than *these*," he said, with obvious disdain. "Or these," he added, choos-ing a different pair. "Or these."

Eric smacked him on the back of the head.

Unfazed, Chase pointed at Eric's shoes. "Or those. And Eric would definitely steal these."

Emma said, "Suit yourself. But Amy's pretty particular about the shoes in her house, and if she sees you wearing those, you'll probably be waiting outside in the car."

"But you can wear yours?"

"Mine," she replied, "are part of the outfit. And I don't wear them outside much."

"So are mine, damn it. I'm wearing *white socks*!"

She raised her eyebrows. "What, white socks in *that* get-up?"

"They're all Eric had!"

"You did *not* get that crappy jacket out of Eric's closet!"

"Kids," Eric said, putting a hand on both of their shoulders. "Could we maybe save this for Amy?"

Emma grimaced. "If you make it a fashion question, Chase might be able to get away with the boots." She shook her head and added, "White socks."

Finding Amy was not as easy in practice as it was in theory, which, given that she always stood out, said something. As Emma was mostly concerned with finding Allison, this didn't bother her too much.

"You recognize all these people?" Eric shouted. Everything, at the moment, had to be shouted, but you expected that at Amy's big parties.

Emma shook her head, because she didn't really enjoy shouting all that much.

"Do you recognize *half* of them?"

She nodded, because it was more or less true. You *also* expected that with any of Amy's big parties. "Just look for Allison."

"What?"

"*Allison.*"

"No, but I see Michael."

"Where?"

He pointed into a crowd so dense there seemed to be more people than floor space. Before she could tell him—loudly, because there wasn't much choice—how helpful this wasn't, he rolled his eyes and grabbed her by the arm.

Two people trying to snake their way through a thick crowd are notably less coordinated than one. Emma, who felt she already knew this, didn't really appreciate the refresher course. On the other hand, she had to admit that it would have taken twenty minutes to cut across this particular room, and Eric had just carved about fifteen minutes off that. He had also almost knocked four people over, although the sound at her back implied that almost was no longer the correct word for at least one of them.

She looked around and realized that he was actually heading toward the large, enclosed sunroom. Or, more accurately, the sliding doors that led from the slate-floored, sparsely decorated room, with its wicker chairs and footrests, to the patio. She realized, again, that Eric was actually taller than she thought, because he could see Michael standing outside in the floodlights. Even in her shoes, she hadn't.

Michael was, not surprisingly, talking to Oliver. He was also, therefore, not paying much attention to anything else that was going on around him. But Allison was standing just to one side of them, out of the worst of the lights' glare, and Emma shook herself free of Eric and ran over to her.

"Sorry," she said. "But you and Michael are still in one piece, so I'm assuming there was no menace to telephone poles."

"And we didn't run any stop signs, either. Philipa's really gotten a lot better behind the wheel of a car. You didn't have any trouble?" There was a slight tinge of anxiety in the question.

"Us? No. We're late because Chase took his time getting dressed."

"Chase?"

Emma nodded in Chase's general direction. "The redhead in the studs."

"I heard that," Chase said. In the bright lights of the patio, he looked even worse. His skin was washed out, and his hair looked like a bad edifice that might just topple if you breathed on it the wrong way.

"Allison, this is Chase. He's a friend of Eric's. Chase, this is Allison, *my best friend*."

Chase immediately put both of his hands up in the universal gesture of surrender. Allison laughed, and to Emma's surprise, Chase—in his black leather—smiled. "I'm not stupid. Eric's afraid of Emma," he said to Allison.

Eric glared at him.

"I'm not technically allowed to embarrass him in public," Chase added, by way of explanation. "Like the jacket?"

"It's . . . interesting," Allison replied.

"I can't stand it either."

Allison laughed again. Emma turned to stare at Chase.

"What, do I have an enormous zit or something?"

"She is staring at you," Eric replied, when Emma failed to answer, "because you are actually capable of charm, and this is the first time you've shown any."

"I figured she's used to no charm." Chase's smile was very smug. "She's spent the week with you, after all."

Allison was polite enough not to laugh out loud at this but amused enough not to be able to keep the smile off her face. "Are you sure you're not brothers?"

"Please," Chase said, at the same time as Eric said "Positive." He turned to glance at Michael, Connell, and Oliver, who existed at the moment in their own world.

"I don't suppose you play Dungeons and Dragons?" Allison asked Chase.

"Not often."

Emma stared at him again.

"What?"

"Fourth edition rules, if you want to join the discussion," Allison said politely.

Emma gave Allison a look, and Allison laughed. "Or not."

"Have you seen Amy at all?"

"Sort of. Her brother showed up yesterday, with a friend from law school in tow."

"Good looking?"

"Very. And impeccably dressed. I think. Do you want to meet him?"

"No."

"Well, then, I suggest we move," Allison replied. "And quickly, because they're heading this way."

"Emma!" Amy's voice—which was, like the rest of her, exceptional—cleared the distance between them as Emma squared her shoulders and fixed a friendly, party smile to her lips. She turned in time to see Amy step through the open doors, followed by the sound of very loud music, Skip, and a stranger.

Amy was wearing a black and white dress. It was cut to suggest, in some ways, a harlequin, but it was fitted, and the black diamonds that trailed from throat to hem glittered; the white was soft and pale in comparison. Her hair framed her face and fell, in a thick drape, down her back. Her shoes were the inverse of the dress; black with a single white diamond.

She looked, in short, fabulous. Emma, who had long since given up any attempt to compete with Amy, repressed a sigh. Which, Amy being Amy, was noticed anyway. "Well?" she said, demanding her due.

"You are *gorgeous*. And I love the shoes!" Emma, on the other hand, was perfectly willing to grant what was due.

"Notice the earrings?"

"No—come here."

Amy did. The earrings were also black and white—but they were the yin and yang symbols, not the straight lines of trapezoids. "Nicely understated," Emma told her.

Amy nodded, satisfied. "I like your dress," she added. Which, to be fair, was a genuine compliment, because if Amy *didn't* like your dress, the best you could pray for was silence.

Because she had perfect timing, Amy paused and then looked at Chase. Whose dress, for want of a better word, she didn't care for. "Emma?"

"This is Chase," Emma said quickly. "He's a good friend of Eric's."

"Really?"

"Eric doesn't dress him," Emma said, with a perfectly straight face.

Chase, on the other hand, had fallen silent. While Emma was used to this reaction when a new guy was put in the vicinity of Amy, it was the wrong type of silence for someone like Chase. She glanced at him and then turned to look at Eric.

Both of them were utterly still. And both of them wore the same expression, or the same lack of expression; it was as if something had sucked all the life and warmth from their faces. What it left was disturbing.

Amy noticed it as well, but, being Amy, she ignored it. She turned as Skip and his friend joined them. "Skip," she said, "this is Eric, a friend from school. He's new here," she added helpfully. "This is his friend, Chase. Eric, Chase, this is my brother. And this is his friend, Merrick Longland. They met at the beginning of term at Dalhousie."

Merrick Longland stepped into the light, standing with his back to Michael and his friends, who remained entirely unaware of encroaching strangers. He was, as Allison had said, impeccably dressed. The dress in question was casual, not formal, but there was something about the crisp lines of a loosely fitted coal jacket and the collarless white shirt beneath it that suggested formality. The shirt was partly unbuttoned, and the telltale gleam of a gold pendant lay across his exposed chest. Emma didn't notice what kind of pants he wore. She noticed that his hair was a short, clean-cut brown, that his cheekbones were high, that his chin was neither too prominent nor too slight; she noticed that his brows were thick.

But mostly, in that quiet moment that exists just after you've drawn and held breath, she noticed his eyes. They were gleaming, faintly, as if lit from behind, and she could not honestly say, then or later, what color they actually were.

Merrick smiled, and it was a deep, pleasant smile; it transformed the lines of his face without exactly softening them.

"Merrick," Amy said, although her voice now sounded quiet and slightly distant, "this is Emma Hall. She's one of the Emery Mafia," she added.

"Emma?" Merrick said. He held out a hand.

Emma stared at it, as if she couldn't quite remember what to do. Shaking her head, she grimaced. She held out her hand in turn, and he grasped it firmly in his.

His hand was *cold*. Not like ice, but like winter skin. She started to pull back, which no amount of apology could excuse or convert into good manners, but his hand tightened.

"Oh, Emma," he said softly. "We've only just been introduced, and I think we have a lot to say to each other."

"I—I'm here with friends," she replied, knowing how lame it would sound even before the words left her mouth.

"Ah. Yes. That could be awkward." His eyes, the eyes that were somehow luminescent, flared in the dark of night sky, becoming what the soul of fire would be, if fire had a soul.

And then the world stopped.

CHAPTER
NINE

I N THE BRIGHT LIGHTS OF THE PATIO, all the shadows cast against the stonework suddenly stopped moving. The music, transformed by solid glass into the thumping of loud bass, continued its steady, frantic beat—but no one was shouting to be heard.

No one, it appeared, was talking much at all. She couldn't tell if they were even trying; she couldn't look away from his face. She knew. She'd tried. But she could see their shadows—Amy's, Skip's. Allison, Eric, and Chase cast shadows that fell past her line of vision.

"Better?" Merrick Longland asked.

"No."

He smiled. It wasn't meant as a threatening smile; Emma was certain he meant it to be friendly. But her hand was cold, and she could have shaved her dog with the edges around that smile. She tried to dredge up an answering smile from somewhere, and she managed. Unfortunately, it was the same as the smile you offered a dangerously furious dog while you were carefully reaching for a big stick.

"What have you done?" she asked, speaking softly because the unnatural quiet almost demanded it.

"I've provided us with a little bit of privacy."

"I don't think we need it." It was hard to keep her voice even.

"It's better. For them," he added. "There are things I have to tell you—things about yourself—that they don't need to hear."

"Need to hear?"

He nodded. "I'll be brief, because I have to be; this is costly. When Skip mentioned that his sister was having a party, I didn't realize I would have to control a small village's worth of teenagers."

She laughed; it was a thin sound, and it quavered too much. "It's one of *Amy's* parties." From his expression, it was clear that there were people in the world who hadn't heard of Amy's parties. And while Emma knew this was in theory possible, it wasn't often that she met them.

"We can explore the delights of Amy's party in a few minutes." He was clearly underimpressed. "What I have to say to you is important. Your life is in danger. I was delayed some few days in my arrival," he added, "but so were our enemies, it appears."

"What do you mean?"

"You're alive. The delay might have cost you your life. There are people who will be hunting you, and if they had found you before I did, you'd be dead. But I have some measure of defense against them."

She nodded carefully. "I'm willing to talk about this, but I want you to let go of my hand."

"I imagine you do. And I will. I mean you no harm," he added. "I traveled here, at some risk to myself, to save your life."

"Who would want to kill me?" But she knew. And it seemed very important at this minute that she keep that knowledge to herself.

"No one you would know. But they know what you are, Emma. And I know what you are. Shall I show you?"

She started to say no. She wanted to say no. But she said nothing, mute, as the hair on the back of her neck began to rise. She felt as if she were at the science center again, one hand on either of two balls that produced enough static to literally make all the hair on her head stand on end.

It wasn't as bad as that. But it *felt* that way.

"Come," he said, in a commanding tone of voice. "Show yourself."

Emma frowned, her brows drawing together. She even started to speak, but she lost the words. Beside Longland, thin tendrils of what looked like smoke began to appear in the air. He spoke a word that was so sharp and curt she didn't catch it. Didn't want to. Eyes wide, she watched as the smoke began to coalesce into a shape that was both strange and familiar. A woman's shape. A young woman.

Her eyes were the same odd shade of light that Brendan Hall's eyes had been; her hair was black, and her skin was pale, although whether that was because of the lighting, Emma couldn't say. She wore a sundress, the print faded, the material unfamiliar—although Emma had no doubt that Amy would recognize it instantly if she could see it.

"Hello," Emma said to the girl, speaking quietly. It was an entirely different quiet than she had offered Longland, because the girl was afraid.

The girl looked at Emma but did not speak.

"You see her, don't you?" Longland asked.

Emma nodded. "Who was she?"

Longland frowned. "Who was she?" It was clearly not the question he expected.

"When she was alive." Remembering that she actually had manners, Emma turned her attention to the girl. "I'm sorry, that was rude."

The girl's eyes widened slightly.

"My name is Emma Hall," Emma continued, lifting her left hand, because she couldn't actually offer the girl her right one; Longland hadn't let it go. "What's yours?"

Longland's frown deepened. He glanced at the girl; it was a cold glance and a dismissive one. "Answer," he said curtly.

The girl remained mute.

Longland's expression shifted again. "Answer her."

"If she doesn't want to answer, it's okay," Emma said, raising her voice.

Longland said, "When you understand your gift better, you will understand why you are wrong." Each word was clipped; he was angry. "*Answer her*." When a name failed to emerge, he suddenly lifted a hand.

"Merrick, don't—"

But he didn't strike the girl. He *yanked*, and when he did, Emma could see a thin, golden chain around his fingers. It was fine, like spidersilk, and she had missed it because it was almost impossible to see. But she *had* seen it, and she was now aware of it and determined to remain so. The strand ran from his hand *into* the heart of the girl. The girl staggered, her face rippling—literally rippling—in pain.

"Emily Gates," the girl replied, and the sound of her voice was so *wrong* Emma almost cried out in fear. Before she could think, she slapped Merrick, and even as his eyes were widening in shock, she reached out for that golden chain, and she *pulled*.

The chain snapped in her hand, and she held its end.

Merrick Longland still held her right hand, however. All smile, all friendliness, was gone. "You will give that back to me," he said, each word distinct and sharp. "Now."

In answer, Emma tried to yank her right hand free. Longland didn't move. She tried harder, and reaching out with his left hand, he grabbed her by the chin. "Give it back, Emma. Don't force me to be unpleasant. No one can hear you," he added, lowering his voice. "And at parties of this type, bad things sometimes happen."

His fingers tightened as he drew closer.

She tried to pull back.

And then she heard a familiar voice in the silence, and she froze.

Michael said, "Leave her *alone*."

Longland's brows twisted in a mixture of confusion, anger, and surprise, but he released Emma, shoving her back before he started to turn.

"Michael! No!"

A familiar and much-maligned book suddenly and unexpectedly connected with the side of Longland's face. It was—Emma could see the title flash by beneath the bright lights—the 4th edition Dungeon Master's guide. She promised that she would never *ever* roll her eyes at that book again.

Noise returned as Longland staggered back. Emma, hands free, began to run to Michael's side, but Eric grabbed her around the waist and yanked her off her feet.

"Allison!" he shouted, "Grab Michael! Grab Michael now!"

Allison's familiar form darted slightly in front of Emma. She didn't grab Michael, but she did touch his arm and his shoulder with both of her hands; he was panting, heavily, his precious book clutched in knuckles that even Emma could see were white.

She saw Chase run past them, reflecting more light than the glass doors did.

"Michael," Allison said, in her steady, even voice, "It's dangerous. Come stand with Emma and me."

"He was trying to hurt Emma," Michael said, still staring at Longland.

"Allison!" Eric shouted.

"He was trying to hurt Emma," Allison agreed, "but he didn't. Emma is safe with Eric. Come back, Michael." She drew him toward Eric and Emma. Emma could see that her hands were shaking. "Emma—what's happening?"

"I don't know. But it's bad. Michael, Allison—" she stopped speaking because Chase had reached Longland. Emma suddenly knew exactly why he had refused to take off his boots; his leg snapped out, and he kicked Longland in the head. Longland staggered and then threw up his arms.

The grass around the patio burst into white and green flame. So did Chase.

"Emma!" Longland shouted. "Come!"

"Fuck," Eric said, under his breath. Had his mouth not been so close to her ear, she wouldn't have caught it. "Emma, stay *here*. Do *not* interfere. Do *not* run away." And then he was gone, racing across the patio stones toward Chase.

For ten long seconds the flames burned in silence. Eric ran, and Emma, watching him, felt the ghost of his arm around her waist, the tickle of his words in her ear. She saw Chase moving through the fire; saw that it followed him like white shadow. She couldn't see his expression, couldn't hear his voice—if he said anything at all. But he moved *slowly*, and she thought she could see the black curl of burning hair rising from his head.

Eric would help him, somehow.

Lifting her hands to her mouth, cupping them on either side of her lips, she shouted. "Oliver, Connell! Come here!" She glanced quickly at Michael and saw that Allison was holding onto his arm.

"Emma?"

She'd forgotten Amy. Under normal circumstances she would have bet that wasn't possible. "*Oliver!*" Turning, she glanced at Amy. Amy was pale, but confusion in Amy seldom gave way to raw fear.

"Tell me," she said, "that our back lawn isn't burning."

Emma swallowed.

"Never mind. Skip, call emergency. *Everyone else*," she added, raising her voice into the stratosphere, "*get back into the house*."

Years of obeying Amy had engendered a purely Pavlovian response to her commands. They all started to head toward the door taking slow, jerky steps, looking at the fight, at the lawn.

But it was Amy who held them up at the door. "Skip?"

Emma glanced at Skip and saw that he hadn't moved.

"*Skip*."

He was standing there, teetering. Amy ran back to him, looked at him closely, and then slapped him across the face. He turned, slowly, to look at her, his brows gathering, his eyes widening in confusion. "Amy?" He spoke slowly.

"Give me your phone," she said, holding out her hand.

"My what? What are you doing here?"

"I live here, remember?"

He blinked. Emma saw the color of his face, and she shouted a warning to Amy just before his eyes rolled to white, like a screen whose projector has just died. He crumpled at the knees, and Amy managed—barely—to stop his forehead from smacking into the flagstones.

"I *do not* believe this," Amy said, under her breath, as Emma ran back to help her. "Tell me my brother's friend is not fighting with Eric and Chase near the hedges."

"Let's just get Skip inside."

"Rifle his pockets for his damn phone," Amy replied, grunting as they each grabbed him under an arm. "My mother is going to murder me if they burn down the garden."

Emma laughed. It was entirely the wrong type of laughter, and she wouldn't have been surprised if Amy had slapped her as well. Hysteria had that effect on Amy.

Longland had retreated to the hedges. Blood trickled down his forehead, and his lip was swollen. His eyes widened as he saw Eric approaching at a run, but they narrowed quickly as he crossed his wrists over his chest.

Chase was caught in the soul-fire, slowed by it; it hadn't yet managed to eat its way past his defenses. But it would if the Necromancer wasn't brought down soon.

Stupid, stupid, *stupid*. Eric hadn't expected to find a Necromancer at Amy's party. He hadn't been prepared. His damn shoes were in the endless hall of shoes that was Amy's vestibule. Chase had kept his head, Chase had stayed focused. He hated it when Chase was right.

Eric slid the one weapon he always carried out of its sheath beneath his shirt. Chase, being paranoid, was probably bristling with knives, but he could only wield two, and even in the stretched warp and weft of space around the Necromancer, Eric could see that he carried one knife in each hand.

Longland hissed a word that broke in three places, and Eric threw himself to the side as the air above the garden grass crackled. He saw night and soul-fire expand in a bubble, stretching and twisting the earth beneath it as it grew. He felt the edge of it catch his arm, and he cursed, shoving himself off the grass and into the air as it spun him around. As he landed, he twisted the dagger around, catching the bubble's edge.

It resisted, and he threw himself back as Longland spoke again.

This time, the hedge itself grew, its branches thickening and widening as they twisted, groping in the air. He felt leaves slice his cheek, and he swore again. He wasn't certain how many of the people at Amy's party had been affected by the Necromancer's first spell. But it encompassed everyone standing outside, and he had held it for some time.

They hadn't sent just anyone to gather Emma; they'd sent someone powerful.

Chase had reached Longland. He didn't throw his daggers, but at this speed, they wouldn't have pierced paper if it was held out as a shield; he kept them close, cutting tendrils of fire, and shedding them as he could. But he was slow.

Eric, trying to avoid the same slowness, grunted as the hedges bit again; he cut the one branch that had secured itself tightly enough to cut shirt and tear skin. It shrank before it hit the ground. Longland, damn it, was *good*. Two to one, and he wasn't panicking. But he was breaking a sweat.

*Come on, Chase,* Eric thought. He cut in to the right, and when Longland brought his arms up for a third time, he caught his wrist with the dagger, breaking the sweep of his arms. Narrowing his eyes, he *looked*. Longland was glowing faintly, but there was no other white shadow surrounding him: no nimbus of death, of the dead.

He jumped and rolled along the ground nearest the base of the hedges, came up and cut through two branches. Six feet. Five.

He swung, low and up, and his dagger clanged off metal.

Longland cursed again, and then, instead of reaching up with those arms, he reached *back*, grabbing the hedge with both hands. All along the row, its carefully cut and manicured lines broken everywhere by the touches of Necromancy, fire blossomed. White fire. And green.

Longland pulled all of that fire *into* himself, absorbing, as well, the fire along the grass and the fire that clung to Chase. Chase screamed—more in frustration than pain—as Longland pulled the entire hedge *around* himself and vanished.

Chase swore. He swore loudly.

Eric pushed himself to his feet. "Well," he said, "that could have gone better."

"Did you recognize him?"

"No."

"He's going to recognize us if he sees us again."

Eric nodded. "But we're going to have other problems," he added.

"What's a problem compared to a prepared Necromancer?"

Eric turned toward the house.

"You're joking, right? You don't intend to go back there. Eric, don't be an idiot. You're not worried about your Peter Parker identity, are you?"

"We're not done here," Eric replied. "And I want to check on Emma."

"On Emma. The *other* Necromancer."

"Don't even think it, Chase."

Chase hadn't sheathed his daggers.

"You gave me a week."

"It's not a game anymore."

"It was never a game. She didn't help him. She didn't even try."

Chase just shook his head. A moment passed, and then, glaring, he put the knives away. "Sorry about your jacket."

"Not a problem—but we're going to have to get those stupid studs repaired."

Chase looked at the jacket; the studs had smeared into running, flattened blobs of silver-crusted iron. "We're going to have to get a different jacket."

"Maybe. And maybe this time you can buy your own."

Eric wished, for just a moment, that he could let Chase take his ire out on the DJ. Chase on the other hand, didn't even appear to notice the sudden increase in volume. Before entering Amy's house, he had carefully peeled off the ruins of his jacket and had folded it in half with the lining facing out.

Not that many people had seen the fire on the lawn, and the fire was now gone. The hedges would probably look a lot worse in the morning light then they did at the moment, but Eric wouldn't have to be there for that. Hopefully, by Monday morning's first class, Amy would be distracted.

Or, he amended, as he entered the sunroom, distracted by something else. Michael was waiting for them as they entered the room, Allison by his side.

"Where's Emma?" Eric asked them. If they noted the tears the leaves had made in his clothing, they stopped themselves from actually mentioning them.

"In the kitchen with Amy and her brother. They asked us to wait here in case you couldn't find it. Chase, are you all right?"

Chase grimaced and reached up gingerly to touch his hair. "I've been better," he admitted. "But I've been a hell of a lot worse. You two are okay?"

"Michael is *not* happy about hitting someone across the side of the face with a heavy book," Allison said. "I'm fine. Confused," she added, in a way that suggested that honesty, however hard it was to get at, was important to her. "But not injured. What happened?"

Eric lifted a hand just as Chase opened his mouth. "I'd rather not have to explain it a dozen times," he said curtly. And loudly. "We can save it until we get to the kitchen." The sunroom was directly adjacent to the very large living room. It was also adjacent to the hall that ran along the back of the house. People filled both of these spaces. "Why are all these people still here?"

"Why wouldn't they be?"

He stared at her for a moment as if she'd just spoken in French. "Because we just had a—"

"Take your own advice," Chase said, swatting him on the back. "It's a big, *loud*, crowded house. Things didn't last that long. I'd bet you even money that most people here didn't even notice; it's not as though they're standing here with their faces pressed against the windows."

Great. The day not only held a powerful Necromancer and a powerful Potential—it also held a moment in which he had to listen to advice from Chase when Chase was right.


Emma looked up as Allison and Michael entered the kitchen through dark, swinging doors.

"Did you find them?"

"See for yourself," Allison said. Chase and Eric entered the kitchen behind her.

Amy was kneeling on the floor with a cold cloth in her hands. Her brother's head was in her lap. The last time that Emma had seen Amy with something wet in her hands near Skip, it was because he had turned the hose on her and she had chosen to retaliate. It was also the last time, Emma thought, that Skip had been home, and the Emery Mafia had, in his words, taken over the entire place. He'd then packed up and left for Dalhousie and law school.

Emma had been solidly part of the Emery Mafia then. Nathan had still been alive.

Amy looked at Eric and Chase. She was, of course, still beautiful—she always commanded attention just by existing—but she was also that peculiar shade of white that comes from anger. Amy was seldom angry.

Even when her parents had, in her own words, ditched her for New York City, she'd only managed to reach annoyed. Or irritated. She was beyond that now.

But Emma understood why. Amy was frightened, and Amy Snitman did not *do* fear.

"What," she said, making a stiletto of the word, "is going on here?"

Chase shoved his hands into his pockets and looked at Eric. "Your show," he said, shrugging.

Eric looked at Amy. He glanced at Emma and Allison and hesitated when he came to Michael. Oliver and Connell, on the other hand, were not in the kitchen, and Michael's book was no longer in his hands. It was in the backpack that was across his shoulders. Emma understood why he hesitated; she would have done the same.

But in the end, she would have surrendered to the inevitable, because in a pinch, Amy was her friend. They might disagree on some things, but when it was an emergency, Amy was a person she could trust at her back. She couldn't make that decision for Eric, and she knew it was a decision he was trying to make for himself.

"How long has he been out?"

He's stalling, Emma thought.

Amy's lips thinned, but to Emma's surprise, she answered the question. "Since just after the fire."

"Did he say anything before he collapsed?"

"He asked me what I was doing here."

Eric glanced at Chase, whose hands were still in his pockets. Chase nodded.

"Why?" Amy asked sharply.

"Did he say where he thought he was?"

"No." The pause between that word and the next few couldn't quite be called hesitation, but only because it was Amy. "But I don't think he thought he was home. He might have thought he was at school," she added, her brows furrowing slightly.

"How far away is his school?"

"On the east coast."

"How long would it take him to get here, assuming he had the plane tickets booked?"

"Hours. I'm not sure. It would depend on where he was, what the traffic was like, how long it took to get his baggage."

"Hours is good enough." Eric walked over to Skip and knelt. He pushed one eyelid up and then lifted a limp arm. "He should come out of this in the morning. He won't expect to be home, though. He'll probably be a bit disoriented, and he'll think he had a very unpleasant dream."

"And his so-called friend?"

"He isn't likely to see Merrick Longland again."

"But you're sure he'll be okay?"

"I don't know what level of compulsion was placed on him. They don't normally do this," he added. "It's costly."

"What would they normally do?" The sharp edge was back in her voice.

"Normally? They'd suggest that he wanted to go home to visit his friends or his family. They'd make it his idea, and they'd just happen to be prepared to go with him. He'd feel like an idiot, after, but he'd remember almost everything."

"Almost?"

"He wouldn't remember the friend in question. He'd just remember the stupid idea—of going home on no notice—and wonder what the hell he'd been thinking."

Amy looked at Emma, who had been watching the conversation in silence. "Is Eric sane?" she asked.

"More or less. I won't vouch for Chase."

"And you knew about this?"

"Me?" Emma lifted her hands, palms out, in front of her. "No. Not this. Not the fire, either. But . . . I'd trust him."

Amy nodded and turned back to Eric. "What you've left out is why."

"Why?"

"Why would someone compel my useless brother to come home? Why didn't Longland just come here on his own?"

"Good question," Eric replied, frowning. "I've been wondering that as well. Longland clearly wanted to be in on this party." The frown deepened. "Chase?"

"Amplifiers," Chase said. If Emma hadn't been standing closer to him than to Amy, she might have missed it. She might also have missed the two words that followed, but they were just swearing. "I'll check."

"Check now," Eric told him roughly.

"Excuse me?" Amy said, and Chase paused in the half-open door.

Eric cursed under his breath. "Amy, it's important."

"How important?"

"He might have needed your brother here to have easier access to your house."

"Which would help him how? We're here alone," she added. "If he could force Skip to leave law school on zero notice—and forget all about it later—he could probably get anyone to do anything he wanted."

"Some people are easier to compel than others," Eric told her, giving her a very pointed look.

She chose to take it as a compliment, but that was Amy all over. "Emma, go with Chase and help him find whatever he's looking for. Don't," she added, "let him find anything he shouldn't be looking for."

"Chase," Eric said, before he could make it out the door, "remember what you said."

Chase rolled his eyes toward the ceiling.

"Where do you want to start?" Emma asked him, when they were finally on the other side of the kitchen door.

Chase glanced at her for a moment and then shrugged. "Any place there aren't four hundred people."

"So you want to start next door."

"Ha-ha."

"We can start upstairs. No one's supposed to be there, and if we happen to interrupt someone making out, Amy will thank us."

"Great. They won't."

"Probably not," she agreed cheerfully. "Besides, you need to get to a mirror and look at your hair."

"My hair?"

"Well, what's left of it." She waved at Nan and Phil, who were closest to the stairs, said hello to a couple of people she vaguely recognized but didn't know by name, and made her way to the main stairs. "Amy didn't even notice your boots."

"Don't sound so disappointed."

They cleared the top of the stairs and headed down the hall. It wasn't a short hall. The rooms that crowded around it weren't small rooms. "Bathroom's over there," Emma said, pointing to the farthest door in the wall to the right. She could feel the bass of the sound system pounding beneath the parts of her feet that were actually against the ground; given that these were dress shoes, that wasn't much. But she walked farther down the hall and then turned to face Chase.

"What, exactly, are we looking for?" It was a reasonable question.

Chase was not in a reasonable mood. "I'll let you know if I see it."

"I'd rather have some warning."

"You probably won't—"

"See it?"

He frowned. "No," he finally said. "You probably *will* see it. But it probably isn't anything that you would recognize as dangerous."

"Do you see the dead as well?"

His brows rose slightly, and then he grimaced. "Can I just say I don't know what you're talking about?"

"If you like lying to my face, sure."

"You don't know what you're talking about." He headed toward the bathroom, and she followed him in. The room was almost painfully brightly lit, but the skylight was dim and dark, although one edge of slanted glass reflected the light. "Yes," he said, as he pushed the door open. "I can see the dead. But not the same way Eric does. Eric's naturally talented; I have to work my ass off for even a glimpse. I'm lazy," he added, just in case this wasn't obvious. "God this room is *huge*."

Since that had been her own first reaction, Emma didn't laugh. Barely.

"What you're looking for," she asked quietly, "could it be planted quickly?"

"If by quickly you mean in less than one day, yes. If by quickly you mean five minutes, no. Not unless the—never mind. No." He stopped to look in the mirror, and froze. The mirror was most of the wall. The parts of the wall that weren't mirror were occupied by a sink with a lot of smoky marble countertop.

"I *told* you," Emma said. And then she realized that he was not, in fact, looking at his reflection—or more precisely, his hair—at all. "Chase?"

"Get Eric."

She looked, instead, at his reflection. It mirrored him; his eyes were slightly wider, and his expression was frozen in place. His hair was a frayed mass of singed ends, and his previously pale skin was the red that usually requires way too much exposure to sun.

"Chase?"

"Get Eric, Emma."

She hesitated in the doorway and then said, "Not without you."

"Emma, I am not joking. Get Eric."

"I'm not laughing, you'll notice. I'm not going to get Eric without you." She couldn't say later why she wouldn't budge. Chase had clearly shown that he was not afraid of much, and that he could handle himself. She forced her face to relax into a smile, and added, "Amy will kill me."

His expression did change, then, to one of frustration and, surprisingly, resignation. On the other hand, he swore a lot as he turned away from the mirror.

Chase and Eric went up the stairs, and Emma followed them as if she were an afterthought. They didn't talk at all. Chase didn't tell Eric what he'd seen, and since Emma had seen nothing, she couldn't fill him in either. But what was most disturbing was that Eric didn't *ask*. He just pushed himself up off the kitchen floor—where Skip was still unconscious—and followed.

But he stiffened as he touched the bathroom door.

"Eric?" Emma asked softly. Eric spun, and what she saw in his face made her take a step back. He reined it in, but she could see that he had to work at it, and it made her nervous.

He had spoken about having to kill her before, and they had been just words to Emma. For the first time since he'd said it, they weren't. He saw that, in her face, as well, and his mouth tightened as he gripped the doorknob and turned away.

Without looking at her, he said, "It's too much to hope you'll go back downstairs and stay with your friends."

It almost wasn't, but she didn't say this.

"But stay in the doorway, Em. Keep your feet on the carpet, and keep your hands on the walls if you have to grab anything. Whatever you do—or see—stay out."

She nodded. She would have asked him why, but in emergencies, why was the first thing to go, and everything about Eric at this point *screamed* emergency. "Wait—what about Chase?"

The tension left his shoulders, and he shook his head. "Chase," he told her softly, "can take care of himself. You've known him for what? Minutes?"

"People I've never met die all the time."

"And you worry about them?"

"They're not standing in front of me. There's nothing at all I can do to help them."

"Believe that there is nothing at all you can do to help Chase. Or me." Eric shook his head. "I give up," he said, to no one in particular.

"You already said that."

"I'm continually optimistic by nature. Shut up, Chase." Taking a deep breath, he entered the bathroom. Chase was standing to one side of the mirror, his arms folded across his chest. The lack of leather jacket didn't detract from the attitude of his posture, which said a lot about his attitude and only a little about the jacket.

Eric stepped up to the counter, looked into the mirror, and froze.

Emma, her feet pressed against the carpet, her hands pressed against the wall, froze as well. She could see Eric's reflection in the mirror; she could see the welt across his cheek, the dark slash of dried blood, but those had been pretty clear in the fluorescent kitchen lighting as well.

What she hadn't seen until this moment were the reflections that had no physical counterparts: the pale, almost translucent profiles of a middle-aged man and a young girl. They stood to either side of Eric, their arms raised above their heads, their eyes open in the glassy stare of people who no longer take in the world that's passing around them.

"Chase?" Eric said, voice both soft and sharp.

"Two. If there's a third, I can't sense him."

"Did you touch the mirror?"

"Do I look like a moron?"

"Usually. Ready?"

Chase nodded, his arms folding slightly more firmly around his upper body.

Eric reached out with his palm and laid it flat against the mirror's surface. The mirror—and Eric's reflection—rippled. Emma felt it; it was as if, in rippling, the mirror had disturbed not only its own surface but the surfaces of every other solid thing in the room as well. Chase grimaced at the same time as she flinched; even Eric clenched his jaws.

Only the two silent people who extended their arms in the mirror seemed entirely unmoved, and Emma knew, then, that they were dead.

But if Eric saw them, he gave no sign; the whole of his attention was focused on the mirror. As the rippling stilled, he withdrew his hand; it fell to his side as if he no longer cared whether or not it was part of him. His reflection was gone. So, too, was the background to it: the tiled walls, the large, in-ground bath, the standing shower stall.

In their place were the walls of an entirely different room, with red rugs, dark-stained wood-plank floors peering out at their edges, globes of light on standing sconces, and one central figure.

Sitting in a tall-backed chair directly opposite Eric, wearing a dress that not even Amy at her most ostentatious could have carried off—too many beads, too much fabric, too many frills, and too much damn *gold*—was a woman Emma had never seen.

Not even in a nightmare.

# CHAPTER
## TEN

NIGHTMARE WAS AN ODD WORD to apply to the woman seated on what was, Emma thought, a throne. Nothing about her suggested the monsters that dwelled across the boundary of sleep. She was not beautiful in the way that Amy was beautiful, but she was striking in a way that Amy was not, at least not yet. She wore a dress that reminded Emma of pictures of Queen Elizabeth I. Her hair was pale, not gold and not platinum, but closer to the latter, and bound in such a way that nothing escaped—no tendrils, no curls.

She wore a thin diadem just above the line of her hair, which contained a single sapphire; this set off eyes that were a remarkable blue. Her lips were, in Emma's opinion, unnaturally red; it was the only thing about her that made her look old.

Or rather, it was the only thing Emma could point at, because no one who wasn't old wore that color. But something about this woman radiated age. Nothing about her seemed remotely friendly. Not even when she smiled. Especially not then.

And she smiled, the left corner of her lips twitching upward, as she looked at Eric. Emma could see only his back, but his whole body had tensed.

"Well met, Eric. Am I to assume, from the unexpected pleasure of your company, that Merrick is dead?"

Chase said nothing. He said it very loudly. Eric's nothing was quieter.

"I thought you might make an appearance," the woman added, when it became clear that no one else would speak. "And here you are. And you've brought your pet with you." Her smile deepened. "If there are two of you, the situation must be dire, indeed. It is seldom that you go hunting these days." The smile slid from her face. "But you will play your games, won't you? Experience teaches you nothing. You should stop, Eric. You should end this game. What can you do, after all, that does not, in the end, add to *my* power?"

He said nothing.

"What can you do at all?" She lifted an arm; it glittered in the globes of light at her back. "Come back to me. Come back. Everything else is dust and illusion." Her expression had changed as she spoke, her eyes rounding slightly as she leaned forward in her chair. Her voice had softened, losing the brittle edge that made it seem too cold.

Eric stood there for a long, silent moment, and then he turned away. Emma saw the expression on his face, and her eyes widened, her mouth opened. But words wouldn't come; she was as mute, in her way, as he was. She would have walked over to him, she would have pulled him away, but he had told her very clearly to stay put, and that much she would do.

But it was hard.

"Eric," the woman called.

He didn't turn back.

"*Eric!*"

Those beautiful eyes narrowed; those red, full lips closed. The arm that had been lifted in what was almost a plea fell once again to the arm of the chair, and even at this distance, Emma could see the way the knuckles of both hands suddenly stood out in relief.

"Chase," Eric said quietly, his back to the mirror, "come on."

Chase, however, was staring at the woman. His back was not turned to Emma, and if Emma had ever needed any proof that Eric and Chase were two entirely different people, she had it here. His expression was as white as the woman's. White with rage.

He took one step forward, just one, and Eric spun and caught the fist he'd lifted before Chase could slam it into the mirror. "*Chase*."

Chase's arm was shaking, and Eric's hand was shaking as well, and they stood there while the woman watched, her fury not lessened by the malice of her smile. But feeding that malicious smile was more than Emma could bear to watch Eric and Chase do.

Keeping her feet on the carpet and anchoring herself with the door-frame, she pivoted into the room and reached for the lights, her hand slapping the wall until she felt the familiar switches beneath her fingers. She turned them off, and night descended through the skylight.

After a few moments of silence, Emma said, "Is it safe to turn the lights back on?"

"More or less."

"I'd prefer the more, if it's all the same to you." She waited for an-other minute, and then she flipped the switch back on. Chase and Eric were no longer locked in a struggle to prevent Chase from punching the mirror. Better, the mirror now reflected them. She waited, watching them look at each other.

*Who was she?* Emma wanted to ask, but given the tension of their expressions at the moment, she couldn't. Had they been Allison—or Michael—those would have been the first words out of her mouth, and they would have been angry, protective words. But Eric and Chase were not friends of a decade; she wasn't sure how they would take it—but she could guess. Badly.

"Guys."

They both turned to look at her.

"Is she what you were looking for?"

"She is *so* not what I was looking for," Chase replied.

"So that means the house search is still on?"

Eric nodded. "I don't think we'll find anything else," he added. "But we might as well be thorough."

He was wrong. He wasn't happy to *be* wrong, but he was wrong.

And it happened that the person who proved him wrong in this case wasn't Chase. It was Emma. Emma knew the house pretty well; it was hard not to know a house that you'd played extended games of hide-and-seek in from elementary school on. Amy's house, it was agreed, was the best house for hide-and-seek because there were so many places to hide, and you could hide on the move if necessary. It changed the whole feel of the game.

So Emma knew the house as well as anyone but Skip or Amy, and once she'd decided to take charge, she led, and Eric and Chase were forced to follow.

She hesitated on the threshold of Amy's bedroom, but that was the only dangerously sensitive area upstairs, and it was, in Chase's opinion, clean. Mindful of Amy's ability to notice when a hairpin had been moved half an inch, Emma supervised Chase like an angry principal conducting a locker search.

Skip's room had never been off limits in the opinion of anyone but Skip, and none of the girls took him seriously anyway. Since Skip barely noticed his closet—and evidence of this could be seen by the shirts and the pants that were nowhere near it, and should have been—she relaxed and let them both poke around.

"Clean," Chase said.

"In a manner of speaking," Eric added.

The room that had been Merrick's was one of four guest rooms. It was almost self-contained, in that it had a bathroom, a small study, and a very large bedroom (certainly larger than any of the rooms in the Hall household) behind a set of off-white double doors. It had a walk-in closet as well. The only thing it lacked was a kitchen. They approached this room with care—enough care that Eric caught Emma's arm as she reached for the doorknob and pulled her back.

"Let Chase open it."

"Why me?"

Eric glared, but Chase was—mostly—grinning. They really were like brothers. Chase opened the doors that led to the guest room. The rooms were empty, which was more or less what they expected. They weren't entirely tidy, but given that they'd been occupied by a so-called friend of Skip's, Emma didn't expect tidy.

The bathroom had the usual things in it—toothbrush, electric razor, deodorant. It had a mirror that was not nearly as dramatic as the one in the hall bathroom, but Emma hesitated at the doorway just in case. Chase, however, didn't seem worried. Eric was that type of quiet that doesn't let much out into the world; she couldn't tell if he was worried or not.

The bathroom was clean. The bedroom contained one very large suitcase and one carry-on bag; the bed was made.

"Was he planning to stay a while?" Eric asked.

Emma shrugged. "I didn't ask," she replied. "But Amy takes something that size on day trips." In case it wasn't clear, she indicated the large suitcase. "Longland looked like he was a bit of a clothes horse, so it might mean nothing."

Eric tried to open the suitcase. It was locked. So was the carry-on.

"Chase?"

"This," Chase told Emma, "is what we call job security." He opened both suitcases, using what looked like long wires.

"Can you unlock doors that way as well?"

"Not easily. A baby could do this, though. At least a baby not named Eric."

The carry-on was full of books. And two large chocolate bars. They were not, however, good chocolate, which said something. Chase pocketed them anyway, which also said something. She looked at the books as Chase lifted them out of the bag.

Eric had opened the larger suitcase. It was, not surprisingly, full of clothing. But this clothing? It was almost like studying geological strata. The first layer? Shirts. One T-shirt, one sweatshirt. Underwear and socks could be found under two pairs of gray pants. No jeans. But beneath the expected layer of clothing? The unexpected.

"What is that?" Emma asked. She had assumed it was either a jacket or a very heavy shirt, but it just kept unfolding as Eric drew it out of the suitcase. In the end, it was a dress. No. Not a dress. A robe.

"Looks like a robe to me," Chase said.

"Seriously?" She reached out for a fold of the draping cloth and saw that it was not quite gray, as it had first seemed. It was a slate blue, embroidered lightly in curling fronds of gray. Gold thread decorated the sleeves and the hem.

"Eric?"

Eric nodded at Chase.

"What, they have a uniform?" Emma asked.

"Not exactly. But my guess? This wasn't meant for his use."

"Whose, then?"

"Yours."

"Why?"

"Because there's another one. Look."

She reached into the suitcase and pulled out a robe that was similar in cut. It was, however, rust red. She held it against her shoulders and watched the hems flap around in folds across the ground. "I think I like the red better."

As a joke, it fell flat. Chase glanced at her and then at Eric; Eric deliberately didn't meet his gaze.

Emma's hands, still clutching red cloth, became fists. She looked at the two of them, and if Eric was avoiding Chase's gaze, he was *also* avoiding hers. Chase followed suit.

"Guys."

They both looked at her, then. "Can we just stop this right now? You know things you aren't telling me, and they're *about* me. You know what I'm facing, and *I don't*. Tell me."

They exchanged a glance, and Chase shrugged. Eric took a breath, held it for a little too long, and exhaled. "Let's keep on looking."

"Eric."

"Emma—"

"At least explain this." She lifted the robe. "These aren't exactly what you or I would call everyday wear. They're not formal, either. I could put that on," she added, pointing to the slate blue robe, "if I were playing a priest in a badly staged school play."

He nodded.

"I could not put it on and just blend in here, for any value of here that didn't include Amy's Halloween party."

"Amy has Halloween parties?" Chase asked. Eric hit him.

"Your point?" Eric asked Emma.

"My point is that I couldn't wear this anywhere here. If I was meant to wear this, where exactly was I supposed to *go*?"

"Emma—"

"Was I meant to go where *she* is?"

Eric flinched. "No," he said, almost too softly. "Never that, Emma."

But Chase said, "God, Eric."

Eric looked at Chase and said, No. But without the sound.

"Idiot. She's right. She's absolutely right. Eric, wake the hell up."

Eric was silent. Chase turned to Emma. "Find us a big room," he told her.

"How big?"

"Damn it, just—*big*."

She bit her lip and nodded. "Come on. There's one up here, and there're two downstairs that might do. They don't *look* as big when they're full of people."

She led them to the master bedroom. It was at the end of the hall, it was fronted by the largest doors on the second floor, and it had always had an invisible sign across it saying: *Keep out or Amy might kill you.* Not that this had always worked.

Tonight was one of those nights when fear of Amy was not as strong as fear of the utterly nameless future that included Chase, Eric, and a man who could suddenly turn the entire backyard into an eerie blaze of silent white and green fire. She opened the doors.

To either side of the doors were large, walk-in closets; beyond those, mirrored vanities with small—for this house—sinks and very large counters. There were also two bathrooms, one beside each vanity. Emma passed between the mirrors and grimaced, but the mirrors were just mirrors. She headed on into the depth of the bedroom. The bed, which was so huge that it would not have fit around the bend in the stairs in the Hall household, looked tiny.

Chase scoped the room out with care, and Emma watched him with growing unease. "Nothing," he told Eric.

"You're sure?"

Chase nodded and then looked at Emma. "Emma," he said quietly, "have Amy clear the house out."

She stared at him. "Chase, it's barely nine o'clock. You want me to tell her to kick everyone out *now*?"

He said nothing.

Eric, understanding Emma's problem, said, "Let's check it out. The noise and the people won't get in the way if we're looking."

"No. Only if the Necromancer comes back."

Necromancer. Emma stared at Chase for a long moment and then turned and headed toward the stairs. "It's one of two rooms," she managed to say. *Necromancer.*

"Any chance any one of those rooms is empty?"

"Depends. If you get the DJ to put on the wrong damn music, he'll either get lynched or people will leave really fast."

There was a lot of quiet swearing. None of it was Emma's. She was still stuck on the word *Necromancer*. She headed down the stairs, clinging to the railing; they followed. She turned one sharp right at the end of the stairs, and came up against the expected press of bodies; this slowed their progress by a lot. This time, however, Eric didn't just grab her arm and drag her through people.

He did catch her hand, and he did hold it, but it was probably either that or get left behind. The music got louder, and the talking was now that level of shouting that's needed just to say hello in a loud room.

"Chase!" Emma shouted

"What?" he shouted back.

"Where?"

"Go to the back of the room. The DJ."

Emma nodded and headed that way. The music got louder; the bass was like a heartbeat—but a lot less welcome—by the time she had made it most of the way there. She'd chosen to try to sidle along the walls, because the people standing there were less likely to accidentally elbow her or step on her feet.

But she stopped well before she reached the DJ. Eric walked into her. Chase walked into him.

Standing against the far wall were four people.

Not a single one of them was alive.

"Emma?" Eric asked, his mouth close enough to her ear that she felt the words trace her spine. "Emma, what is it?"

"Can't you see them?" She lifted her hand and pointed. When Eric failed to answer, she turned—and it was hard—to look at him. His eyes were narrowed, and he was scanning the back wall, but no shifting expression told her that he saw what she could easily see.

"Chase?" She had to shout this.

Chase shook his head slowly. He moved closer, which meant that they were all standing on almost the same square foot of floor. "What do you see?"

Emma didn't like the words "dead" or "ghost" because they didn't look like her preconceived notions of either. They were, for one, too solid; there was a faint luminescence around their eyes, and even their skin, but without it, she might have mistaken them for living people.

Although perhaps not in those clothes. She hesitated, then said, "The dead. There are four, two women, one boy and one girl. Eric—I don't understand why you can't see them. They're dead."

Chase closed his eyes, and his shoulders tensed. Eric finally let her go so he could put a hand on one of those shoulders. "Not now, Chase."

"Fuck, Eric—" He took a breath, steadied himself. "You can't see them?"

Eric shook his head.

Emma said, quietly, "They're chained."

Eric looked at her. "Chained?" She almost couldn't hear the word.

She nodded.

He swore, but it was background noise, now. She started to walk again, and after a minute, he followed. The DJ shouted something and pointed at the floor, but Emma couldn't see what he was pointing at. She smiled at him, and he grimaced and shrugged.

She passed him, reached the wall, and approached the closest of the dead women. She was, Emma thought, a good deal older than her mother—older and stouter. She wore a dress that might have been acceptable business dress twenty or thirty years ago, and her hair, which might once have been a mousy brown, was shot through with gray. She didn't appear to see Emma, which, since Emma was standing in front her, was a bit disconcerting.

Emma lifted a hand, waved it in front of her eyes. Nothing.

She felt Eric's hand on her shoulder and turned. "They don't see me. Eric, why are they here?"

He didn't answer. But Chase said, brusquely, "Tell her, Eric."

"Not here."

"Tell her, or I will."

Eric reached out and grabbed Chase's shirt, Chased shoved him, and Emma snorted. "*Guys,*" she said, through clenched teeth. "While I would love to see you pound each other senseless, it's not actually *helpful.*"

They both looked at her.

"You really are brothers. I don't care what you say." She took a deep breath and stepped up to the woman until she could touch her. Her hand hovered just above the rounded contours of the pale cheek, before she let it fall. It wasn't—wouldn't be—like touching her father; it would be like touching a corpse.

Instead, she looked at the chains. They were slender, golden chains, much like the one Merrick Longland had held. She'd snapped that; she thought she could snap these as well. "I'm sorry," she said to the woman, who might as well have been a statue for all she seemed to notice.

"Emma, what are you doing?" Eric asked her.

"Not trying to strangle Chase," she replied curtly. The chain was thicker, and she could see that it was like rope and that the woman was bound several times by its length. Those loops disappeared into the wall and emerged out the other side, gleaming faintly. One strand—only one—passed from this woman to the next, and from her to the two children. It seemed to be looped several times around each person.

"Emma?"

"Just let me figure it out." She touched the chains that bound the woman to the wall; they were pulled so tight they had no play at all. Fine. She walked to the woman's right, and put both hands on the taut, single strand. It was slightly warm, and although it looked metallic, it felt . . . wet. Slippery. If the chain that had bound Emily Gates had been slippery, Emma hadn't noticed. That was one of the advantages of adrenaline.

She tugged at it, and all four of the trapped people shuddered. She pulled her hand back as if she'd just grabbed fire.

Eric must have seen her expression. But he had come to stand by her side, and he said—and asked—nothing. Chase came to stand on her other side; they were like bookends. Probably better that she was standing between them, though. If they *did* start pounding on each other here, Amy would kill her later. Amy put great stock in civil behavior when it wasn't her own.

But that was people: you could always justify what *you* chose to do, because you made sense to yourself.

"I'm really, really sorry," she said softly, to four people who didn't seem to be aware she existed. "I'm sorry if this hurts. I don't know what I'm doing."

She put her hands on the chain again, both hands this time, and she tried very hard to keep the strongest of the pressure between her hands. She saw the chain stretch and thin, saw the four shudder again, but this time she kept going.

The chain snapped.

Eric swore. As the chain unraveled slowly, the women began to blink. They looked at Emma, and Emma exhaled.

"I see two," Chase told her. Or Eric; she didn't look at them.

"There are two at the end. They're younger." She left the slowly waking women and walked to the children. She found the single strand that stretched between them and broke it.

They blinked, recovering more quickly than either woman had.

"Are you okay?" she asked the girl. A girl who looked to Emma to be about six years old. She was very viscerally glad that the dead didn't look like their corpses.

The girl blinked again and then looked at Emma, her eyes that faint and odd luminescence that seemed to contain no color. She nodded slowly but didn't speak. Neither did the boy. He was taller than the girl, and his hair was an unruly dark mass that suggested hairbrushes had been no part of his cultural norm; he didn't, however, look significantly older. Emma worked her way through the slowly building rage their presence here invoked.

She didn't reach out to touch them; she lifted her hands and then forced them back down to her sides, remembering what had happened the last time she had touched her father. Four very oddly dressed strangers appearing out of nowhere in the middle of the room was probably not going to cause a big stir in a place this loud and crowded, but if it did, she'd be at the center of it.

Instead, she asked them all to follow her, and they nodded again in silence.

"Follow you where?" Eric asked her, as he and Chase fell in behind.

"Outside. We can check on Skip and pick up Allison as we go."

Picking up Allison was a bit of a production that involved literally lifting Skip and dragging him up to his very messy room first. Chase and Eric did the heavy moving, and Amy came along to stage-manage. Michael, Allison, and Emma hovered behind the hard work, glancing at each other. Emma's arms were firmly folded across her chest.

"Bad?" Allison asked.

Emma nodded. "And confusing."

"More confusing than anything else that's happened this week?"

"Good point. Maybe. Certainly not less confusing." She glanced at Michael. She had expected Michael to be fidgeting—and he was—but he wasn't yet possessed by the all out frenetic movements that meant he had outlasted his best-before date and needed to be gently nudged home.

"Michael, do you want to go talk to Oliver and Connell while we figure things out?" Emma asked.

"No." He had the slightly vacant expression that meant he was thinking. It was harder to stop him from thinking than to stop a moving subway train by standing in front of it and pushing.

"Okay, then."

Eric, Chase, and Amy descended the stairs. Emma, seeing them coming, headed out to the backyard. It was too much to hope that Amy wouldn't follow, so she didn't bother. She did, however, hope that Amy wasn't as angry as she looked. But she did look angry, and when Amy was *that* angry, it was very hard not to cringe when she did anything. Like, say, speak. Or look at you.

When they were safely outside—and this took a few minutes as people approached Amy, saw the look on her face, and hurriedly backpedaled—Amy shut the door and then turned, hands on hips, to glare at them all.

Eric took this moment to tell Michael, gently, that it would probably be best for him to go inside and join the party. Michael stared at Eric blankly.

"Emma, help me here." Eric said, out of the corner of his mouth.

Emma grimaced. "He's staying."

"I don't think this is going to be helpful for him."

"It's probably not going to be helpful for me, either." She exhaled. "He's not an idiot, Eric. He saw what happened with Longland. He saw more, I'm guessing—I don't think anyone else was moving until after he hit Longland with the book."

"They weren't moving," Michael said. His hands were slightly balled fists at his sides, and his feet didn't stay in the same spot for more than a few seconds. "No one was moving but Emma and Skip's friend."

Emma nodded but continued to speak to Eric. "This is strange for all of us, and we all want explanations. Michael does more than want: he needs them."

"He doesn't need these."

"Yes," Amy said, quietly coming to the rescue—not that it was needed. "He does. Don't bother to argue with Em about this. She won't budge."

Chase started to speak, and Allison cut him off by simply raising her hand. The funny thing was that Chase actually paid attention. Allison then added her voice to the discussion. "He's always processed information differently than the rest of us do—it might be why he wasn't completely affected by whatever it was Longland did. Because he knows he doesn't understand some of the same things we do, he needs the explanation; if we don't give him one, he'll come up with one on his own—one that doesn't resemble reality."

"Which can be even more frightening than the truth usually is. If he knows what's actually happening, he can work with it." Allison reddened slightly. "Sorry."

"And he clearly doesn't mind being talked about in the third person, as if he weren't here," Eric observed.

Michael frowned. "But I am here," he told Eric. "Everyone knows it."

"Yes?"

"Then they're not talking about me as if I weren't here."

Emma almost felt sorry for Eric. Almost. "He's staying, Amy's staying in case you were about to be stupid enough to suggest she leave, and Allison's staying because I'm going to tell her everything anyway, and it's just easier not to get who-said-what confused. That about covers our side of things." She glanced at Allison. "Did you fill Amy in on everything?"

Allison nodded, looking slightly relieved.

"Then we're good to go with *your* side of things."

Eric and Chase glanced at each other; Chase shrugged.

Amy cut in. Given the number of sentences they'd managed to get through uninterrupted, this was more than expected. "What exactly did Longland do to my brother?"

"We're not sure. Not exactly. Which is to say, we don't have a good way of explaining how it works. We've seen it before," Eric added, speeding up slightly as Amy opened her mouth, "and as I said, it's a compulsion. A control."

"You said he normally wouldn't do something like this—he'd just make it look like it was Skip's idea. Skip's not the brightest guy in the world. This is the type of stupid he might believe could be his own."

Eric nodded, wary now. Emma liked that, about him. He wasn't stupid.

"But if he needed to do something in the house, he'd do something worse. Which he clearly did."

"More or less." On the other hand, he looked distinctly uncomfortable.

"So Chase and Emma went upstairs to search the house, and Chase came back and pulled you in. What did you find?"

They looked at each other again, and any sympathy Emma felt for either of them evaporated. Michael, however, had stopped fidgeting so badly. She reached out and put a hand on his shoulder.

"Nothing."

"Nothing?"

"Nothing upstairs," Emma interjected. "Chase, you called Longland a Necromancer. Maybe we can start with that."

# CHAPTER
# ELEVEN

AMY TURNED TO LOOK AT EMMA. "A . . . Necromancer."
"Pretty much."

"So . . . what Allison said about your dad in the hospital—that had something to do with Necromancy?"

Emma frowned. "I don't think so. I think he's just dead."

"Oh. Okay then."

Emma winced. "Yes, yes, I know it sounds insane."

"It sounds worse than insane, but at least it hasn't descended into B-movie badness. Yet. We checked the hedge while you were upstairs; Longland broke a few branches. The grass is mostly okay."

"How mostly?"

"I *think* I'll survive. I'm not sure Skip will, if we don't have an explanation that won't get us both thrown into an insane asylum. And no, before you ask, I am *not* telling my parents about any of this unless they absolutely need to know." She added, "You haven't told your mom, have you?"

Emma shook her head.

"Allison?"

"No."

They all turned to look at Michael. Michael looked mildly confused. "I told my mother about Emma's dad. Why aren't you telling your parents?"

"Our parents will worry so much they probably won't let us out of the house again, except for school," Emma told him. "What—what did your mother say?"

"Not very much. She asked me not to tell my dad. She told me I must be mistaken. I told her she could ask your mother. Did she?"

"No." Emma thanked god for small mercies. "But she probably doesn't want your dad to worry." *Because she doesn't believe you, and she's pretty certain he won't either*, Emma thought. This was not, however, something you could say to Michael unless you wanted to upset him.

"When the rest of you have finished, you can tell me when you'd like me to start."

The girls turned to look at Eric. He lifted his hands in instant surrender.

"Start with Necromancers, if you can't start with Longland. What, exactly, is a Necromancer, anyway? Some special type of—of dead person?" Emma tried unsuccessfully not to rest her hands on her hips; she was aware that this made her look a little bit too much like her mother. Or an Amy wannabe at this moment.

"No. They're not dead. They're very much alive."

"Alive and something that no one else has ever heard about."

"Not and survived, no. Possibly not and died; they don't really feel the need to explain their existence to ordinary people."

"So . . . they're like a secret society?" Amy walked over to the patio furniture, snagged herself a chair, and dragged it back. She sat down.

Chase and Eric exchanged another glance. Chase was clearly torn between finding this hilarious and finding it infuriating, and he hadn't decided which.

"Ye-es."

"And people who can see the dead, for whatever reason, are naturally

Necromancers?" Emma decided that a chair was a good idea. She did not, however, move.

"No," Eric said, as Chase said, "Yes."

"Eric can see the dead. Eric is, I'm assuming, not a Necromancer." Silence.

"We all saw your dad," Michael offered. "I don't think I'm a Necromancer. Eric, what is a Necromancer? I know what they probably are in D20 rules," he added, to be helpful.

"They're not like that. They can't summon an army of zombies or skeletons. Science will get there first. And no, Michael, you are definitely *not* a Necromancer. Neither is Mrs. Hall or Allison or the other people who probably saw Emma's dad."

"But Emma?" he added, with just a trace of anxiety.

"Emma," Chase said, while Eric was struggling for words, "is a Necromancer."

If, as they say, looks could kill, Chase, or what was left of Chase, would have fallen over on the spot. Chase, however, squared his shoulders and met Eric's furious glance without blinking. "She is," he said quietly, shoving his hands into his pockets.

"Are you telling this story, or am I?"

"You are, of course. If I were, I wouldn't have taken this long to get to the damn point."

Emma thought Eric was going to punch him, and Chase, judging by the way he shifted his stance, thought so too. "Eric," she said.

He lowered his hands. He didn't manage to uncurl them.

"I'm a Necromancer?"

The look he gave her made her turn away for a moment. Sometimes you couldn't look too closely at another person's pain.

"Yes."

"And this means you have to—" she broke off, looking at her friends. "Tell me."

"The headaches weren't headaches. They weren't a concussion. Some people have a lot of trouble adjusting to what they see when they're first coming into their power. Your brain builds new channels, new ways of assimilating visual information, but it's complicated and it hurts. While you're doing this, you can often hallucinate, hear voices, see things. It's both painful and confusing, but if you have no guide, if you have no information, those will shut down on their own as your brain learns to ignore the incoming information. It's almost natural."

"That's what you were hoping for."

He nodded, closed his eyes, turned his face away.

"He knew it was too late," Chase told her. "He just doesn't want—"

Eric stepped on his foot, hard.

"What is it that Necromancers can do that makes them so dangerous?" Emma found it easier to ask this of Chase. Possibly because it didn't seem to hurt him so much to answer, and possibly because he was still recovering from the very necessary stomping.

"You can ask that after tonight?"

She grimaced. "Good point. But—how can they do it?"

"They take their power from the dead."

"From the dead." Emma's eyes widened. "You mean like the dead in the room?"

"Like the dead that are following you, yes."

Amy said, "Allison, do you see any dead people?"

"No."

"Michael?"

"No."

"Okay. Just checking, because *neither do I.*" Amy shifted in her chair. Emma had to give her this: when she wasn't in the mood to be impressed, it took a lot to impress her.

"With the dead you have following you," Chase continued, "you could probably destroy this whole block without blinking and still have power left to go home."

"I can walk home from here."

"That's not the home I was talking about."

"It's the only home I have." But she turned to look at the dead. Because Chase was right. They were following her. She frowned. "Emily," she whispered.

A fifth ghost appeared, almost shyly. "Yes?"

"Sorry. I—I almost forgot about you, and I wanted to see if you were still here."

"I can't leave," the girl replied.

"Why not?"

"You hold me."

"Emma," Amy said sharply, "You are creeping me the hell out. Who are you talking to, exactly?"

Emma grimaced. "I don't know if this will work," she said.

Eric said, "Don't. Em. Don't."

But Emma reached out with her hand, palm up, to Emily, who hesitated for just a minute before she reached out and grasped Emma's hand with her own. Hers was *cold*. To Emma's eyes, nothing had changed.

But Amy's intake and Allison's soft rush of breath—exhale or inhale, Emma couldn't tell—told her that things had changed for her friends.

Michael said, "She doesn't look dead."

"No. Thank god. I don't think I could stand to see corpses everywhere. This is Emily Gates. Emily, these are my friends. This is Michael," she added, because Michael had walked toward Emily. He was tall, certainly taller than Emma, Amy, or Allison.

"Hello," Michael said quietly. He held out his hand.

Emily looked at it and then shook her head. "I can't," she told him.

"Oh." He let his hand drop. "It's okay," he added because she seemed to be unhappy about the admission. "Emma, why can we see her now?"

"I don't know. But in the hospital—I touched my dad."

"No, you didn't."

"She did," Eric replied. His voice was very quiet. "But not in a way you could see, not then. Until she touched him, you couldn't see him."

"Why does her touch make them visible?"

"It doesn't. Not exactly. She's using a very, very small part of their power to make them visible to you. To everyone here."

Emma's hand tightened slightly, and then she let go. "Emily, how do I let you go? What am I holding?"

Emily frowned. "I don't know."

"It doesn't matter." Eric's voice was rough. "You can't let them go here, even if you could figure out how to do it. Longland's still alive, and he's still out there. You let them go, he'll probably be able to pick them up again, and we cannot face him when he's wielding that kind of power. It's not *easy* for him to pick up the dead this way. It is not trivial."

Emma nodded and turned to the other four. She introduced herself, and she received their names. The children were hard for her. They were just too young to be caught up in all of this. Too damn young, she thought, to *die*.

But they were dead. "Do you want to meet my friends?" she asked them softly.

"Don't." Eric again. "Emma—don't do this."

Setting her jaw, she touched each by the hand, and she introduced Georges, Catherine, Margaret, and Suzanne, to her friends. She introduced the two women, Margaret and Suzanne, first, and then the children, because she knew what effect they would have on Michael.

Michael liked children, possibly because there was something in children that was not yet entirely fettered by social convention, and he responded to it. Her hands—she introduced Georges and Catherine at the same time—were numb by the time he had finished asking them questions, because he did ask. They answered, slowly at first. But as they talked, they grew more animated, and Michael, forgetting for a moment that they were dead, started to play, to make faces, to try to get them to laugh.

It was heartbreaking to watch him. It was worse to watch them absorb this playfulness, because they wanted it so badly, and this fact was completely obvious to Emma.

It was obvious, Emma thought, glancing at Allison and Amy, to all of them. Allison approached them as well, but she was more reserved. She retreated because Michael was making them laugh, and when they laughed—they didn't seem dead.

But when Allison turned to Emma, her eyes were filmed with tears that she was trying not to shed. "Em."

Emma nodded.

"How can we help them?"

"I don't know."

"There's got to be something we can do. Is the little boy in the burned out building like this?"

"I think he would be, if we could get him out of the fire."

"And if we don't?"

"He'll be a four-year-old trapped in a burning building at the moment of his death for decades, if not forever."

Amy said, "What four-year-old?"

Allison told her.

"You were going to tell me about this, right, Emma?"

Emma shrugged. "It sounded crazy," she said. "But I probably would have; we need really big, solid ladders, and a car that can carry them, without the parents that would probably insist on coming along."

"Right. Ladders. Car. Parents out of town. Check."

"Emma."

She turned to look at Eric. "Michael, I have to let go of their hands, now. I can't feel mine at all."

"Oh. Why?"

"Their hands are very, very cold. It's like grabbing ice, but without the wet bits."

"I don't think they want to go away."

They didn't. She knew they didn't. She managed to nod, but she had to force herself to unclench her jaw. "Eric, I'm using their power?"

"Yes."

"Does it hurt them?"

"Ask them," he replied.

"Georges? Catherine?"

They failed to hear her, the way children who are having fun frequently fail to hear the parents who want them to leave the place in which they're having it.

"I'm going to take that as a no," Emma told Eric. "I'll let go when I can't feel my arms."

"Emma—"

"Did Longland come here to find me?"

"Yes."

"How did he know where I was?"

"Probably the same way we did. It's not exact," he added, "but the dead . . . some of the dead know."

"And he expected me to just pick up and go wherever he wanted me to go."

"That's what usually happens."

*Unless you kill the Necromancer first.* She wanted to say it, but didn't. Throwing murder into the mix, while her friends were standing around her, was something she wasn't up to doing.

"Michael, don't do that, you'll get grass stains on those pants." Emma shook her head, because Michael, like the two six-year-olds, wasn't really listening.

"And the four in the dance room?"

"They're amplifiers," Chase replied. "I think that room was meant to serve as a road."

"A . . . road."

"A road."

"To where? Hell?"

"Pretty much. That's not what they call it," he added.

"What do they call it, and what *is* it?"

"I don't know what they call it."

Emma suppressed a strong and visceral urge to strangle Chase. She probably wouldn't have managed if she weren't still holding onto two children who were leeching the heat out of her body by inches. "What do you call it?"

"The City of the Dead."

"Great. And Longland thought he could just come here, screw around with my friends, and cart me off?"

"He doesn't know you very well, does he?"

"No, Michael, he certainly doesn't." She paused, then said, "If I had gone with him, what would have happened to these four?"

"He would probably have sucked all the power out of them at that point. Creating a road like that takes a lot of power."

"And this power—if it were gone, what would happen to them?"

Chase just stared at her, as if she were making no sense. "What do you mean, what would happen?"

"What I said. I can try to use smaller words, if it'd help."

"They're dead. They'd still *be* dead."

"Sucking the power out of them can't be good for them. They must need it for something. What do they use the power *for*?"

"How the hell should I know?"

"Eric, I'm going to kill Chase now."

Eric just looked at her. "Emma—" He exhaled, and then shook his head, lifting his hands as he did. "I give up."

To her surprise, she started to smile, and it was a genuine smile, even though her hands ached, and her arms were now tingling. "You say that. A lot."

"Without their power, they still exist. You might even see them, although it's not a given. They can't *use* the power they have, not on purpose. Andrew Copis *is* using power, but not consciously. They can't use it to defend themselves. They can't use it to free themselves. They can't use it to manifest and play with Michael on their own.

"To do any of that, they need you."

"They need a Necromancer, you mean."

"No. A Necromancer would never, ever do what you're doing now. Any of it. I meant you." He smiled, and it was the smile that she liked best. It was warm, if slightly weary, and it changed the lines of his face. Made him look more open. "Chase."

"Is she crazy?" Chase asked.

"Oh, probably."

"And the rest of you," Chase continued, looking at Amy, Allison, and Michael, although Michael was not paying attention. "Are you all crazy, too?"

"Dude, you see the dead and you talk about Necromantic magic and the City of the Dead, and *we're* crazy?" Amy shot back.

Eric walked over to Emma. "Emma, you are letting go of the children. Now."

"But they—"

"You can always let them out to play with Michael later. But you need to let go now."

"Why?"

"Because your teeth are starting to chatter, and you're turning blue." He reached out and caught her hands, and he forced them out of their numb, frozen curl. "We can come back and visit Michael again tomorrow," she told Georges and a crestfallen Catherine. "I promise."

His hands? Weren't cold. They were so very, very warm. And he cupped them around both of hers and held them.

*　　*　　*

"Is the house safe?" Amy asked Eric.

He nodded. "We can search the rest of the rooms if it makes you feel better."

"Not really. If it's safe, I have a party to attend." She stood, scraping concrete with the legs of her chair. "Emma?"

Emma nodded.

"I'm going to check on Skip. I don't see any reason to kick people out. So far, no one's called the police to close us down."

Chase's eyes almost fell out of his head, which made Emma laugh. "What?"

"You're going to keep the party going?"

Amy shrugged. "Why not? Longland won't be back tonight."

"How the hell can you say that?"

"He's not an idiot. Allison and Emma make a habit of trying to see—and say—only good things. I don't."

"No kidding."

She rolled her eyes. "He didn't like the odds or he wouldn't have run in the first place. You're still here. You know who he is now, or what you think he is, at any rate. Eric said he can't gather his power base at all quickly. He's not going to come back to face the same odds. Because I think you'll kill him, if he does. Or try. You can correct me when I'm wrong," she added. "Not that it happens often. Emma, did he wear those boots upstairs?"

"Sorry."

"Never mind. I'll kill him myself if I find dirt. Speaking of which, you should take Chase upstairs and do something about his hair." Amy grimaced. "Which, at this point, would probably involve shaving his head. We can talk in the morning, maybe go to this burned-out house you saw earlier."

Emma nodded again. Amy, in her perfect mock-harlequin getup, slid the doors to one side, letting noise out and herself in. Only when she was gone did Emma turn to Chase and Eric. "You're sure the house is safe?"

"Where did you find her?" Chase asked.

Eric, on the other hand, nodded.

"Good. We might as well go inside and see if there's any food left."

He shook his head. Emma caught it out of the corner of her eye as she turned to face Michael, who was standing, head bent, hands at his sides. He wasn't moving around too much, which was either a good sign or a very bad one.

"Michael?"

Michael nodded. "I want to go with you," he told her quietly.

She could have pretended to misunderstand him, but if she had, he would have asked again, with more words. "We won't go without you."

He nodded again, and this nod went on in a little bobble of head and hair. Allison touched his shoulder, and he stilled.

"I want to help them," Michael told her. "They shouldn't be here."

"No," she agreed softly. "They shouldn't. But I don't think Eric or Chase know where they *should* be. And I don't know how to get them there."

"But there's someplace they should go?"

"I think so, Michael."

He paused, but she knew him well enough to know he wasn't quite finished. "Will they be happy there?"

Remembering her father's words, Emma nodded. "Happy and safe."

"Then we should help them go there. Can you see it?"

"No. I think only the dead can."

"I don't want you to die, Emma."

She nodded again.

"But I guess sometimes what we want doesn't matter. You can't make them alive again, can you?"

She felt Eric's hands stiffen as they covered hers, as if he'd been stabbed or struck, hard. Her own tightened, catching his fingers.

"No," she told him softly. "I can't. If I could—" She closed her eyes. "I can't. I don't think anyone can."

"Would you?"

"Yes."

He nodded again, but this time, she thought he was done. He surprised her, but he often did. "What should I do?" He asked her quietly, in a voice she hadn't heard since he was twelve.

"Go find Oliver and Connell. And your books. We're going to stay here until one, and then we'll head home. But we'll call your house in the morning. Try—try hard—to finish your homework in the morning."

"But I watch—" he stopped, swallowed, and nodded. "I'll do homework in the morning."

"Michael?"

"Yes?"

"You did good. Georges and Catherine were happy, and I don't think they've had much to be happy about for a long time."

He smiled, then. Michael's smiles were always some mix of heartbreaking and beautiful, partly because they had their roots in a childhood he could still reach back and touch. It wasn't the same as Emma's or Allison's, because he saw it more clearly.

Only after he had shuffled inside did Allison speak.

"So, Eric. You and Chase hunt Necromancers."

They glanced at each other, and Eric winced slightly. This was probably because Emma had just crushed one of his hands in hers, in warning. Even Chase, who didn't seem, to Emma, to be the sharpest knife in the drawer, hesitated before he nodded.

"And you kill them, if you can."

"Ally, it doesn't matter," Emma said urgently.

"Yes, it does. Because if I'm not mistaken, Chase thinks you're a Necromancer."

The silence was notably chilier. Allison let it go on for a bit before she started again. "Longland was looking for Emma. But so was Eric, the 'new student.'"

"Ally."

"Were you looking for her to kill her?"

"Ally, *please.*"

"Is that a yes or a no?" When Eric didn't answer, she looked at Chase. "Well?"

"Yes," Chase replied. "She's a Necromancer."

"She's a Necromancer who *hasn't done anything wrong.* You were just going to kill her because in the future she *might?*"

Chase's eyes had narrowed. "We were planning to kill her before she figures out how to use the power she has and starts killing hundreds of *other* people, none of whom have our training."

"Because you could just assume that she's going to turn into a mass murderer?" Allison's face had gone from the healthy side of pink to the unhealthy side of crimson. "And how many other times have you *saved the world* by killing someone who is *entirely* innocent of any crime?"

"Have you ever met a fucking Necromancer?"

"Apparently yes—I have one for a best friend!"

"So maybe she's a freak!" Chase was also red now. The color didn't suit him.

"So *maybe* other budding Necromancers were freaks too—and you'll never know it because they're dead!"

"Allison," Eric said, shaking his hands free from Emma's and turning toward her, "don't judge him. You don't know what he's been through."

"I don't know what he's been through?" Allison took a deep breath. It was not a cessation of hostility, however. She needed it. "You're right. I don't. And you know what? I'm not going to kill *him.* He has *no idea* what Emma's been through, and he intended to kill her."

"When he speaks of hundreds dead, he speaks from experience. He's seen what Necromancers can do."

"Fine! Then kill the Necromancers that *do*. Killing Emma means there's one less decent person in the world! Or does he only try to kill Necromancers who can't do anything to defend themselves first?"

"Ally, he did go after Longland."

Allison looked at Emma, and then shook both her head and her hands to prevent a familiar half-shriek of frustration from escaping. "Em, this is serious."

"I know. Believe that I know. But Eric? He's not going to kill me."

"Chase?"

Chase had shoved his hands into his pockets, and his shoulders were at about the same level as his ears.

"Well?" Allison's hands were in tight fists at her sides.

"No," he said, as if the word had been dragged from him, and judging by his expression, had broken his front teeth on the way out. "No, I am not going to kill Emma. Satisfied?"

"Not really."

"What *would* satisfy you?"

"Help us."

"Help you do what?"

"Free the dead. You can start with the little boy on Rowan Avenue."

Chase gave the little shriek that Allison had managed to swallow. "What's the *point*? He's *dead!*"

Allison just stared at him. After a moment, she said, "I would rather spend eternity wandering up and down an empty street than burning to death without actually dying. I'm assuming that the same is probably true of a *four-year-old*."

Chase stared at her for a moment and then turned to Emma.

"Don't look at me for support. I'm so much in Allison's camp we might as well be sharing a brain."

"Eric?"

"You can go back if you want; I know enough to know this is going to be hard on you. But I'm staying until this is resolved, one way or the other."

Chase opened his mouth. Closed it, shoved his hands into his pockets. Opened his mouth again. Emma liked that Chase was always so expressive, except when she didn't.

Before he could say anything—or before he could figure out which of the many things he was going to say first—a phone rang.

Emma recognized the ring.

"Fuck." So, apparently, did Eric.

"Are you going to answer that?" Allison asked him.

Emma almost laughed.

"No."

"At this time of night? It could be an emergency."

"If I answer it, it will be. Come on, let's get something to eat."

Chase shrugged as the phone stopped ringing. They made it to the door before it started ringing again. "You know he's just going to keep trying."

"Let him. It's loud enough inside I won't hear it."

"Answer it, Eric."

"No."

"If you don't answer it, he'll just call *me*."

"You don't have a working phone."

Chase laughed. "You think of everything."

"Someone," Eric said, sliding the door to one side, "has to."

They dropped Michael off first, swung around to Allison's house, and then dropped Emma off by her front door. The time was just a little past one-thirty, which in the Hall household was still within the bounds of "on time."

Emma stopped by the driver's window, and Eric opened it.

"Do you have my number?" she asked him.

"No."

"Do you want it, or do you just want to come by in the morning?"

Chase said something about morning, which Emma pretended not to hear.

"If you come, I'll feed you. I might even feed Chase. I don't know when Amy will call, so you might be cooling your heels for a while."

"Any chance she won't call?"

"None."

"We'll drop by. When's good?"

"Any time after eight-thirty." She turned toward the house, stopped, and turned back. "Thanks."

"For what?"

"For tonight. You can thank Chase, too."

"You could thank me yourself!"

"Too much trouble," she said, but she smiled. She was tired, and even the hot and stuffy house hadn't taken the edge off the chill in her hands. "We need to find Maria Copis, and we need to get her to Rowan Avenue. I don't think all the ladders in the world are going to help us get that child out if she's not there."

"Let us figure out where she went after her house burned down. You get some sleep."

She nodded, and headed to the front door. The walking, black alarm system was already gearing up on the other side of it.

When the house door had closed on the glimpse of a frantically barking rottweiler, Chase turned to Eric. "Do you have any idea what you're doing?"

Eric shrugged. After a moment, he said, "Do you really want to kill her?"

"I think we should. You didn't tell her that she's now carting around more power than most Necromancers *could*."

"No." Eric was restless enough to open the car door; the lights went on. "They're not power, to her. There's no way she's going to *use* them."

"She didn't even have to *try* to get the dead to show. She just did it."

"I know, Chase. I was there, remember?"

"You didn't warn her about Longland, either."

"If I had warned her about Longland's power, she'd've figured it out. She's crazy but she's not stupid. And warning her wouldn't give her any useful information." He looked at Chase, got out of the car.

Chase sighed—audibly—and slid out the other door.

"Do you want to kill her?" Eric asked again.

"Does it matter? I'm not going to try."

"Yeah, it matters."

"I think we should."

"Not an answer, Chase."

"Asshole." Chase slammed the car door shut, turned his back, and after a minute, walked around the back of the car and slammed the other door shut as well. He leaned against the driver's door, his back to Eric. "I understand why you didn't. Kill her, I mean. She seems so *normal*."

"Yeah. Normal. Happy. Has friends she actually cares about who are actually still alive. So."

Chase pushed himself off the car. "You want me to take the first shift, or do you want to take it?"

"Up to you."

Chase detached himself from the car. "I need a new coat." He glanced at the house and added, "Any chance that dog won't go insane if I park myself inside?"

"He's a rottweiler."

"Figures."

"You sure you want the first shift?"

"Yeah. I don't want to go back and hit the radioactive button on the answering machine."

Eric grimaced. "Fine. I'll be back in four hours."

"It'll probably take at least that long to wade through the messages."

"Thanks. Don't," he added, "do anything stupid. If Longland does show up here, he's not going to kill her. He will, however, kill you without blinking."

"He'll try." Chase smiled. Even in the scant light, it wasn't pleasant. But it was, Eric had to admit, all Chase.

# CHAPTER
# TWELVE

EMMA'S MOTHER HADN'T WAITED UP, which was probably for the best. The lights were off in the house; the only light in the hall was the light that shone in through the little decorative windows in the front door. Emma doused that when she shut off the front door's light. She stood in the hall, absently patting Petal's head until her eyes had acclimated to the darkness; the only place it was ever truly dark was the basement.

When everything had become a dark gray, she slid out of her shoes, picked them up by the back straps, and headed up the stairs. The stairs were carpeted, but the house wasn't exactly new; they creaked as she walked. They creaked as Petal walked, but he jingled anyway. No one in the Hall house could be easily woken up by either sound. Not if they actually wanted to get sleep, ever.

She made her way to her room, dropped the shoes in front of her closet, and began to fiddle with the straps of her dress. Her hands were cold; she rubbed them together, but it didn't help. Bed—and the large, down duvet—might. Petal jumped up on the bed, somewhere near the foot, and waited, his head resting on his forepaws.

"Sorry, Petal. I know it's late." She slid out of her dress, grabbed pajamas, slid into them, and sat on the side of the bed, scratching behind his ears.

Something made her look up. It wasn't sound, exactly, and it wasn't light—but it caught her as if it were both, and loud and bright.

Her father stood in the center of the room. "Sprout."

She wanted to get up and run into his arms. She didn't. She was cold enough, and she knew that there was no warmth waiting. Love, yes, and affection—but also cold. She pulled the duvet up and around her shoulders, resting her hands in her lap.

"Dad." Petal tried to get under the covers as well, but as he was sitting on the outside of one end, he had no luck.

"Sleep, Em."

"Why are you here?"

He shook his head and looked out the curtained window. What he saw, given that the curtains were drawn, she couldn't tell.

"To see you, Emma. To see that you're okay."

She smiled, shivering. "I'm fine," she told him.

He stared at her and then folded his arms across his chest. If hands-on-the-hips when angry came from her mother, this folding of arms—and raising of one brow—was definitely learned from Brendan Hall.

"You need to let them go, Em."

She could have pretended to misunderstand him, but that had never gone down well. "I don't know how."

"How did you bind them?"

"I didn't! They were already bound."

"They're bound to you."

"How do you *know*?"

"You're my daughter," he replied.

His words made her yearn for the days when she was four years old, parents lived forever, and her father knew *everything*. The yearning was so strong that she was out of bed and almost across the room before she caught herself and froze. He'd opened his arms as well, and at the last moment, stepped back, failing to catch her.

"It's hard, being dead," he told her, his lips curved in an unfamiliar and bitter smile.

"Is it worse than being alive when the people you love go and die on you?" She stopped speaking and looked away. After a moment, when she could trust her words again, she added, "Sorry, Dad."

"Nathan?" he asked her softly, and she startled.

"You know about Nathan?"

"Daughter, remember?"

She tried really, really hard to believe that he hadn't seen anything that would embarrass her. Or him.

If he had, he was kind enough not to mention it. But he'd mentioned Nathan. She went back to her bed, pulled enough of the duvet free of Petal, who'd begun his midnight sprawl, and wrapped it tightly around herself. "I miss him.

"I keep hoping—I keep *wanting*—to see him." She looked at her father, then. Waited until her voice was steady. That took a while. "Just to talk to him. Just to hear him again." And to touch him again, even if her hands numbed at the shock.

"But . . . what if he's like the others? What if he's on some golden leash, and he's being drained of any power he might have that could— that could bring him *back* to me?"

"Emma." Her father started to say more, and stopped.

She was cold, cold, cold. She couldn't, at this moment, remember what being warm felt like.

"You need to let go of them. At least a couple of them. Chase and Eric didn't say enough. Maybe because they don't understand it. I can see it in you, now. It takes power, to hold the dead. If you can't pull power from them to do it, the bindings take power from you."

"How do I let go?"

"Unwind the chains, Emma."

"I broke them."

"Yes. And no. You couldn't break them; you grabbed them. You're holding them."

"Oh." She looked at her hands, at her empty palms. "Dad?"

"Yes?"

"What else can you tell me about being a Necromancer?"

He said nothing.

"What can you tell me about the City of the Dead?"

His arms, which had fallen to the sides in his abortive hug, now folded themselves across his chest again; his hand curled, for just a moment, around the bowl of a pipe that he couldn't smoke. When she had been young, he had called it his thinking pipe. "Not very much," he finally said. "But it's there."

"Where?"

He lifted an arm, his sleeves creasing slightly, and pointed.

"Give me something I can Google."

That smile again. She hated it.

"Can the dead at least talk to each other?"

"Some can. It depends."

"On what?"

"Power, Emma."

"But Eric and Chase said—"

"They're not dead."

She was shivering, and the duvet didn't help. His arms fell to his sides, and then he walked across the room to the side of her bed and knelt there, as if she were four years old again, and sick, and awake in the middle of a long night.

He touched her forehead with his hand, and his hand passed through her. Or it started to. She reached up and grabbed that hand. And *yes*, it was cold. But she felt something at the heart of that ice, something that shed warmth the way the sun sheds light. She brought her free hand around, caught his, held it, and felt her hands, without the painful tingle, for the first time since she had introduced the dead to her friends.

And then she cried out, and pulled both of her hands back, as if the warmth had scorched her. "Dad, no!"

"Emma, you won't survive a week otherwise. I'm dead," he added softly. "And in this world, that means only one thing: sooner or later. Someone is going to harvest whatever power I have. I would rather give it to you now, because when I give it to you, I'm saving the life of my very stubborn, very precious daughter.

"I can't do anything else for you. Let me do this."

"You can. You can talk to me. You can come to me more often. You can tell me I'm not insane."

"Talk is cheap."

"Fine. It's cheap. It's better than *nothing*."

He flinched.

But she wouldn't touch his hands again, and she realized that she had to be the one who initiated the touch. He could touch hers, but there was no actual contact. She knew this because he tried. "I'm not cold now," she whispered, and it was true. But she felt like a—a vampire. Or worse. The cold had to be better than this.

Eric and Chase came by at 8:30 in the morning.

Had it not been for Emma's father, her first clue would have been Petal jumping off the bed, running down the stairs, and barking in an endless loop. But even in her sleep, she was aware of Brendan Hall, and he returned at 8:00. Which was good, because on a good weekend, her mother didn't lever herself out of bed until 9:30 or 10:00. Given the shock of seeing her dead husband, Emma expected that this would be a *bad* weekend. For her mother.

Which would be useful, but made Emma feel guilty.

Swinging around the bottom of the banister she headed to the kitchen, checked milk, eggs, and bread with a slightly anxious frown.

All there. She also checked sugar, brown sugar, maple syrup, cinnamon, coffee, and tea. That done, she fed Petal, who was as usual slightly anxious because she'd done things in the wrong order. If he could talk, he would say *feed me* pretty much all day long.

It was too early to phone anyone, and she had no idea exactly when Eric and Chase would show up, so she sat in the living room, legs curled beneath her on the couch, Petal's head in her lap. Thinking about Necromancy. About Necromancers. And about the dead, her absent, longed-for dead. It wasn't a cheerful way to spend the time, but it was also the way she frequently spent a lot of the weekend. Except for the Necromancy part.

When Petal bounced off the couch and headed to the door, she rose and went with him. She didn't bother to tell him to be quiet, because it never worked; instead she inserted her legs between as much of his body and the door as she could, while opening it.

Chase and Eric were almost at the front step.

"Can you guys hurry?" she said. "I don't want Petal to wake up my mom."

"She can sleep through that?" Clearly skeptical, Chase looked at Petal, who could be heard barking through two closed doors and a stretch of walk.

"Not for more than ten minutes."

They hurried into the house as Emma slid a Milk-Bone into the palm of her hand. The rottweiler stopped barking and started chewing instead. Eric crouched down and patted his head. Because Petal was a very sweet-tempered dog, he didn't assume that Eric was trying to steal his food, and Eric got to keep his hand.

She busied herself in the kitchen and was surprised when Eric and Chase ambled in.

"Can we do anything to help?" Eric asked.

"The answer to that is no, trust me," Chase told Emma. "Because I see the table is already set."

Emma, breaking eggs, spared Chase a glance. "Oh?"

"He can set the table and dry the dishes. And take out the garbage, if you nag him. He can't, on the other hand, be trusted with food."

"Because he eats it?"

"Because he ruins it. I've had eggs he's forgotten were in boiling water; you could bounce them off walls."

"That happened *once*," Eric told Emma.

"Because we never let him try it again."

"Chase likes cooking because it gets him out of cleaning up."

Chase grinned. "Also true."

Emma looked at the two of them and laughed. Felt a pang of only-child sneak up on her, even though they weren't actually brothers. It was hard not to like them, even knowing what they did. On the other hand, if she needed a reality check, Allison would be coming sometime soon. She glanced at the clock. Not time to call Michael yet.

Chase picked up an apron.

"No, honestly, I don't need help."

"Don't get all kitchen territorial on me," he told her cheerfully.

"Why not? It's my kitchen."

He turned enormous, puppy dog eyes on her. Petal would have been jealous, if he'd noticed. Chase's hair was a good deal shorter—and a good deal less frizzled and sooty—than it had been the previous evening, although a tiny, red braid trailed down the side of his neck.

She laughed in spite of herself. "That's not an answer."

Eric leaned against the counter and stretched.

"Well," Chase told her, "We hardly ever get the chance to cook like this. Mostly, we fight, drill, buy ugly jackets we can modify, fight some more, bleed a lot, and narrowly avoid dying."

"And kill people?"

"That, too."

"Chase," Eric said, "Don't be an asshole."

"What? I'm asking Emma for a chance to pretend—for, like, half an hour—that I'm a normal person."

Eric grimaced as Emma glanced his way. "Half an hour is the most he can manage."

"You're better at it?"

"Mostly. Sometimes I forget my manners."

"Your manners are good."

"Yes. Often too good."

She thought about that for a minute, and nodded. "Fine. Make the pancakes." She regretted this about two minutes later, because apparently Chase had strong religious issues about using an instant pancake mix. He also had some issues with the lack of bacon, and when Emma said "Nitrates," he snorted and sent Eric to the store.

Emma called Michael after breakfast and asked him to wait for Allison. She called Allison next and asked her to pick Michael up on the way. Eric, who was standing beside the phone, handed her a folded piece of paper. She opened it. It was an address.

"What's this?"

"Maria Copis' address. Her phone number's unlisted."

"How did you get this?"

"Don't ask."

She set the phone down almost hesitantly.

"What's wrong?"

"I'm afraid."

"Of what, exactly?"

She waved the address in the air. "We don't know what we're doing," she told him, as if this needed saying. "And if we go and get Andrew's mother, and drag her to Rowan Avenue, and we can't even reach her son, we'll have hurt her for no reason."

"And if you can reach him, somehow, and she's not there, there's no point?"

"Something like that."

"I think you're taking too much of a long view."

"Why?"

"Because you're going to need to get her there first. Work on that," he added.

"I think we can only get her there once."

Chase appeared from around the kitchen. "Eric, dishes?"

"Don't worry about the dishes." Emma told them both.

"What? I cook, he cleans. Those are the rules."

"You didn't *have* to cook, and he doesn't *have* to clean."

"If I don't want to listen to Chase bitch about this for the rest of the week, I do." He headed back into the kitchen. Emma started to follow him, but Chase positioned himself in the arch.

"Chase, I helped you cook. I can help him clean."

But Chase's expression had shifted, the smile that accompanied his banter deserting his face so cleanly it was hard to imagine that it had been there at all.

"I understand what Eric sees in you. In all of you."

"And that's a bad thing."

"For us? Yeah, it is. It reminds us of the life we don't have." His face tightened, jaw clenching a moment as he closed his eyes. "My sister," he said, eyes still closed, "would have liked you." Something went out of him, then. "Allison reminds me of my sister. Same unexpected temper. My sister would have said the same damn thing she said last night. But," he added, slowly opening his eyes, "she would have smacked me."

She swallowed. "Chase—" Reached out to touch him, and then pulled back. "Your sister's . . . not alive."

He shrugged, shirt creasing and draping again in a way that suggested silk. "No." He turned, and then turned back. "You're right. You don't know what you're doing."

"I know."

"What you don't know? It can kill you."

Remembering the heat of the fire, she nodded.

"It can also kill anyone you take with you. Your friends. Michael. Allison."

"Amy?"

"I don't think anything can kill Amy." He grimaced. "Look, you're what you are. I can't talk you out of it—and I'm not Eric. I'm not going to try, because unlike Eric, I have no hope. But Michael and Allison are *not* what you are. You drag them into this, they have no protection. You might think on that," he added, "because you seem to care about your friends."

"They—they want to help." Her mouth was dry.

"A toddler wants to play in the middle of the road, too. I'm not telling you what to do, Emma. I'm pointing out that it has costs."

"But you and Eric aren't Necromancers, and you do this all the time."

"Emma, what you're going to try? We've never done that. We've never tried it. And what we are? This is our *life*. If Michael and Allison had led *our* lives, they wouldn't be *your* friends." He swore. "And it wouldn't make it safe for them anyway."

"So . . . you're saying both you and Eric are at risk."

"Anyone there is at risk." He looked as if he would say more, but he didn't, and this time when he turned and headed into the kitchen, he didn't turn back.

Michael and Allison arrived less than half an hour later. Petal was all over Michael two seconds after the screen door opened—Emma knew this because she counted. She had to nudge them both out of the doorway so that Allison could actually get into the house without having to step over the huddle of rottweiler and Michael, but Emma took a minute to watch them. Michael would probably have a small fit if someone walked up to him and licked his face, but he barely grimaced when Petal did it. And she knew what her dog's breath smelled like.

Still, watching Michael with Petal was normal. She needed a bit of normal.

She handed Allison the piece of paper that Eric had handed her; Allison knew what it was immediately. She also had the same concerns that Emma had. But she had more faith in Emma than Emma did at this particular moment.

"Are you worried about getting her there?"

"No. I can do that."

Allison didn't ask how. "It's not just Andrew, is it?"

"Mostly."

"Em."

Emma grimaced. She had learned, over the years, that she could lie to Allison about little things—probably because Allison didn't care enough to pick at them—but never about anything big. Why she still bothered to try, she didn't know. "Chase thinks you're all in danger if we do this."

"We probably are. So?"

"Life-threatening danger."

"Emma Hall, do not even think of leaving us behind. You promised Michael you wouldn't," she added.

"I know. I just—I shouldn't have promised him that. I wasn't thinking."

"Yes, you were. You were thinking that you go through enough alone as it is. You don't need to prove anything. You don't know what you're doing, and neither do the rest of us—but we've always managed to come up with something when we work at it together. Besides, you're going to phone Amy and tell her you don't need her help?"

"Chase says that nothing can kill Amy."

Allison laughed. "Probably not."

Amy called at 10:00. She dropped by the house with a loaded SUV at 10:30 and honked, loudly. Emma, flipping the drapes back, saw the big gray vehicle they affectionately called the Tank, and motioned for everyone to head out.

Amy was not, however, alone. In the passenger seat, elbow hanging out the open window, was Skip. He looked better than he had the last time they'd seen him—he was at least conscious—but not by much.

"This is not a fucking barbecue," Chase muttered under his breath.

"Hi, Skip!" Michael said. He was cheerful in part because Chase's comment and Skip's presence seemed entirely unrelated to him. "Emma, are we bringing Petal?"

"No." Emma headed over to the driver's side of the car and glanced pointedly at Skip. Amy shrugged. "He wouldn't give me the car keys unless I brought him."

"If we were the secret service," Emma said, "the country would be doomed. How much does he know?"

"Enough," Skip replied, before Amy could—and given it was Amy, that was impressive, "not to have to be talked about in the third person."

Since ignoring Skip was a bit of a specialty, Emma said, "We always talk about Skip in the third person." She didn't, however, stick out her tongue.

"I'm coming along to keep you guys out of trouble."

"Oh, like *that* ever worked."

He grimaced. "Fine. I'm coming along because I'd like proof that my sister has lost her tiny little mind. I have a camera. I'll take pictures." When Emma hesitated, he added, "I'm going, or the car and the ladders aren't. You can take Amy."

Amy rolled her eyes at him in the mirror. "If you're finished? He can help with the ladders," she added. "Where are we going first?"

Emma grimaced. "We're going to get Maria Copis."

"That's the mother?"

Emma nodded. She gave Amy the address, waited until Amy had fiddled with the talking map, and then took it back.

\*     \*     \*

Maria Copis lived well away from the downtown core, in a neighborhood of semi-detached homes with uniformly neat lawns and trees that
had grown to a reasonable height, obscuring the boulevards. Emma
looked at them as the car slowed, and Eric said, "Her mother's house.
Number sixty-two."

"Oh."

"Where did you think she would go?" Chase asked.

Eric took one hand off the wheel to slap his shoulder.

"No," Emma told Eric. "It's fair. I didn't think."

"Listen to Emma," Chase told Eric. To Emma, he said, "Did you
think about what you were going to say?"

When Emma didn't answer, Chase snorted. As the car rolled to a
stop, he opened the door.

"No, you don't." Eric grabbed his shirt. "You're not going anywhere
near that house. Emma, Allison, this is all yours."

Emma nodded and glanced at Allison, who nodded back and opened
her door. She got out first, waiting for Emma to join her. Emma's hand
was shaking on the car's handle as she pushed the door open. She got
out slowly.

*I don't want to do this.*

"Emma?"

Emma glanced at Allison.

"I think we should get Michael."

"We look more harmless without him."

Allison said nothing, and after a moment, Emma nodded. She almost regretted it, but it bought her time. *I don't want to do this.*

Allison walked over to Amy's car as it pulled up, and after a minute,
she returned with Michael. "She's got kids," Allison told him. "An eighteen month old and a baby. We might need you to help with them while
we talk."

Michael nodded and looked at Emma, who hadn't moved.

Emma shook herself, took a deep breath, and started up the driveway. Yes, she didn't want to do this.

But she couldn't let that stop her.

As she walked, she thought of how she would feel if two strangers—of any age, any description—had shown up at her door, promising her they could take her to Nathan. Telling her that unless she believed them and went with them, Nathan would be trapped in a miniature version of hell for a long damn time.

She knew that she would stand in that door, Petal practically under her feet, staring at them as if they were either insane or unspeakably cruel. Knew, as well, that while most of her would want to slam the door in their faces, some stupid part of her would *want* to believe them. Not about hell, but about the necessity of *her* involvement.

And that part of her?

That stupid, selfish part would want to believe it because then she'd see him again. Just once. Just one more time. She could say good-bye. She could tell him she loved him. She hadn't been able to do that. He hadn't survived long enough for Emma to reach the hospital.

"Em?"

"Sorry." She'd stopped walking. Wrapping her arms around herself, she started again. But she was aware, as she walked, that it was the stupid, selfish part of herself that she needed to understand here: the part that hoped in the face of the worst possible loss even when it knew all hope was pointless.


Emma approached the bright red door. Flecks of peeling paint showed that it hadn't always been bright red, and this was exactly the type of detail she noticed when she was nervous. She cleared her throat, straightened her hands, reached for the doorbell and hesitated for just a moment.

Allison said nothing. Emma was fiercely glad that Allison was beside her; if she'd been Amy, she would have already pushed the doorbell and taken a step back. "Sorry, Ally," she said. "I'm just—I'm not certain what to say."

Allison nodded. Because she wasn't, either. But she had just enough faith in Emma that Emma *could* push the doorbell. Heard from the wrong side of the door, the chime was tinny and electric.

They waited together, listening for the sounds of footsteps. They heard the sound of shouting instead, and it got louder until the door opened.

A woman with a red-faced child on her hip stood in the doorway, dark strands of hair escaping from a ponytail and heading straight for her eyes. She was younger than Emma's mother; she looked as though she wasn't even thirty. The child's voice gave out in the presence of strangers, and she—Emma remembered the eighteen-month-old daughter—shoved a balled fist into her mouth.

"We're sorry to bother you," Emma said quietly, "but we're looking for Maria Copis."

The woman's dark eyes narrowed slightly. "Why?"

"We're not trying to sell anything," Emma said quickly. "Are you Maria Copis?"

The child reached out and grabbed a handful of her mother's hair, which took some effort, and made clear why so much of it had escaped its binding. "Don't do that," the woman said and, catching the perfect little fist, attempted to retrieve her hair without tearing it out. "Yes, I'm Maria Copis. As you can see," she added, "I'm a little busy. What can I do for you?"

"We just want a—a moment of your time," Emma replied. "I'm Emma Hall, and this is Allison and Michael. Do you mind if we come in?"

The answer was clearly yes. Maria set her daughter down inside the hall. The child immediately grabbed the edge of her mother's shirt and tried to drag her away from the door. "I really don't have time to talk right now," Maria said. "Maybe you could come back when my mother's home from work."

"I'm afraid we won't be here, then," Emma told her.

Before she could answer, her daughter let go of her shirt and walked in that precarious way that toddlers do, half leaning forward as if taunting gravity. She reached the edge of the front step and pointed up—at Michael. Michael knelt instantly, putting his hands in reach, and she leaped off the step to the sound of her mother's quiet shriek. Michael caught her, and she caught his nose. He laughed and said ouch, but not loudly enough to discourage her.

"Cathy, don't pinch people's noses," her mother said.

"I don't mind. It doesn't hurt," Michael told her. Cathy grabbed his ear instead, and he stood, lifting her off the ground. He also let her pull his head to the side until she was bored, which, since she was eighteen months old, didn't take too long. She went on to discover the pens Michael sometimes carried in his pockets, when he was wearing shirts that had them. She grabbed one, and they had a little tug of war over it.

Maria Copis stood in the door for a minute, watching Michael with her daughter. Her shoulders relaxed slightly, and she glanced at the two girls, shaking her head in wonder. "She's going through a shy phase. She won't even let my mother pick her up."

"Michael likes kids," Allison said. "And they've always liked him. Even the shy kids."

"I guess so." She exhaled. "You might as well come in, then. It's not going to be quiet," she added. "And the place is a mess."

The place, as she'd called it, was undeniably a mess, and they had to pick their way over the scattered debris of children's toys just to get out of the doorway. Michael tried to put Cathy down, but she grabbed his hair. So he sat crouched in the hall, surrounded by toys that were probably hers. He picked up a stuffed orange dinosaur and tried to exchange it for his hair.

When she ignored it, Michael made baby-dinosaur noises, which was better seen than described, and Cathy laughed when the baby dinosaur tried to lick her face. Emma glanced at Maria Copis, who was watching while a smile tugged at the corner of her lips. It was a tight smile, and it faded into something else as Emma watched.

She wanted to leave, then, because she knew what the expression meant, and she hated invading this woman's privacy—and her grief. But still, watching her daughter play with Michael was peaceful, and Emma remembered watching Michael play with Petal in just the same way. Life went on.

Some lives.

She let it go on for a while, because she was a coward and she still didn't want to do this: bring up Andrew, her dead son. Add to the pain.

But Andrew was waiting, and he was waiting for his mother. Emma found courage from somewhere, and she spoke.

"I know this is going to sound bad," she said quietly, and Maria started slightly and turned to face her. "And I want to apologize for that up front. I almost didn't come here today."

The woman looked confused. Not suspicious, not yet; that would come. Emma glanced at the living room, which was also mired in toys, and after a pause, she walked toward it, forcing Allison and Maria to follow. Michael, absorbed in little shrieks of laughter, would notice eventually, and even if he didn't, Maria could still keep an eye on him if she wanted.

"What did you want to talk to me about?" Her eyes narrowed. "You're not reporters, are you?"

"No! I mean, no, we're not. We're still in school," Emma added.

"I'm sorry," the woman replied. "The only strangers recently who've wanted to talk to me have been reporters. Or ambulance-chasing lawyers. And no," she added, again looking at Michael, or more accurately, at her daughter's face, "you really don't look like either."

Emma bit her lip. "We might as well be," she replied quietly. "Because we *are* here to talk about your son."

THE EASE—AND THERE HADN'T BEEN MUCH OF IT— drained out of Maria Copis' face. What was left was raw and angry. Emma flinched, even though she'd been expecting it.

"I think," the woman said evenly, "you'd better leave, now." Her hands, Emma noted, were balled in fists, and they were shaking slightly.

Emma raised both of her hands, palms out. "Please, hear me out. Please. I don't—I wouldn't do this to you, I *would not* be here, if there were any other way. I lost my father a few years ago. My boyfriend died this past summer in a car crash. Both times people let me grieve in peace. They gave me privacy, and I needed it. I *know* just how much I'd hate me if I were in your shoes.

"Please, just let me say what I came here to say. If you—if it makes no sense to you, if you don't believe it, we'll leave and we will never, ever bother you again."

The edge of anger left Maria's dark eyes, but her hands were still clenched, still shaking. Michael, behind her, was crawling around the floor on all fours, barking like a dog.

"Your boyfriend died last summer?"

It wasn't what Emma had expected to hear, and she flinched again, for entirely different reasons. But she swallowed and nodded.

"Were you there?"

"No. I would have been, if I could have. I went to the hospital the minute his mother called me to tell me—but none of us made it there in time." She closed her eyes and turned her face away for a moment, remembering the industrial gloss of off-white halls and the klaxon sound of monitors in the distance. She shook herself and looked back to Maria Copis.

"I'm sorry to hear that," the woman said quietly. As if she meant it. Her eyes were ringed with dark circles, and she lifted a hand and pushed it through her hair. No fists, now. No obvious rage.

"It was the worst thing that's ever happened to me," Emma replied. "And even so, I can't imagine what it must be like for you. I can try. I can *think* I understand it—but I don't." It was hard for her to say this, because she wasn't even certain it was true. Just one week ago, she would have said that no loss was greater, or could be greater, than the loss of Nathan. But . . . for just a moment, she thought Maria Copis' loss might be.

"Why did you come here, Emma?" The question was quiet, weary.

Emma took a deep breath. "I can see the dead."

Cathy shrieked with delight; it was the only noise in the house. It was followed by Michael's voice. Neither of them erased the heavy weight of the words Emma had just spoken.

Maria Copis said, "Pardon me?"

"I can see the dead," Emma repeated. She swallowed. "I know it sounds crazy. I know it sounds stupid, or worse. But I'm not pretending to be a medium or a—a whatever. I'm not going to tell you that I can reach the afterworld and put you in contact with your son, or offer to do it if you pay me. I don't want your money, and I'll never ask for it."

"You . . . can see the dead."

Emma nodded.

"And you're going to tell me you've seen my son."

"Not—not exactly."

Maria Copis lifted a hand. "I'm crazy tired," she said, and she obviously meant it. "And I'm either hallucinating, or I've lost my mind. I need a cup of coffee. Would either of you like one?"

"No, thank you," Emma replied. Allison didn't drink coffee.

"Come into the kitchen with me."

"Should we tell Michael to follow us?"

Maria lifted a hand to her eyes and rubbed them a couple of times. "No," she said. "My mother would call me an idiot, but—he's not going to hurt her, and he's not going to let her hurt herself. And this is as happy as I've seen her since—since. She deserves to play in peace while he's willing to play with her." She turned and walked into the kitchen, and, stepping around toys, Emma and Allison followed her.

She made coffee in silence, opening the various cupboards to find filters, coffee, and a cup. She kept her back to Emma and Allison the entire time, grinding beans first and then letting coffee percolate. When it was done, and when she'd added cream and sugar to the cup in very large amounts, she turned to them, leaning her back against the kitchen counter as if she needed the support.

"So. You two can see the dead."

"Oh, no," Allison said quickly. "Just Emma."

Maria's eyes reddened, and she bit her lip. She rubbed her eyes again with the palm of her hand. Emma looked at the floor, because it was hard to look at someone whose grief was so raw and so close to the surface she was like a walking wound.

Hard because Emma had been there. Had hidden it, as much as she could, because she *needed* to hide it. She'd told everyone she was fine—everyone except Petal, because Petal couldn't talk. When Maria Copis spoke again, however, Emma looked up.

"So, Emma, you can see the dead. But you haven't seen my son."

Emma grimaced. "Not yet."

"And you're trying to see him for some reason?"

"No." She swore softly. "Yes."

"Which is it?"

"Yes. We're trying to see your son." Emma spread her hands, again exposing her palms. "I—I heard you," she whispered. "From midtown, I heard you shouting his name. Drew."

Maria stiffened.

"And I followed it. The shouting. It was—" Emma took a deeper breath. "I'm sorry. Let me try this again. I *can* see the dead. Some of the dead are strong enough that I can see where they are. Or where they were when they died. Some of the dead are strong enough that they think they're still there, and I can see and feel what they see and feel."

Maria put the coffee cup down on the counter and folded her arms across her chest, drawing them in tightly.

"I could hear the shouting while I was in school, and I followed it, while a friend drove and took my lousy directions. When we finally got to Rowan Avenue, I tried to go into what was left of the house. I couldn't. Fire was gouting out the windows."

"There's no fire there now," Maria said.

"No. In theory there wasn't any fire when I went, either. No one else could see it," she added quietly, "because no one else can see the dead. Only me. It singed my hair.

"I didn't know who was trapped in the house. I only knew that the fire was recent because it looked recent, and the buildings were still standing. I went home, because I couldn't get into the building, and I looked the address up, because I hoped it would tell me what had happened or what was happening." She swallowed. "And when I read his name—Andrew—I realized that the shouting I'd heard wasn't his. It was yours."

Maria lifted a hand to her face for just a moment. When she dropped it, she wrapped her arm around herself again. She didn't speak.

Emma did. "He could hear you. He could hear you shouting. He still can.

"He thinks the house is burning. I couldn't get to him because I couldn't get through the fire, not then. So, no, I haven't seen your son."

Silence.

"I am *trying* to see your son," Emma continued, her voice thickening, "because I think he's trapped in the burning building. I'm not even sure we can safely get into the building; I'm not sure if we can reach wherever he's standing. But I have to *try*. And I came to you because—" She couldn't say it. She couldn't say the rest of the words. She turned to Allison, and Allison was blurry, which was a bad sign. Emma Hall didn't cry in public.

Allison caught her hands and squeezed them, and Allison saved her.

"We think," Allison told Maria Copis, "that Andrew won't—or can't—come out of that building if you're not there. He's waiting for you," she added quietly. "He has no idea that he's dead."

And there it was. When Emma could see again, when she could see clearly—or as clearly as she was going to be able to see—she could see the hunger in Maria Copis' eyes as plainly as if it were her own. She could see the suspicion, as well; she could see the way Maria's expression shifted as she tried to figure out what their angle was. What they wanted.

As if to quell those suspicions, she walked to the edge of the kitchen and glanced out into the hall where Michael was still playing with her toddler. She stood there for minutes, and then, arms still tightly wound around her body, she turned back.

She was crying now, but she didn't raise her hands to wipe the tears away; they fell, silent, down gaunt cheeks. "Why should I believe you?" she whispered.

This, too, Emma understood. But she could do something about this. She lifted one hand, and she whispered a single name. *Georges.*

In the air before Emma, a golden chain extending from the palm of her hand to his heart, Georges shimmered into existence. The sunlight through the kitchen windows shone through his chest, casting no shadows. But he looked at Emma almost hopefully, and she cringed.

She held out her hand to him, and he took it in his own.

Maria Copis gasped and covered her mouth with one hand. She swore into her palm, her eyes widening, her brows almost disappearing beneath the fringe of loose, dark hair.

"Georges," Emma said, "I'm sorry. Michael can't play right now, but I wanted to introduce you to Maria Copis. Maria," she added, "this is Georges."

"He's—" Maria hesitated and then took two firm steps toward Georges, who looked dubious but stood and waited. Georges didn't look like a ghost. He felt like one, to Emma, whose hand was already beginning to sting at the physical contact. Maria tried to touch Georges and her hand passed through him, as Emma had known it would.

"Oh, my god. Oh, my god."

Georges turned to Emma. "Where's Michael?"

"He's babysitting right now."

The look of disappointment across those delicate features was its own kind of heartbreak, in a day that had already exposed too much of it.

"I'm sorry, Georges," Emma said, kneeling so that she was closer to his eye level. "I promise as soon as I can, you can see Michael again. But we're trying to help another little boy—"

"They caught him?"

"No. No, Georges. He's trapped inside a burning building."

Georges frowned. "Did he die there?"

Emma nodded.

"I don't think you should go there."

"We have to try to help him," Emma said quietly. "He's a little boy. Much younger than you."

"Oh." Georges nodded. And then, while Emma watched, he quietly disappeared.

And Maria Copis looked at Emma.

"I'm sorry," Emma said, rubbing her hand. "Even dead children like Michael."

The woman's laugh was brief and brittle.

Emma swallowed air. "I can't promise anything," she told Maria Copis. "And I won't try. I'm not sure we can even get past the fire—but I can't leave him there without trying. We came here to ask you to come with us—but we might not be able to reach him at all. It might all be for nothing."

"When are you going?"

"We're going now. If you give me your phone number, I can call you if we can actually get far enough into the building to reach him."

Maria laughed again, and it was the same thin laugh.

"But we have two cars," Allison told her, correctly interpreting that laughter. "If you can't find a babysitter, we can all go. Michael would stay if we asked him."

"I can call my mother. I can ask her to come home from work. I can—" she stopped as Emma stiffened, but Emma said nothing. ". . . I can sound like a crazy, grief-stricken, hysterical daughter."

Emma winced. But she didn't disagree. "I could ask Georges to come out again for your mother," she began.

"No. You're right, even if you didn't say it out loud. We could call her, she could come home, and she could be terrified enough that she wouldn't be fit to babysit, if she even let me out of the house. How long do you think—" She lifted a hand. "No, sorry. I'm just being incredibly stupid. I can't call anyone else, either. Do you have enough room for two car seats?"

Emma nodded. "We have two cars—and a couple of other friends as well."

"There are more of you?"

"We needed help with the ladders. You'll come with us?"

"Yes. He's *my son*. There's no way I'm going to stay here just waiting beside the phone while you try to help him. Yes, Emma. I'll come. Maybe Michael can help with the kids while we're there."

If Emma's world had changed overnight—and, with the appearance of Longland and the ghosts, it had—Rowan Avenue had continued in blissful ignorance. If, by blissful, one meant a raging fire and billowing dark smoke from all the downstairs windows. Emma got out of the car slowly, and approached the sidewalk, where she surveyed the ruined buildings. Only one of them was burning, which made it a bit easier to spot, given the lack of numbers on the front facade.

She glanced at Allison, who had also emerged, and at Michael, who was half in and half out of the car, struggling with the straps of a car seat and a toddler who did not, apparently, like being stuck in one. Amy had pulled up by the curb, parked, and flipped the back hatch of her vehicle up; she was already giving Skip—and Eric and Chase— instructions about the ladders.

Maria Copis emerged last, holding her baby while Michael carried Cathy. She stayed beside Michael, possibly because Cathy was attached to him with that toddler force that allows for no quiet separation, and possibly because it was hard for her to approach the ruins of her home, the place where her son had died.

Emma glanced at her and found it hard to look away. Maria was holding her baby as if the baby was some kind of life buoy and she was on the edge of drowning.

"Maybe this wasn't a good idea," Emma said softly to Allison.

Allison shook her head. "It's going to be hard for her. Even if she weren't here with us—even if she weren't trying to help her son. Her oldest child died here. I don't know if Cathy remembers the house or not—she's still glued to Michael—but . . . Maria had to walk out of the house without Andrew and pray that he followed."

"I know—it's just . . . the look on her face, Ally."

Allison didn't tell her not to look. Amy would have, but Amy was busy shouting at Skip. Skip, not shy, was shouting back. Eric, not stupid, was quietly avoiding getting between two siblings who were arguing, and Chase—well, it looked as though Chase was *trying* not to be stupid and mostly succeeding.

Emma spread her hands out, palms up. "I feel like I should say something to her or do something for her, but I can't think of a damn thing I could do that won't somehow make it worse."

"Except this," Allison said quietly.

"Except this."

"What do you see, Em?"

Emma grimaced. "Smoke. Black smoke. And fire."

"Can you hear anything?"

Emma frowned. After a moment, she said, "Beyond the fire? No."

"No shouting?"

"No. It's the first time—" She grimaced again and wondered if the expression was going to be stuck there permanently, she'd used it so often lately. "Not that I've been here that often. But . . . no. I don't hear her voice."

"Is that a bad sign?"

"I don't know."

"Emma!" Amy, hands on her hips, had turned. "Are you going to sit there chatting with Allison all day, or are you going to get this show on the road?"

Allison touched her shoulder. "We needed the car and the ladders," she whispered.

Emma nodded, shoved her hands into her pockets, and headed toward the facade, where Chase and Eric were now positioning ladders. Or trying to keep them in position. The front of the building was not entirely cooperating, because there was a small porch on the second floor that hovered just over the door. It wasn't terribly wide, but it was—almost—in the way of at least one of the ladders.

They did, however, manage to set the ladder against the wall just to one side of the overhang. How, Emma had no idea, and she wasn't about to look a gift horse in the mouth. No one lived here anymore, so any external damage to the building wasn't likely to get them in trouble.

"Eric," she said instead, as she approached him, "I think something's changed."

He raised a brow, and left Chase and Skip. "What's wrong?"

"I—when we were here last time, I could hear his mother shouting his name. I can't hear her now. Is that because she's here?"

"Emma, please don't take this the wrong way, but I don't know. I've never done this before. Chase sure as hell hasn't, and neither have any of your friends. This is a first, for all of us." He glanced over his shoulder at Amy and then back. "On the other hand, at least one of us isn't fazed by it at all."

"Amy doesn't believe in dwelling on difficulties."

"There's a lot Amy doesn't believe in. I'm surprised she believes in the dead."

Emma laughed. "If she's seen it, she believes in it. And if she believes in it, it's not safe to question her."

"I think I got that." He smiled, but it faded. "Can you see the fire?"

Emma nodded. She glanced at Skip, and winced. "I don't think I've ever seen Skip so angry."

"He's not gaining much traction with Amy."

"No, but he's lived with her all her life; he's got to be used to that. He mostly trusts her. If he's pushing, he knows she'll push back, and *he's* the one who's skipping Dalhousie to come to Amy's party."

"That's not his fault."

"His parents won't care, unless he can convince them—and no one's in a hurry to drag parents into this." She failed to mention Michael. "They can't do anything but die." She turned back to the fire, although she'd never really left it; it was loud.

"Bad?"

"It's bad. But firefighters did get in through the upper windows, and the worst of the fire seems to be coming out of the downstairs ones. If it's true that I'll be in whatever Andrew sees, I should be able to get to him through the second story as well."

"Without the asbestos and the oxygen."

"Thank you, Eric."

He grinned, but the grin didn't reach his eyes. "You don't have to do this," he told her, reaching for her hand and gripping it surprisingly tightly.

She looked over her shoulder at Maria Copis, still clutching her baby. Then she looked back, and briefly squeezed his hand. "Sorry. You don't have to, though."

"As if." He shook his head, but he hadn't expected a different answer, and she wondered why he'd tried. She would have asked, but Maria now approached her. Emma made way for her at the base of the first ladder.

"What do we do, now?" Maria asked.

"I go up the ladder," Emma told her, striving for certainty. "I'll take a look around."

"And what do you want me to do?"

"Give the baby to Amy or Allison. Or Skip. You can climb up on your own, but you won't see the fire—at least I don't think you will—until I find Andrew."

"You don't think?"

Emma winced. "I'm not entirely certain how this part works. I'm fairly new to all this—"

"Is there anyone here who isn't?"

Emma didn't answer that, but continued, "—but new or not, we all feel we need to at least try." She tried to keep her voice smooth.

Maria Copis frowned. "This isn't safe, is it?"

"It should be."

"For you. This isn't safe for you."

Eric, bless him, said nothing.

"Does it matter?" Emma asked Maria, squaring her shoulders slightly, and taking the meager scraps of courage she could from defiance.

"Yes. You're not dead. He is." Maria swallowed and glanced away, but only for a second. "I don't want to be responsible for—for killing you."

"You're not. This was my decision, start to finish, and we're going up there with or without you."

Eric cleared his throat. "I think you're getting left behind," he told them both.

Emma frowned and turned toward the ladders. Chase was already at the top of the rightmost one. He turned and blew her a kiss, and she grimaced. He missed it; he'd already braced himself against the ladder—with a pause to shout instructions to Skip and Amy, who had managed enough of a truce to hold the ladder steady between them—before crawling in through the window. "Chase," she told Maria, "is very easily bored and has no sense of self-preservation."

"Chase," Eric corrected her, "is testing the floor to see if it'll hold weight. It probably won't," he added quietly, "and if it doesn't, you're going to have to hold her hand before she enters the building."

"But the fire—"

"Yes. She'll see it, too."


Maria's glance bounced between Eric and Emma a few times. She didn't speak. Instead, she withdrew for a moment. Emma almost asked why, but she stopped when Maria pulled up the edge of her shirt and nudged her baby awake.

"I'll feed him," she told Emma quietly. "And change him. Hopefully he'll sleep until after—after we've finished."

"What if he wakes up?" It was Allison, who had joined them quietly, who asked. Which made sense, since it was Allison who was going to be holding him.

"Walk him around. Or bounce him—gently." She didn't ask Emma how long things would take. She didn't ask anything. Instead, she told Allison, "There's a bottle for Cathy in the diaper bag and a couple of teething biscuits; if she's fussing—and she won't until she's tired—have Michael give her both." She took a breath, held it, expelled it. "I don't suppose any of you have changed diapers?"

Eric raised a hand. "I have."

"If she needs—"

"We'll take care of her. If we're down here."

Chase came down the ladder and found Eric and Emma.

"Well?" Eric asked him.

Chase grimaced. "It held, at least part of the way in. I'd recommend that you let Maria risk it," he told Emma, "but make sure she's standing almost on top of you. If the floor buckles, grab her hand or her arm, and pull her in. Unless the fire doesn't seem too bad when you get up there. In which case, just pull her in right away."

He hesitated for a minute, and then he addressed Maria. "I'm going to go up with you both, if that's okay. I'm crap with babies, and Eric's practically a wet nurse, but without the breasts. If Emma has problems, I'm going to have to pull her out. I'll be walking behind you, hopefully far enough back that my weight won't be a tipping point if the joists are going to collapse. But I'll need to risk a bit, because I won't be able to reach her if she needs help.

"She'll be walking into the burning house," he added. "It won't look like that to either of us, but . . . she might catch fire, her hair might burn. I don't know if the effects of the—of—" he had the grace to flush. "I'm sorry. I don't know if your son is strong enough to actually burn her clothing."

Maria nodded gravely. "If she looks like she's being burned, or if she starts to cough or choke, you'll pull her out?"

"Got it in one. But I might need help. Don't try to help me unless I ask for it; stand your ground, because the floor's not solid. When I touch Emma," he added, "the floor will be solid for *me*. But so will the fire. If you can avoid that, avoid it. Wait for my word.

"Got it, Emma?"

Emma nodded. "Maria, was he in his bedroom?"

Maria swallowed. The words were slow to come, and they came in a heavy rush. "Yes. I left him there and headed to the stairs. It's the room to the side of the hall, not the back room. These windows open onto my bedroom. If you head out the door into the hall, his is the first room on the right."

"Good. It's not far."

Chase said, "Far enough."

Eric stepped on his foot. "Here, Em. Maria. Take these." He handed them damp towels. "Cover your mouths, if it comes to that. I don't know how much time you'll have; I don't know how much time you'll *need*. Buy what you can."

Emma nodded.

"Come out the same way you entered, if you have that much control."

"We should be able to do that."

"Yes. You should. But right now, Andrew is in the driver's seat, and it may mean you won't have the choice." He hesitated and then added, "Even if you can touch him, and she can see him, she can't touch him, Emma." The words were soft and final.

Emma, who had not thought of it until that moment, felt the world shift—in a bad way—beneath her feet. His mother couldn't touch him, and couldn't pick him up, and he hadn't moved the first time when she'd shouted and pleaded with him. He had waited for her to carry him out.

And that had killed him.

\*    \*    \*

They started up the ladders. Emma went first, and she moved slowly, covering her mouth and nose with a damp towel. It was hard to see much, because the smoke from the lower windows was so dark and so acrid; it stung her eyes, and clung—she was certain—to her hair. She felt the heat, but the actual ladder was cool to the touch. It wasn't much of a comfort, but here, you took what you could.

Beneath her, struggling in her own way, Maria Copis followed. Chase was climbing the other ladder in parallel, shouting encouragement. At least, that's what Emma thought he was trying to do; what he was actually achieving was more irritating. Then again, an irritating Chase was a whole lot better than a deadly fire if she had to choose something to dwell on.

There was still broken glass in the window frame. Only the bottom of the frame, which was black with smoke, was an issue, if they were careful. Emma, who had dressed to visit a bereaved parent, winced— she had old painting clothing, most of it her mother's, and after she'd finished here it was going to look a whole lot better than what she was wearing now. And she *liked* these clothes.

Chase helpfully told her to be careful of the glass.

She helpfully told him that she was; she might have said more, but Maria was here. Maria, whose face was a little like the shards of glass that nestled in what was left of the window's frame; you could cut yourself on her expression if you weren't careful.

Emma was careful enough to hold the cloth to her face and to partially cover her eyes, and then she wasn't worried about Maria anymore. The room wasn't burning, but smoke was wafting up the stairs and through the open door. It was hard to avoid the glass when she couldn't clearly see it, but she came up on the window's edge on the soles of her shoes before jumping lightly down. The floor held. It was hot, but it held.

Chase had told her to wait for Maria, but it was hard. This was where Andrew had died, and this was almost when—and what killed him, could kill her. She dropped to the ground, staying as close to the floorboards as she could to avoid the smoke.

Maria came up through the window next, and she took a lot more care getting down from the frame. Chase, in the window beside hers, was doing the same. "You're okay?" he asked. Emma wasn't certain who he was asking; she couldn't see, clearly, where he was looking.

"Emma?" Maria said.

"Avoiding the smoke," she barked back. "Hurry, please."

But it wasn't as easy as that; it never was. Maria was stepping gingerly across the boards, testing how much give they had; she was stopping to listen to Chase, and she was following his directions. He was less careful than she was.

Emma couldn't see what Maria was stepping on; she could only see what she herself moved across, and she wondered just how different they were. Grinding her teeth, and staying as low to the ground as possible, she crawled along the same path that Maria Copis was walking. She crawled faster.

By some miracle, they reached the hall door, then the hall itself. Emma didn't bother to get to her feet, because the smoke here was at its thickest. Instead, she scuttled across the floor, holding her breath; she could only barely see the dim outline of the door in the hall; she couldn't tell what color it had been painted. She thought, at first, the poor visibility was due to smoke, but then she realized that it was night in Andrew's world. The fire had occurred at night.

Breathing through her nose and keeping her lips tightly pressed together, she made her way to his bedroom door. She couldn't and didn't look for Maria; there was too much smoke, and she was too afraid. She had never been in a fire before, and if she survived this one, she would never, god willing, be in one again.

The door was slightly ajar, and over the crackle of burning, she heard Andrew Copis for the first time.

He was screaming.

# CHAPTER
# FOURTEEN

EMMA HAD TO FIGHT THE URGE to get to her feet and run into the room; she crawled toward the door and nudged it open just enough that she could fit through it. Andrew Copis was standing—in his bed—screaming for his mother. It wasn't a scream of pain; in some ways, it was worse. He was utterly terrified, and his voice was raw with the weight and the totality of that terror.

As long as she lived—and she wondered how long that would be—she would remember the sound, the feel of it; it passed right through her, leaving some of itself behind.

She didn't fight to stay on the floor after that; she couldn't. She got to her feet, and she ran to the bed, and to the child who stood there, his eyes wide with the horror that came from a growing realization that he'd been utterly and completely betrayed—and abandoned. He had, she realized, his mother's dark hair, and part of it was plastered to his face; the bangs were wet with either sweat or tears, and gathered in clumps near his eyes and across his forehead. Emma reached out for him.

He was *cold*. He was so damn cold to the touch she pulled back as if she'd been burned. He didn't seem to notice that she'd touched him; he didn't seem to notice that she was there at all.

She heard footsteps behind her, and shouted. "Chase, shut the damn door! Keep the smoke out!"

The door did close. She heard his muttered apology.

"Emma?" She also heard Maria's voice. It was hard to listen, though; Andrew had not fallen silent, and Emma thought, short of exhaustion, he wouldn't. No, not short of exhaustion. Short of death. This was how he had died.

She felt it like a blow, and she almost turned to throw up. But turning, she caught sight of his mother's face, and that was just as bad.

She looked at Chase instead. Chase, whose face was shuttered, whose expression was grim and closed. She wanted to ask him to help, but she couldn't force the words out. Or not all of them.

"Chase . . ."

He grimaced, which cracked his expression. "What is it?"

"He's so damn cold. I can't—" She lifted shaking hands. Numb hands. "It's not like—"

"Emma," Chase said, cursing. He walked to her, caught her hands in his. Crushed them, briefly. "He's powerful. You *knew* that."

"I didn't know what it meant." She swallowed. Chase was angry. And, she realized, he probably should be. Andrew was here—and he was in worse than the hell she'd imagined. She'd tried to touch him once, and she was almost in tears. How pathetic was that?

"Sorry, Chase," she told him. She squeezed back, feeling her fingers.

And then she squared her shoulders, took as deep a breath as she could, regretted it briefly, and approached Andrew again. This time, she held out her hands slowly, waving them in front of his open, sightless eyes. Nothing. If he was aware of her at all, he made no sign.

"Maria," Emma whispered, aware that the smoke was thickening in the room, aware that—for herself and Andrew—there was a growing lack of time, "brace yourself."

She didn't know how Maria responded, wasn't really certain she'd been heard at all. Emma reached out with both of her hands and grabbed both of Andrew's.

The cold was so intense it defined pain; she forgot about fire, about heat, about the smoke of things consumed by either. She tasted blood and realized that she'd bitten her lip. Knees locked, she stood, rigid, in front of him.

But even with his hands in hers, the screaming didn't stop. Emma realized she'd bitten her lip to stop from joining him. She dropped to her knees by the bedside, coughing; she'd dropped the cloth during her first rush to reach him, and she couldn't hold it anyway; both of her hands were in his.

"Drew!"

*Emma.*

Maria could suddenly see her son. And Emma could see her father.

"Drew!" Maria darted forward, closing the gap between them. She blinked, coughing, as the truth of fire rushed in, along with the lack of sunlight that spoke of night. If her son was trapped here, so, now was Maria Copis—but Emma understood, from the look on her face, that she had been trapped here ever since the night her son had died. She reached for Drew, and her hands passed through him. Emma shuddered; she couldn't help it.

Maria reached for Drew again. A third time. A fourth. There was no fifth, but there were now tears, leaving a trail across her cheeks. "Emma—he doesn't see me."

It was true.

"I don't know why," Emma forced herself to say. The words were shaky and uneven, but she managed to get them out clearly. "This has never happened before." She turned and looked up at her father.

*Emma.*

"He can't see her. He can't see his mother. I—I don't even think he can see me, and he's so *cold.*"

*Sprout.* Brendan Hall stood in the wafting smoke. He watched Maria and her son, and after a moment, he closed his eyes. *I was spared this*, he told his daughter softly.

"You were never in a fire."

*No. That's not what I meant. I was spared your death. I got to die first. This—* he shook his head. *This is our worst nightmare, Em. As parents, there* is *no fear that's stronger. It's still my worst fear. If it were up to me, you wouldn't—* But he opened his eyes again, and he looked at Maria Copis' face. He didn't bother to say the rest.

"Help me, Dad. I don't know what to do. I can't leave him here—"

Her father glanced at Chase.

"I honestly do not give a damn what Chase thinks or what he's afraid of right now. We'll all die here if I can't get him out. His mother's not going to leave him a second time."

It was true. It hadn't occurred to her until this moment, but it was true. She could tell Maria that she had two living children who needed her, now more than ever, and she knew that Maria, like Andrew, would be deaf.

Her father reached up with both of his hands, and he cupped her cheeks. His hands were not cold. Emma remembered what he'd done— what she'd taken from him—and she tried to pull her face away. "No, Dad—"

He couldn't touch her unless she touched him first. She remembered that. He couldn't touch her unless she *wanted* him to touch her. But he did, and maybe that said things about her that she'd never wanted to admit. She said no, but she let him do it anyway.

Chase started forward, hand outstretched. But he stopped, and he dropped the hand, where it curled in a fist at his side. "Emma—"

"Shut up, Chase. Just—shut up."

"Is he trying to *give* you power?"

She said nothing, because what she wanted to say would have irritated the hell out of her father. At least it would have when he was alive.

*Sprout,* he said quietly, *let me help you.*

"I don't want—"

*Sprout.*

"I don't want you to leave."

He smiled, the indulgent smile that had always been given only to her. And sometimes Petal. *I won't leave. I've nowhere else to go.*

"But I—"

He bent down and kissed her forehead gently. Where his lips touched her skin, warmth traveled, carrying with its slow spread something that felt like the essence of life, which was strange, because he was dead. She tried to hold on to the cold, but she couldn't. Maybe she was that selfish. Maybe, in the end, all children were. But this warmth reminded her of what love, being loved, felt like, and she leaned into it.

The cold drained out of her hands, although she still held onto Andrew Copis. Andrew, who still wailed, unseeing and terrified.

Chase was watching her in silence. Watching, she realized, her father as he stood, bent over her. When her father unfolded, he vanished slowly; for Chase, Emma realized, he had vanished the instant his lips had left her forehead.

She met Chase's gaze and said, "That was my father." Her voice was thick. She swallowed, then turned back to Andrew.

"Your father."

"He came to help me. He—it *does* help me. Even if he didn't—even if I didn't—" She couldn't force herself to say the words. "It helps me to know he's there. And that he's always been there, watching me." But she flinched as he continued to stare. "I think I know why you hate Necromancers," she whispered. "Because I'm afraid. What he gives me, Chase—I take it. I'm afraid I'll take it *all*. I'll use him up, somehow. There'll be nothing left."

Chase was utterly still. After a moment, he slid his hands into his pockets and swore. Neither Maria nor Andrew noticed; Emma couldn't make out the actual words herself. She could make out the smoke and the heat of the floor. Time was passing in Andrew's world, and time here was not kind.

Finally, Chase said, in a flat, cool voice, "You need more power."

She shook her head.

"You do. And it's standing there screaming on the bed."

This was a test. Emma thought it, and wanted to slap him. But she couldn't withdraw her hands. Even if they were no longer so cold she couldn't feel them. Perhaps especially then.

Instead, she turned her attention to Andrew Copis, who was choking. He might have been choking because he'd screamed himself raw. He might have been choking because of the cost of that screaming in a house that was filling with smoke. It didn't matter.

"Andrew," she said, raising her voice as his sputtered, momentarily, out.

He stared straight ahead. He stared *through* her. Through his mother, whose hands were shaking. She'd not made fists of them; she still held them out, palms up, as if to show how empty they were.

Emma turned to Chase, still holding the boy's hands, and said, "Chase, I don't care if you think you'll have to kill me. I need you to tell me what I need to do here."

"If you keep this up, I won't. Have to kill you," he added. He looked around the room. "It'll just be a matter of time."

"I notice that you're standing here anyway."

"It was me or Allison."

"Allison wouldn't—" she bit her lip.

"Or Michael. Emma, I'm not what you are. You need to pull some of his power."

"I'm doing that now, according to Eric—if I weren't, his mother couldn't see him at all."

"If what I'm seeing is any indication—and remember, not an expert— you're not doing it *at all*. You're giving him whatever *you* have. Emma, he has power for a reason." He grimaced. "He's stuck here. It's that power that will unstick him, and the only person who can use it is you."

"He's not exactly *giving* it."

"No. But you can—exactly—take it."

"And what the hell am I supposed to *do* with it?"

"Fuck, Emma! You came here without even thinking?"

"I came here because I *was* thinking—about him! It's not like there are a lot of experts I can just ask to show me what to do!"

Maria Copis cleared her throat. Loudly.

Emma and Chase both startled, and both had expressions of similar guilt as they looked at her.

"I need to be able to touch him," she said quietly.

"Lady," Chase said, "he's *dead*. There's no way—"

"I can't bring him back to life," Emma told Maria. "And I am *not* letting you die. I'm not even sure the dead can touch each other."

"I need to be able to touch him," Maria said, in the same reasonable, flat voice.

Emma took a shallow breath and counted to ten. She got to eight, which is about as high as she ever reached in her own home. But it wasn't words or temper that killed the count; it was sensation.

The hands that were holding Andrew began to tingle, and as Emma looked down at them, they began to glow. The glow was golden, but it wasn't even; her hands looked as if she'd slid them into delicate, lace gloves. She could see her fingers beneath the winding strands of light; could see, beneath the forming lattice, the veins on the back of her hands and the slight whitening of her knuckles where her hands were clenched that little bit too hard.

She glanced at Maria Copis, but if Maria noticed at all, she gave no indication. Chase, on the other hand, was watching her hands with narrowed eyes.

"What do you see, Chase?"

He shook his head.

"Andrew," she whispered. But Andrew, like his mother, was in a different world, a different time.

"It's not Andrew," Chase told her.

She frowned. Then she looked at her hands again. The strands of light were strands of gold; they were the chains that she had broken and wound around her palms. She could follow them, now, tracing filigree from skin to the air around her.

Georges materialized first, pulling himself slowly into the world. He reached out to touch Emma, and Emma let him.

Maria Copis flinched. That was all. Whatever pity or kindness she had to spare for the dead was being entirely absorbed by her son. Georges was not her problem because he wasn't *hers*. Following Georges came Catherine, and she appeared in the same slow, almost hesitant, way. But she also touched Emma gently.

"Margaret and Suzanne can't come unless you call them," Georges told her. "And neither can Emily. She's almost here," he added, "but she's kind of stuck."

Chase stared at the two children. "You came here for Emma on your own?"

Georges nodded solemnly. "Margaret didn't think Emma would call us," he added. "I told her we could come. And," he said, with the serious pride of a six-year-old boy, "we *did it*. The fire can't hurt us," he told Chase. "We're already dead. But it *can* hurt Emma. We like Emma."

"But she's a Necromancer."

Georges shook his head forcefully. "No, she's *not*."

Chase lifted both hands in surrender. "This is fucking *insane*," he told Emma, out of the side of his mouth.

"We can still hear you," Catherine told him, with all the vast and vulnerable disapproval a six-year-old girl has in her arsenal. Having been one, Emma was familiar with the tactic.

"I thought . . . you couldn't talk to each other."

"We couldn't, before," Catherine condescended to tell him. "We couldn't until Emma. But now we can talk to each other. Georges can talk to Emma's dad," she added. "I like *him*."

Georges faced Emma. "You need to call the others," he told her. "Margaret is really smart. She can help you. She's been in the City of the Dead for a long time."

"Does she want to come?" Emma asked him. She tried to keep hope out of her voice.

Georges nodded. "She says it's dangerous, though."

"Why?"

"Necromancers."

Chase swore. A lot.

"Chase, do you want to go?"

"Fuck." He reached into his pocket and swore more loudly. "The fucking phone! If we survive this, I'm going to kill Eric."

Emma grimaced. "I've got mine," she told him. She glanced significantly at both of her occupied hands. "It's in the left pocket. Dig it out."

He did as she asked, although it was slightly awkward, and when he'd flipped it open, he punched the buttons hard enough it was a small miracle they didn't come out the phone's back. "If Eric doesn't answer this—Eric?" He moved a little away from Emma, and covered his mouth. "Emma, get this show on the road—we don't have time. Yeah, it's me. Who else?

"We might have a problem. No, shit for brains, a serious problem. One of the ghosts says we've got Necromancers. No kidding. No, they're not talking about Emma. No, how the hell should I know? They're not talking to *me*. You want me to leave?" He glanced at Emma.

Emma called Margaret, Suzanne, and Emily. They came quickly, and far more easily than either Georges or Catherine had done. But they came because Emma summoned them.

"Maybe. How the hell should I know? Look—you need to get the others the hell away from the house. Yes, I'll stay. I think it's a waste, but

I'll stay." He looked up at Emma. "Emma—when your ghost said Necromancers, plural, was that just a figure of speech?"

"I don't know. Give them a sec, we can ask."

"A second is about all the time we have. We didn't manage to kill Longland."

"Margaret?" Emma's voice was soft and shaky. She couldn't reach out to touch the older woman because she didn't want to let go of Andrew, even if touching him didn't seem to be doing any good. Margaret, who was not six, made no attempt to touch her.

Margaret was the oldest of the four who'd been trapped along one wall in Amy's ad hoc dancing room. Her hair was an austere blend of gray and brown, and her eyes were the same noncolor, the slight odd glow, that the eyes of all of the dead seemed to be; she wore clothing that would have suited businesswomen thirty years ago. Or more.

She looked at Chase. "It was not," she said, in a deep and precise voice, "a simple figure of speech. But you may tell your hunter that one of those Necromancers is Merrick Longland."

Chase looked back. Margaret was visible to him, even though Emma couldn't touch her. "How do you know?"

One gray brow rose. Emma had seen teachers with less effective stares.

So, apparently, had Chase. "How long do we have?"

"Minutes," Margaret answered. "Possibly ten."

"How many?"

"I can be certain only of Longland. And Emma."

"Then you're not certain there are more."

"There are more. At least one other, possibly two. I can't tell you who they are, but I can tell you they're with Longland."

"Fine. Eric, you still there? No, it wasn't a figure of speech. Yes, we're screwed. You still don't want backup?" The silence lasted a minute too long, and Chase flipped the phone shut. "Emma—go. Whatever you need to do, do it *now*."

"Chase—"

"Because if the fire doesn't kill us, the Necromancers will. Eric's our best," he added. "But even Eric can't stand against more than one Longland. Not alone."

"Then go. Help him. You can't do anything here anyway."

Chase hesitated. "He'll kill me."

"Probably. And I'd like him to be alive to do it." She turned only her face—her body was aligned with her hands—and added, "Maria's children are out there. Allison and Michael. Skip and Amy. You were right," she added, her voice dropping. "*Go.*"

Chase shoved the phone back into her pocket and then sprinted for the door. Smoke billowed in when it opened, and the air seemed to be sucked out, into the hall. He slammed the door shut behind him, for all the good it would do.

"I'm of two minds about that boy," Margaret told Emma. She then glanced at Andrew, whose screaming had quieted. It hadn't stopped; he'd just lost volume as the minutes passed. "But I think you'll win him over, in the end."

Emma clenched her teeth. She'd met women like Margaret before, however, and she forced herself to speak politely and clearly when she trusted herself to speak at all. "Margaret, if we don't manage to reach Andrew, we're—Maria and I—not going to leave this place. Not alive."

Margaret nodded, and her expression softened; it added years to her face, but those years weren't unkind; she had the bone structure that made a lie of youthful beauty. "Can you bind him, Emma?"

"Can I what?"

"Bind him. Bind him the way we're bound to you."

"How do I do that?"

"How did you bind us?"

"You were already tied to a wall. I just—I broke the chains around you and they kind of stuck to me."

Margaret closed her eyes and shook her head, and Suzanne gently touched the older woman's shoulder. "Well?" Margaret said, opening her eyes and looking to Suzanne. Suzanne glanced at Andrew, who was standing and shuddering on the bed. "I don't think so," she said, after a pause. "He's too young, Margaret, and too new."

"He is very, very powerful, though."

"He is."

"Emma, can you touch that power at all?"

"I can touch him. I—no." She gave up on excuses. "No. I can't."

"Well, then." Margaret turned to Maria Copis. "I'm sorry for my lack of manners, but the situation is somewhat dire," she said, speaking slowly enough that the words seemed to run counter to their content. "I'm Margaret Henney. You are Andrew's mother?"

Maria managed to pull her glance away from her son. Her face was streaked with trails, and those trails were now dark gray. "I am. I—"

Margaret lifted a hand. "I know, dear. My son drowned in a crowded lake at the height of one summer. I understand guilt. And loss. I also understand that you wouldn't be here at all if it weren't for Emma.

"But neither would we. I am about to suggest that we try something that may not work. And it may leave some permanent scars."

Maria Copis laughed. "You think I care about *scars*?"

Emma, listening, shook her head. "She's not talking about that kind of scar," she told Maria. "I think she means it might change you somehow."

"Will it get my son out of here?" Maria said, still looking at Margaret.

"It might. It's the only thing I can think of that has any chance, unless you're willing to wait another ten years."

Maria's eyes widened. Answer enough. "Emma, what is she suggesting?"

"I'm not sure." Emma hesitated, thinking. It was hard, because Andrew had found a second—or third, or tenth—wind. "Is it something you can do, Margaret?"

"No, Emma. Not I."

"Me, then."

The older woman nodded. "What do you see, when you look at us?"

"The dead." Emma shook her head. "No. Truthfully, you wouldn't look dead to me at all if it weren't for your eyes." And the fact that they could appear out of thin air.

"What do you see when you look at Maria?"

"I see Maria." Emma started to describe her, and stopped as Margaret's words finally came into focus, over the endless wails of a bereaved four-year-old boy. She swallowed, coughed. "Margaret—"

"Look at her, Emma. Look *carefully*."

Emma shook her head, almost wild. "She's *alive*, Margaret." She glanced at the door, as if seeking some kind of guidance from Chase, who was no longer in the room. "I can't—" pause. "Do Necromancers—can they—"

"What you are, and what they are, are not yet the same. You can become them," Margaret added, in her crisp, clear voice. "Or you can become something different. But, yes, Emma. If they were willing to pay the price, they could touch the living."

"What price?" Maria asked Margaret. She was pale, the way old statues are pale.

Margaret looked at Maria, and her expression gentled again. "You cannot pay it for her, although you may suffer in the process. You are willing to suffer; I don't doubt it, and in the end, neither does our Emma. But Emma is afraid of losing what she is."

"Will I?" Emma asked starkly.

Margaret didn't answer. But Georges came to stand by Emma's side, and he wrapped his arms around her, briefly. Catherine did the same, looking first to see whether or not Georges' gesture was met with disapproval.

"Margaret, will it kill her?"

Margaret said nothing for a long moment. When she did speak, she said, "Trust yourself." Which was so far from comfort, she might as well not have bothered. "Catherine, dear?"

Catherine detached herself from Emma. "Yes?"

"Please. The young boy?"

Catherine nodded. "He's very loud," she said. But she walked over to Andrew Copis, and she put both her arms around him, as if she were his older sister. He started, looked at her, and then screamed *MOM* at the top of his little lungs.

The world slowed, then. The smoke seemed to freeze in place.

Margaret looked at Emma again, as if this had been some sort of proof, at the end of a long theorem. In a way, it was. Because Emma now thought she understood exactly what Margaret hoped she could achieve. She took a deep breath, nodded, and then let Andrew Copis go.

Maria darted forward and stopped. She took deep, deep breaths while she stood rigid.

Emma looked at Maria Copis. She saw a woman who was not quite thirty, in a sooty shirt, baggy jeans. Her hair was dark, her eyes were dark, and her face was that kind of gaunt that makes you feel like a voyeur just seeing it. Emma shook herself, took a much shallower series of breaths than Maria had, and looked again.

Her eyes were dark, yes. Her cheeks were stained. This wasn't helping. She was alive, her son was dead; they were divided by that state. Just as Emma and her father had been divided, as Emma and Nathan had been divided. Death was silence, loss, guilt. And anger.

But life led that way, anyway. From birth, it was a slow, long march to the grave. Who had said that? She couldn't now remember. But it was true. They were born dying. If they were very lucky, the dying was called aging. They reached toward it as if they were satellites in unstable orbits.

And when they got there, they were just dead. Like the unfamiliar student in the cafeteria. One moment in time separated the living from the ghosts. Emma looked for that moment now.

She tried to age Maria in her mind's eye, the way she avoided aging her mother. It didn't help, and she discarded the attempt, wishing—briefly—that she'd brought Michael with her. Michael, with his rudimentary social understanding and his ability to see beyond almost all of it, would have had a better chance of arriving at something useful than she did.

Michael would have asked her the important questions. *What is death? What are the dead? Why are they here? Do people have souls, Emma? Can you prove it?*

Well? Did they have souls?

She glanced at Margaret, at Suzanne, and at the two children.

Did it matter? They looked as they must have looked in life. Not in death; the death itself didn't seem to define them. But the life they'd lived? That did. In the clothing, the names, the style of their hair, the way they spoke to her. They remembered what they had been; it was, in essence, what they still were.

If Maria Copis died now—today, here—this is what she would look like, to Emma. Because this is what she would look like to herself. It was *there*. It was in her. People couldn't predict death most of the time. Maybe ever.

"Maria," Emma said. "Give me your hand. Just one."

Maria held out a hand. She hesitated for just a moment, then firmly gripped Emma's in her own.

Emma *looked* at her. Not at her face, her hair, or her clothing; not at her expression. "Georges," she said, not taking her eyes off Maria, "come here and take my other hand."

Georges shuffled along the planks, and then she felt his hand in hers. It wasn't cold, but she knew why. Her father's gift. She used it now, without pause for regret or guilt.

When she touched the dead, the living could see them. Eric had said this was because she was using some of their power—some very small part—to make them visible. To give them a voice. But now, just now, she tried to see *how* she was taking that power. What she was actually touching when she reached for what looked like a hand.

She closed her eyes, because actually looking wasn't helping her to see at all.

She heard Maria say, "Hello, Georges."

She heard Georges reply. Where, in his words, was Emma's power? Where, in that quiet, child's voice, was some evidence of her work? There. In the palm of her hand. A small tendril, a string, a chain. Something that bound him to her, but something that also bound her to him. It went both ways.

It was cool; the way ice was cool when touched through thin gloves. Colder when she pulled, because she could pull at it if she concentrated. She tried, and Georges said, "Yes, Emma?"

She hadn't built it. It had existed before her. But she'd used it. She was using it now, in some ways. She let go of Georges' hand in the darkness, and whispered, "Dad."

She couldn't see him, but she could feel his sudden presence growing. With it came memories, some good, some bad. They were hers, but they were his as well, seen on opposite sides and from different angles.

*Sprout.*

"Dad, take my hand?"

He did. She heard him say, "Hello, Maria. I'm Brendan Hall, Emma's father."

She touched her father. If she tried, she could feel the cold—but it wasn't as sharp as Georges; it was the difference between a winter day and solid ice. She tried to pull at him in the way she had pulled at George, and it was harder. But it was—barely—possible.

But his power had flowed *into* her when he wanted it to.

*We're bound, Em,* he told her, and she could hear the affection in his voice so strongly it almost hurt. *I love you.*

She looked at him, then, and her eyes teared. She started to tell him it was the smoke, then stopped and smiled instead. It was a weak smile, and she added, "I'm fine, Dad," before she could stop herself. "I miss you."

He touched her face for just a second, and his smile deepened.

She looked, last, to Maria. Maria, whose chain she didn't hold; Maria, whose love she didn't have. The only thing they had in common was the desire to save a four-year-old boy from decades of terror and pain—and Emma knew her desire was nowhere near the equal of Maria's.

But the desire to try was as strong, and that would have to do. She took a breath, and she tried to reach for Maria Copis. All she felt in her hand *was* Maria's hand.

She reached for her father again, and she felt the cold. This time, she was more careful. She approached the fact of his death slowly, as if he were not, in fact, dead at all. She could see him. She could speak with him. She could, if she wanted, hug him. He still loved her. He still worried about her.

What he couldn't do, she didn't think about—not now.

She felt the cold. But instead of shying away from it, she reached into it, and then, as if it were a wall, she pushed beyond it. For a moment, the cold was sharp and cutting, and then she felt a slow and steady warmth. She opened her eyes and stared at her father, who said, and did, nothing.

"I think," Margaret said in the distance, "she might have it, Suzanne."

"He's dead," Suzanne very correctly replied. "The boy's mother is not."

"No. You make a point. But still."

Emma let go of her father's hand, and the warmth receded. She wanted to call it back, because in it, for a moment, she felt safe. She felt safe in a way that she couldn't remember feeling, even as a four year old; what pain could touch her, there? What worry, and what loss?

"Maria," she said, and she held out her free hand.

Maria took it.

"Think," Emma told Maria, "of the good things. The good things about Andrew. Not his death, not his loss, but all the reasons you feel the loss so strongly. Can you do that?"

"I . . . I don't know. I'll try."

Emma had never doubted it. She watched Maria's face, and after a moment, Maria grimaced and closed her eyes; she'd been staring at the spot in midair where Andrew stood because she could no longer see—or hear—him. And this was probably for the best, because there was no way she could have done what Emma asked, otherwise. As it was, climbing Everest with toothpicks for pitons would probably have been easier.

Emma watched Maria's face. Her eyelids flickered and trembled, and her lips turned at the corners, tightening and thinning. The smoke was thick in the room, and Emma sat; she wanted to lie flat across the floor, remembering her elementary school lessons about moving in fires. But she crouched instead, waiting, and trying not to feel the passing time.

Bit by bit, Maria's expression relaxed, her lips losing that tight, pained look, the lines around her closed eyes slowly disappearing as she bowed her head toward Emma. Emma, both hands locked around Maria, just as they had previously been locked around her son, closed her eyes as well.

She reached out for Maria Copis the way she had reached out for her father; she didn't move her hands, didn't open her eyes, didn't try to physically grab anything.

And doing so, she remembered the first night that she had seen—and touched—her father. Her *body* had been in a chair, beside Michael. But *she* had been standing in the middle of the waiting room in front of Brendan Hall, her hands outstretched, her palms and fingers splayed wide to catch him before he vanished.

That part of her—it was inside her now, and had been ever since that first night. Maybe it had always been inside her. Maybe what she saw, somehow, was not actually what was *there*. Maybe it wasn't something eyes could actually see—but her mind was doing the translating and giving her images that she could recognize and hold.

Eyes closed, she looked for her father.

And she saw him, standing in the darkness, limned in light, his face bright with that smile that meant she'd done something that made him proud. She looked for Georges, and she saw that he was standing beside Catherine; they were holding hands, and where their hands met, the light was bright and unfaltering.

She nodded at them but didn't speak; instead she moved on, searching now for Maria Copis.

She saw Andrew first, his face tear-stained, his hair matted to his forehead, his eyes wide and wild. He wasn't solid; he wavered in her vision like a—like a ghost. But he stood in the way, and she felt that if she could move past him somehow, she would reach Maria.

Instead, for the first time in this darkness of closed eyes that had nothing at all to do with her living, breathing body, she held out a hand. Or at least that's what it felt like she did; when she looked, she couldn't actually see her hand. Or her arm. Or anything at all that looked like Emma Hall.

But for the first time, Andrew seemed to sense her. Chase had called him powerful, and maybe he was—but not here. Here, he was weak, wavering like a heat mirage in the air before her; here he was so damn lost it was hard to see him at all. She held out her hand again.

This time, he reached for it.

*Come on, Andrew*, she told him, as gently as she knew how. *Let's go find your mom.*

"AMY. SKIP. GRAB THE LADDERS. They're not coming down any time soon." Eric turned to speak to Allison; he turned back when he realized that the ladders weren't coming down. "We need to move. Quickly."

"And if they need to come down in a hurry?" Amy's hands lodged themselves on her hips, and she shifted her stance.

Eric resisted the urge to point out that she was not, in fact, holding the ladder at this moment. "Skip," he said, over her, "it sounds as though your friend Longland is going to make an appearance. I'd suggest you get ready to hightail it out of here with your sister, if you can get her to leave."

Skip let the ladder go and turned to his younger sister. For the first time, Eric saw the similarities between the siblings, not the very obvious differences. Amy was obviously angry; on her, it looked good. "Amy."

She turned so her back was squarely facing his voice.

"Amy, we're leaving."

"I'm not leaving Emma—"

"Eric's staying."

"Eric's barely known her for a month. I'm not—"

Skip grabbed one of the arms that was attached, by her hand, to her hip. "You're leaving. You can carry a ladder, or we can leave the ladders behind—but I'll be carrying you."

Her eyes rounded in an almost operatic way; Eric thought she was going to slap her brother. "The kid's dead." Skip spaced the words evenly and slowly, as if English were not Amy's native tongue. "If what you said about last night is even halfway true, you're going to join him if we can't get away before Longland shows. I personally don't give a shit if you die here," he added. "But it'll kill Mom and Dad."

"Amy—" Eric began.

She lifted the arm that wasn't gripped by Skip. "Fine," she told her brother. Skip pulled the ladders down as Eric turned to Allison.

"Allison, take the baby. You and Michael get as far away from this house as you possibly can." He glanced at Michael, who was in Cathy's world and had failed to hear anything, and he decided that Michael and his compliance were going to have to be Allison's problem.

"I'll take Amy and Skip," Allison told him, after a small pause.

"Michael's not—"

"Michael is the only person who seemed to be unaffected by whatever it was Longland did at Amy's."

Which was interesting. "Probably because his brain's wired differently. It'd be worth some study—at another time. This is not that time. If Longland is aware that Michael somehow resisted the very, very expensive compulsion that affected everyone else in that house, he won't bother with subtlety. He'll kill him, probably quickly."

"Once he's committed to that, he'll kill all of you," Eric added.

"But Emma—"

"Emma has Chase."

"Why is Longland here?"

"If I had to guess? Andrew Copis has a lot of raw power, and Longland has, at the moment, a need for raw power."

"He—"

"If he's adept, he can sense it. He can't sense the rest of us; we're probably not his target here. That'll change when he arrives, and I'd rather not risk any of you." He slid his hands into his pockets. Nestled against his thigh were iron rings, warmed by constant contact with his leg. He pulled them out and slid them on. "If he's done any research at all, he'll have some idea of what he's facing."

"Could he go into a burning building and drag Andrew out?"

The fact that Emma, Maria, and Chase had failed to emerge passed without comment, but the worry was there on her face.

"Hard to say. It wouldn't be his first choice, if our own records of Necromancers are anything to go by. If we're away from the building, and he sees the same fire that Emma sees, he might try to find a different power source. He probably hasn't had the time to gather any."

"But you're not coming with us. You don't think he's going to leave."

"If he decides to risk it—" He shook his head. "If he decides to risk it, he'll have safer passage than Emma did; he knows how to use the dead, and he only has to reach Andrew. No, I'm not coming with you. Emma isn't close to his match yet, but she has *all* the others. Even if he gives up on Andrew, Emma's got what he needs—he can just take that. I'll hunker down out of sight, and I'll see what he does. But the rest of you have to leave *now*.

"Ally," he added, when she failed to move, "I'll have enough to worry about. If you all stay here, you'll slow me down when I can't afford to be slowed."

She hesitated again, and Eric looked, very pointedly, at the baby she held in her arms. He could see that she wanted to argue. She didn't. But she shifted her grip on the baby, and she bent to grab the diaper bag before she retreated as far as Michael. She tapped Michael on the shoulder, and he looked up instantly; Eric couldn't hear what she said. But he saw Michael's expression darken in utterly open concern.

Eric understood why Emma valued them both so highly. Why, in fact, she loved them, even if that word was out of vogue among the young. He had thought, watching Emma, Allison, Amy, and the rest of Amy's mafia, that Michael was simply a burden they'd chosen to adopt.

But he watched Michael pick up Cathy, as if Cathy were his baby sister, and he watched as Michael's mouth moved over words that distance silenced, and he understood that the burden of care, if that's what it was, was not by any means shouldered on just one side.

He could see only Allison's profile, but she was, at this distance, measured and calm for someone who was also, clearly, in a hurry.

Michael lifted Catherine, and they headed down Rowan Avenue. Skip and Amy joined them, and Amy's denunciation was the clearest sound in the street. Skip was ignoring her, rather than engaging. Arguing was, admittedly, hard to do when they were both lugging ladders.

He hoped they weren't heading in the wrong direction. He couldn't be certain. He didn't have time to check; Longland would come to number twelve. Now if only number twelve weren't lacking anything remotely useful behind which he could hide. If, he thought grimly, hiding would do any good at all. Longland wasn't alone. He wouldn't feel the need to be that cautious.

There were no bushes here; no obvious cover, no neighbor's yards, and no roof that he was certain would bear his weight, if he could climb that far up. Eric glanced at the boards nailed in a large X across what remained of the doorframe. He grimaced and started to pull them off.

They splintered from the inside as he worked, and he jumped back, pulling daggers. He got both a face and an ear full of pissed off Chase for his troubles.

"Chase, what the *hell* are you doing here?"

"Same old, same old," Chase replied, looking past Eric's shoulder. "Someone moved the fucking ladders. Where were you going?"

"In." Eric bit back every other angry comment he wanted to make, because, in the end, he was happier to have Chase than to stand alone. "They're not here yet, and outside is a total bust."

The hair on his neck started to rise, and he swore. "Scratch that," he said, pushing Chase back into the house, and flattening himself against the wall with its shattered windows. "They're here."

Andrew's hand wasn't solid. But even insubstantial as it was, Emma could reach out and touch it. She did, and he allowed it.

*The house is on fire*, he told her, the last syllable stretching out as if it were about to birth a scream.

"Yes, I know." She kept the words simple and forced them to be gentle. Here, she missed Michael, because Michael could have distracted—or better, calmed—Andrew.

*I want my mom.*

"I know. She's here, somewhere. But it's smoky and she's lost. Let's go find her."

He reached up for her, then, and she tried to pick him up. He stiffened, and the scream that she'd managed to subvert started in earnest. She didn't so much hear it as feel it. As gently as she could manage, she put him down again.

*Only Mommy.*

She nodded. "Let's find your mother. She's been very worried."

*I waited for her.*

Emma's eyes were already closed, or she would have closed them. She held out her hand again, and when he placed his palm in hers, she closed hers over it gently.

This time, she reached for Andrew, while she held this small part of him. She reached for him, and then, she reached through him. All she felt was a little boy who was close to hysteria—on the wrong side. Four years old.

Since the day her father had died, so many years ago, she had accepted that life wasn't fair. When Nathan died in the summer, she had hated it. Life. The grayness. The ache. The loss of future. All of it.

Watching other people's happiness, other people's dreams, had been so damn hard, she'd withdrawn from most of her life. Only Allison and Michael had remained a central part of that life because they wouldn't let her go. Everyone else had made space for her grief; they'd given her the room in which to mourn.

They could give her *years*, and it would never end.

*Are you crying?* Andrew asked, in that curious but detached way of children everywhere.

"A little."

*Why?*

"Because it's dark, and it's scary, and I'm lonely."

*Oh.* The pause was not long, but it was there. *Me too. Are you a grown-up?*

Two years ago she would have answered yes without hesitation. Now? "Not quite. Almost."

*Can you get out of the fire?*

"I think so."

*It'll kill you, you know. If you don't.*

"I know."

*Where's my mom?*

"She's here." Emma took a breath and looked down at her non-hand. This time, when she reached out, she reached out for Maria Copis.

She felt the skin of the older woman's hand in her palms, and knew that that was a real sensation; it was distinct, almost overwhelming in its sudden clarity. Andrew cried out, and she flexed her hands; felt Maria's response.

*Don't go!*

"No, Andrew. I'm not leaving." She took another breath. It hurt.

"Emma?"

"Margaret?" She blinked. Margaret stood in the shadows, Suzanne by her side.

"Yes, dear."

Emma hated being called "dear" by anyone under the age of seventy. She grimaced but said nothing.

"You're almost there, dear, but I wanted to warn you—you don't have much time. You've reached the boy, and the fire has slowed; you've got his attention. But . . ."

Coughing, Emma nodded. She reached for Maria Copis again, but this time, eyes closed, she reached out with her other self. With the self that had left her body in a chair in a hospital emergency triage room.

"Hold on, dear. Hold on for as long as you can."

She would have asked Margaret what she meant, but she didn't have time. Fire engulfed her hands, searing away skin, sinew, tendon. She bit her lip, tasted blood, stopped herself from screaming—but only barely, and only because she was also holding Andrew, and Andrew was terrified.

Andrew had never stopped being terrified.

The soul-fire came to sickly green life in the frame of the door, lapping around the sharp edges of newly broken boards.

They were out of its range, but only barely, and the floors here looked suspiciously unstable.

"Where did the fire start?" Chase hissed.

"Basement. Back of the house one over." Eric rolled along the floor against the wall. The wall would have provided more than enough cover had it not been for the large gap a windowpane had once occupied. Here, everything was blackened; paint had peeled and curled, and just beyond the windows, the carpets were the consistency of melted plastic.

But the soul-fire didn't burn in that particular way. Something to be grateful for. "Chase?"

"I'm clear."

Eric felt the soul-fire bloom just above his head. These damn homes with their huge windows. Even the cheap homes had them all over the place.

"I'd say they know where we are," Chase added.

"No kidding." Eric drew daggers.

Chase pulled a mirror out of his shirt pocket. "You've got yours?"

"No."

"Fuck, Eric, what were you thinking?"

"Never mind. It'll only piss you off."

Chase angled the mirror so that it caught light through the ragged hole that was now the door in these parts. "Three."

"Longland."

"Yeah. Two others."

"Dressed?"

"Street clothes. No robes."

"They were already in Toronto, then."

"Either that or the old lady's getting lax."

Eric winced. "Don't call her that, Chase. You know it pisses her off."

Chase shrugged and pulled the mirror back. "We've got trouble," he told Eric grimly.

"How much trouble?"

"Longland has Allison."

Emma had never been terrified of fire. It had always fascinated her. Candlelight. Fireplaces. Bunsen burners. Even the blue flames of the gas stove. But all of those other times, she'd been far enough away to feel only warmth.

Here, there was no warmth. Warmth was too gentle.

She'd broken her arm once, and that snap of bone had been quick and comfortable compared to this. She almost let go, but she realized that the fire burned only her *hands*.

No. Not even her hands, not her real hands. The fire had not yet reached this room. She dimly remembered that Andrew had died of smoke inhalation; it was possible that this type of fire would never reach these rooms.

Remembering Margaret's words, she held on. It was like holding on to a stove element when it was orange. It was almost impossible, and she would have screamed and pulled back in defeat, opening her eyes and falling back into her body and the grimness of reality, if it had not been for Andrew Copis, who waited by her side in the darkness, where the pain was strongest. For his sake, she held on.

But it wasn't enough just to hold on.

She realized it, tried to cling to the thought, until pain washed it away, again and again, as if she were the shore and pain was the ocean that reached for her. It wasn't *enough* to hold on. Hold on. No, it's not enough.

It was like breath, like heartbeat, this pain and this realization, but it wore grooves in her thoughts, until the pain couldn't dislodge it anymore. And when that happened, she reached into, and through the fire, as she had reached into, and through the cold.

On the other side of the fire, she finally found the warmth she hadn't even realized she was seeking.

"Maria."

The urge to throw herself into that warmth, and away from the fire itself, was so strong it was like the gravity that takes you—quickly—to the bottom of a cliff from its height. But she'd stood on the edge of a lot of cliffs, and she'd never once thrown herself off. She heard, in the distance, the sudden gasp of shock or pain in Maria's voice, and she knew what the warmth was.

Emma had never tried anything like this before, but she had a pretty good idea that throwing yourself entirely into another person's life—any other person, no matter how you felt about them—was not a good thing. But it was hard. She'd tried it once before, and then? It had been joy, until it was loss, and pain. Finding boundaries, with Nathan, had been so difficult; accepting the boundaries he sketched for himself, more so.

She didn't love Maria Copis. She didn't even know her.

But not loving, not knowing, she was still drawn into parts of her life. The parts were good, because she had asked Maria to think about happy things—as if she were the Disney channel—and Maria had done her best to oblige. Emma could feel love, fear, and frustration for her children, and all of these were mixed and intertwined. She couldn't, in her own mind, see what the joy of changing a dirty diaper was, but apparently, Maria could.

She could hear Andrew's first words, although she couldn't understand them at all. Maria could. Or thought she could. Parents with small children were often stupid like that. She could see Andrew take his first steps. See him run—and fall, which he didn't much like—and see him insist on feeding himself.

Cathy came next, but Andrew was entwined with Cathy, and a brief glimpse of someone Emma had never met and yet now both loved and hated intruded. He was taller than Maria, and he was young, even handsome, his hair dark, his eyes dark, and his smile that electric form of slow and lazy that can take your breath away. The children loved him. Maria loved him.

And him? He loved them, maybe. He loved himself more. Emma watched the expressions on his face when he thought no one was looking. Saw the phone calls that he took, the false joviality of casual conversation no blind at all to Maria. The easy way he lied.

The hard way the truth came out.

Shadows, there. Anger. Loss. The slow acceptance of the death of need. Or love. It was complicated, and Emma tried very hard not to look at it, and not only because she was afraid of walking unannounced and uninvited into the Copis bedroom.

But she could see the man leave—and that still hurt—and she could see the struggle to be a reasonable, sane parent with almost no money and two children with a third on its way. The struggle to find the joy in the townhouse, with its narrow walls and its crowded, cluttered rooms, was both hard and somehow rewarding. Emma felt it, but she didn't understand it.

But she saw the turn happen, and she knew that she couldn't withdraw; she followed Maria, holding on as lightly as possible and riding her back like an insect. Andrew was walking. Talking. Arguing. Saying a lot of unreasonable *No*. Andrew was trying to stick six slices of bread, side by side, in the toaster. Andrew was grabbing Cathy's toys, and Cathy was pulling his hair, a trade that didn't seem fair to his outraged, little self.

Andrew was trying so hard to be a Big Brother, even if he didn't quite understand what that meant when it came to toys.

Andrew was standing in the line-up to junior kindergarten, glancing anxiously back at his mother before the doors opened to swallow him and the other twenty-six children. Andrew was—

Andrew was—

Dead.

Just like that, the warmth twisted; Emma held it, but it was *hard*. Because to hold it, she had to hold on to the fire, and the smoke, and the screams of her daughter and her son; the baby was sleeping, thank god, the baby was hardly awake. She had to pass through the smoke, the thickening of it, the heat of the floors, the sudden, horrible realization that she had slept through death, and death was calling.

But Emma had done despair, and loss, and guilt. She'd lived with grief until it was silent unless she touched it or poked it. She'd lived with its shadow, lived at its whim, gone through the day-to-day of things that meant nothing to her anymore—the gray, pointless chatter of her friends, the endless nothing of her future.

Emma knew these things well enough that she could endure them, because she already had. Even if this was *worse*.

The baby was sleeping in her room. Cathy was down the hall—at the farthest end—in her crib. Andrew was in his bed in the room midway down. She grabbed the baby, and she ran, covering her mouth, the panic sharp and harsh. She woke Cathy, she grabbed Cathy, lifting her in one arm, lodging her on her left hip; the baby was cradled, awkwardly and tightly, on her right.

She kicked Andrew's door open; Andrew was waking, and Andrew *never* woke well. Andrew woke, crying. Disoriented, the way he often was when wakefulness didn't come naturally. She kept her voice even— god knew how—and she told Andrew to follow her quickly.

He stood up in bed, and he saw smoke and his mother's harsh fear, and he froze there, in the night, the glowing face of a nightlight the only real illumination in the room. *Andrew, follow me—the house is on fire!*

Andrew, understanding her panic, was terrified.

She'd done it *wrong*. He could hear the raw fear in her voice, and he could see—oh, he could see—that she carried Cathy and the baby in her arms. He was a *child*. He could see that she carried *them*, while the house was burning. He could understand what this meant about her love for *him*.

And as a child, he started to cry, to whimper, to lift his arms and jump up and down on the spot, demanding to be carried. It wasn't petulance; she saw that clearly. It was terror.

She'd done it wrong. If she had just stayed *calm*—

But she hadn't. She tried to lift him somehow, Cathy screaming in her ear, the baby stirring. But she couldn't do it. She couldn't—she shouted at Andrew, told him to follow, begged him to follow, and she realized that he couldn't do it either. Not newly awake. Not in the dark with the fire eating away at the promise of life.

She turned, ran down the stairs. Fire in the living room, fire in the hall. The front door clear, but covered by the smoke shed by burning things. God, she had to get them *out*. Just—get them out, come back in before it was too late, get Andrew, bring him out as well. Running as she'd never run, through the smoke, past the fire, coughing, as Cathy was coughing in between her cries.

And then, night air, smoke rushing after her as she raced along the path in her bare feet, picking up small stones and debris. Her neighbors, she could see, were standing in the darkness, except it wasn't dark; it was a bonfire. Not her house, not her house—

She handed Cathy to the lady next door, handed the baby to the lady's husband, turned to the house again, ran back up the path.

And fire, in the hall, near the door, greeted her—

Emma broke through the fire, the memory of fire, the scream that was swallowing all thought and all rational words. "Maria," she said, in a voice that was outside of memory, but strong enough to bear the pain and the despair, "Come. It's time to rescue your son."

She held out a hand—a hand she could actually see—to Maria, and Maria stared at her, her face white and blistered from heat, and she paused there, on the crest of the wave, and realized that all hope was already lost.

She was not in the fire.

She was in the daydream of the fire, the one to which she returned, night after night, and in every waking minute: the one in which she had done things *right*, or the one in which fire hadn't spread so damn fast, the one in which she could make it up the stairs to her son's small room, to her son's terrified side, the one in which she could pick him up and carry him. Not back to the door; that was death.

But to the window that overlooked the gable above the porch. To her bedroom, where he'd slept until he was almost a year old. To those windows, which she could break and through which she could throw one screaming child because even if he *broke something*, he'd still be alive.

And standing beside her, Emma Hall was also in her daydream.

Maria looked at Emma's hand and understood in a second how damn much Emma had seen.

Andrew was screaming.

Emma's hand was steady.

Maria grabbed it, and together they walked through the fire and up the stairs, where smoke lay like a shroud. They walked into Andrew's room and saw Andrew standing on the bed, screaming and coughing, and his eyes widened as he saw his mother.

Emma opened her real eyes to Maria's real expression, to the wet and shining veil of tears across both cheeks. Maria opened her eyes on Emma, and then she looked past Emma's shoulders, and her eyes widened.

"Andrew!" She could see him, although Emma wasn't touching him.

"Mommy!"

Maria pushed herself off the floor and ran to him, arms wide; she picked him up, and he hit her face and shoulders before his arms collapsed around her neck, and he sobbed there while she held him, her lips pressed into his hair, her body the shield through which nothing—nothing at all—would pass.

"We have to go," Emma told her softly.

Maria swallowed and nodded. "The fire—"

"I think—the fire won't kill us now."

"You're not sure."

"No. But we need to leave."

Maria's arms tightened around her son. "What happens when we leave?" she asked Emma.

"I don't know. I'm sorry."

Maria nodded again, and Emma understood why she hadn't moved. This was her son, her dead son, and these might be the only moments she would ever have with him again. They were a gift—a terrible, painful, gift—and she wanted to extend them for as long as she possibly could, because when she opened her arms again, he would be gone.

Emma Hall, who didn't cry in public, struggled with her tears, with the thickness in her throat, as she understood and watched.

"Emma," Margaret said at her back.

But Emma lifted a hand, waving it in a demand for silence. For space.

"Just . . . give them a minute," she finally managed to say.

Maria, however, turned, her eyes widening. "Margaret?" Her voice was soft; it was the first time since she had lifted her son that she'd taken her lips entirely from his hair. "I can see you."

Margaret nodded. "Yes."

"But Emma's not—"

"No. You will be haunted all your life by glimpses of the dead. I'm sorry, dear."

Maria's arms tightened around her son. "I'm not." She kissed his hair, his forehead, his wet little cheeks, held him, whispered mother-love words into his ears until he told her she was tickling him.

"Emma," Margaret said again.

"What?"

"Longland is here."

Emma closed her eyes.

"And Emma?"

She didn't want to hear more. But she listened, anyway.

"He has Allison and Maria's baby."

# CHAPTER
# SIXTEEN

"H OW—HOW DO YOU KNOW?"

Margaret said nothing for a long moment, and then she glanced at Emma's father. He slid his hands into his pockets—it was odd that the dead would have pockets, since they couldn't actually carry anything—and said, "Someone else is also watching."

Which made no sense.

"I know what happens to you," Brendan Hall told his daughter. "I watch you. I'm not—yet—like Margaret, but I have some sense of what you've seen, what you're worried about."

Emma lifted a hand and looked at Maria. Maria looked mostly confused, but an edge of fear was sharpening her expression. Emma hadn't bothered to mention little things like Necromancers to her, because it hadn't occurred to Emma that they would actually meet them.

The only child that was in danger here was supposed to be Andrew, who was already dead. But the baby that Allison carried was alive. And in the hands of a man who, if you believed Chase, and, sickeningly, Emma did, had no trouble at all killing anyone.

She took a deep, steadying breath. Panic was not her friend, here.

"Margaret," she said, as her father's words finally sunk in. "Someone you knew in life is out there as well?"

"Yes, dear."

"Can he help them?"

She didn't answer.

Emma ran to the door and pulled it open; the doorknob was warm but not yet hot. She yanked the door wide, and smoke billowed into the room; it was all she could do not to turn and shout at Andrew. *We've brought your mother here, she's carrying you, damn it—*

*Damn it, he's four years old, Em. Think. Just think.* She headed down the hall to Maria's bedroom, which was only a few short steps away; the door was ajar, as they'd left it. Fire was playing out against the height of the stairs, but how much of the stairs had been consumed, she couldn't say.

It didn't matter. She made her way to the front windows, the bedroom windows, and some instinct made her flatten herself against the floor. The air here was cleaner, but at this point not by a whole lot. She rose slowly to one side of the window frame, and she looked out into Rowan Avenue.

She could see Longland in the street. His hand was on Allison's arm, and Allison's arms—both of them—were curled protectively around the baby.

No Michael, no Amy, no Skip. Emma felt sick, literally sick, with sudden fear. Where were the others? Were they even alive? Chase had warned her. Chase, who'd been so angry, so self-righteous, and so damn *right*.

*Emma.*

She looked up and saw her father standing in the center of the room. Beyond him, Maria stood, her son in her arms, her face so pale her lips were the same color as the rest of her skin. The others were nowhere in sight.

Emma swallowed. "Dad," she said, her voice still thick. "What do I do?"

"Just think, Em."

She wanted to scream at her father, and screaming at her father was something she'd done, in one way or another, since she was the age of the baby in Allison's arms. But it wouldn't help anything, and it wouldn't change anything.

"Maria," she whispered. "Stand to one side of the window; don't stand in front of it. Don't let them see you."

Maria hesitated and then nodded, crossing the room to where the windows, open to night, let in air that was breathable and relatively clean. "What's happening? Who has my— Allison and my son?"

"His name is Merrick Longland, but his name doesn't matter. He's a—" Emma grimaced. "They're called Necromancers. I don't know a lot about them, but I do know a couple of things."

"Share."

"They feed on the dead."

"But—"

"Not on their corpses. I think they'd be called ghouls. Or zombies." God, she could say the most idiotic things when she was frightened. "They feed on the spirits of the dead."

Maria was not a stupid woman. Her arms tightened around her son. "What does it give them?"

"Power."

"Power?"

Emma nodded. "And with that power they can do a bunch of things that we'd technically call magic."

"Please tell me he's not here for my son."

"I'd like to. But I don't know why he's here, and your son—" she swallowed. "Your son could maintain a fire that could burn me even if I couldn't see him and couldn't touch him."

"What does he want with Allison?"

"I don't know. But if I had to guess, probably me."

"But—but why?"

"I have something he thinks of as his. He probably wants it back."

"Can't you just give it to him?"

"No. No more than you could just give him Andrew."

Maria really wasn't stupid. "You're talking about the others," she said, her voice flat. "Georges, Catherine, Margaret—and the other two. I'm sorry, I don't remember their names."

Emma nodded. And then, because she was a Hall, added, "Suzanne and Emily."

"He can use them because they're dead."

"Pretty much. It would be like handing a loaded gun to a man who's already promised to kill you." She grimaced, and added, "Sorry, Margaret," aware that it was all sorts of wrong to talk about people as if they were simply strategic objects. *That* made her more like Merrick Longland than she ever wanted to be.

"Emma?"

From her position on the floor, Emma glanced up at Maria.

Maria could see street in the narrow angle between the wall and the window. Her gaze was now focused in that distance. "I think your two friends are out there as well."

"Who?"

"Eric," she said. "And Chase."

"What—what are they doing?"

Silence, and then, in a much quieter voice, "Burning."

"Is the fire green?" Margaret asked.

They both started, but Maria nodded. "It's green, yes. It *looks* like fire, but filtered badly."

"It's soul-fire. They've some experience with that fire," Margaret said at last. "It may not kill them yet; it is not, technically, fire at all."

"Maria, is Allison—"

"I don't know. Longland—that's the name of the one who's holding her, right?" When Emma nodded, Maria continued, "Longland is speaking. Or shouting; I think I can almost hear his words."

So could Emma, but the fire made it difficult; it was louder.

"Emma, dear," Margaret began.

Maria said, "Eric and Chase have stopped moving. They're carrying knives," she added. "But they're not approaching Longland."

"Has he done something to—"

Maria's breath was sharp and clean as the edge of a knife. She didn't speak. She didn't have to.

Emma rose. She stood, forgetting any warning she had given Maria, because she had to *see* and had to *know*. Longland had his hands on Allison, yes, but Allison was struggling because he was also now touching the baby. He frowned and then almost casually lifted his hand from the infant's chest and slapped Allison, hard, across the face. Allison staggered, and were it not for his grip, she would have fallen.

It would have been a bad fall; she still held tightly to the child. Would hold tight until the end of the world—or the end of her life. It was Ally all over. It was why Emma loved her.

She swallowed, and she looked, hard, at Longland. Looked at the two people who stood to either side of him. One was male, and older; the other was female, perhaps Maria's age, if that. Emma's gaze narrowed as she watched them all.

"There's at least one ghost," she said out loud. "Maybe two. Longland doesn't have one."

"How can you tell?" Maria asked. Her voice sounded soft—but it wasn't. It was strained, as if speaking loudly would break it.

"The Necromancers bind the dead somehow, and to me it looks like—like a golden chain. I can't see the dead, but the links are pulsing," she added. "They're using that power."

"They would have to, dear. Against Eric, in particular, they would have to. Longland must have recognized him at some point."

Emma shook her head. "He talked to some lady in a mirror. *She* recognized him."

Margaret was utterly, completely silent. Emma would have glanced back, but she couldn't force herself to look away. She had felt helpless before, but never like this.

"They'll kill Eric," she said, almost numb. "They'll kill Chase."

"If Longland has Allison, yes," Margaret said. In a much gentler voice, she added, "You've always had a rather large amount of power on hand, dear."

"Margaret?" Emma swung away from the window and lifted her hands, palms curved and empty, as if she were begging. Which was fair; she was about to start.

Margaret turned to confer, briefly, with the other ghosts—all save Brendan Hall, who stood, arms folded, expression watchful. She turned back to Emma. "You know you don't have to ask," she began. She lifted an imperious hand when Emma opened her mouth, and Emma snapped it shut again in deference. "But you do ask. It's the difference," she said quietly, "between making love and rape.

"We'll let you take you what you need."

"Georges—"

"He's not a child, dear. He's dead."

"I saw him with Michael," Emma replied.

Margaret shrugged, a motion that was at once both delicate and crisp. "You know what to do."

"But I don't—"

"You don't know that you know. But you managed to walk the narrow path when you altered Maria's perception. And you changed very little—in her. What you've done to yourself remains to be seen, but that's for another time. Touch the lines, Emma. Touch all of them."

"Lines? You mean the chains?"

Margaret nodded.

Emma frowned, and then she turned to Andrew, still lodged in the safety and heaven—for him—of his mother's arms. "Andrew," she said, without looking up at his mother, "there are men outside. I don't know if you can see them, but they're—they're not good men. One of them wants to hurt your baby brother. And he will hurt us—all of us—if we're not very careful."

"Emma—" Maria began, her voice as sharp and cutting as only a mother's can be when her child is threatened.

Emma forced herself to ignore this. "If they try to reach your mom, you need to look at the fire," she told him.

He buried his face in his mother's neck, and Emma looked away. "I'm sorry, Andrew," she said softly. "But the fire—it's doing what you want it to do, even if you can't see it, yet. If they come, try—try really, *really*, hard."

She turned back to her ghosts, and this time, when she lifted her hands, she lifted the right one in a loose, grasping fist. From that fist, streaming from her folded palm to the five who now watched her in silence, ran lengths of golden chains. They stretched, as they had the first time she'd seen them, from her hand to their hearts, glowing with a faint luminescence, just as their eyes—all of their eyes—did.

She swallowed.

"Your friends will die, if you don't, dear."

She hesitated, because she knew these lines and their life force, if it could even be called that given they were dead, were the dividing line. If she did what she *must do*, she *was* a Necromancer. What she'd done for Andrew, what she'd done to Maria—it was different, and she knew it.

This? This was using the exact same power that the Necromancers did. It didn't matter, in the end, why. All of the Necromancers must have believed they had their reasons, and all of them must have believed those reasons were *good* reasons, because people were just like that. They could justify anything they did themselves. Things only looked wrong or evil when seen from the outside.

She turned to look out the window in desperation. She saw green fire lapping at Eric and Chase and saw it distorting the green-brown of the lawns on the boulevard; she saw Longland, both hands on Allison, and she saw the other two Necromancers, both hands splayed out in the air, as though the fire that surrounded Chase and Eric was coming directly from their hands.

Eric. Chase. Allison.

She didn't know what had happened to her other friends.

She took a deep breath to steady herself, and then she opened her hand.

"Emma—"

The chains lay against her palms. "I can't," she said starkly. "Not this. But I *can* break the power they're using, the way I did with Emily."

"If you try, he'll kill Allison."

"If he kills Allison, he'll die." Emma said nothing else, because there was nothing at all she could say. And as she started to find a handhold on the windowsill, to lever herself up onto it, she felt her hands began to pulse. With warmth. With heat that was both intense and intoxicating.

"You'll do, dear," Margaret said, her voice a bit deeper. "You'll do."

"Margaret!"

"Oh, hush. You've said what you had to say, and you even believed it. That's all we could ask for. Suzanne?"

"I agree."

"We would have let you take the power," she said. "But we can also—like your father—give. Go, dear. Do what you have to do. We'll be with you."

Because they didn't have any choice.

The warmth stretched up from her hands, traveling through her arms, her shoulders, and from there into the whole of her body. She closed her eyes for just a minute because the sensation itself was so powerful it was almost embarrassing.

And when she opened her eyes again, the whole world looked different.

\*     \*     \*

The street was dark, although it was the middle of the day. The sky was an angry red—not the red of sunset or sunrise; it was too deep for that, and there was no other color in the sky. It took a moment to understand why, in that light, the street was so dim.

The grass was gray. The trees were gray. The cars—which were translucent and ghostly—were also gray. Even the clothing they wore— the pants, the shirts, the jackets—were different shades of the same damn color.

Emma pushed herself up into the window's frame and balanced there a second.

Only the people—Eric, Chase, Allison, Longland and his two companions—looked normal. Even the baby was a dull shade of puce, because he'd woken, and he was not happy about it.

She balanced a moment in the window, looking down at the small roof that covered the porch. It wasn't much of a roof; it covered the door and a few linear feet of concrete, no more. The ladders had been placed beside it, and one had run up to the first window, with only a little difficulty. The second window had been clear. There were no ladders now, however.

She slid out of the window and landed on the roof of the porch so hard that her knees buckled. The small roof, however, held her weight. She took a deep breath and looked at the street again, now somewhat closer to it. Chase was in pain, and he was breathing hard. Eric's face was a mask. If it had ever had any expression at all—and it must have, because she remembered his gentle smile so clearly—he'd shed it completely. Emma couldn't tell if the fire, which still surrounded him, caused him any pain at all.

He watched Longland as if Longland were the only thing in the street.

"Emma," Margaret said. Her voice drifted down, carried by a breeze that smelled faintly of cinnamon and clover.

Emma nodded.

"Look at the soul-fire. Look at it carefully. Longland doesn't see you yet—but the minute you act, the minute you use power, he will. Eric has the whole of his attention," she added.

"Does Eric know I'm here?"

There was a brief hesitation. "Almost certainly," Margaret finally admitted.

"But he's not looking—"

"No, dear, please try to pay attention. If Eric looks here, so will Longland. Eric is a bright boy, and he—and Chase—are buying you time at some cost."

"But—"

"He's willing to trust you. I don't know why. He's sensitive enough that he knows there's a lot of power behind and above him, and if he knows where, he's almost certainly guessed whose power it is."

Emma nodded, only partly because it made sense. The other part wanted Margaret to stop with the lecture. She didn't ask, because the lecture had followed useful information. Instead, she acted on that information, and she looked with new eyes at green fire.

It was no longer, strictly speaking, green. It wasn't exactly gray, either; it looked at base like gray, but as she watched it, she realized that it was almost opaline. The colors grew brighter as she watched them, and she realized they were responding, in part, to the movements of the Necromancers, who were concentrating from some distance away on maintaining them.

And when she looked at the Necromancers again, she could see the chains, not as chains but . . . as the attenuated bodies of the dead. Long, thin, their forms stretched out around the Necromancers, as if they were on a rack; they were pale, as if they'd never seen sunlight—which wasn't surprising in a ghost, or wouldn't have been had Emma not seen any.

But as she watched, she saw that the color was being leeched out of them for the sake of that fire.

She saw, as well, that the fire was clinging to Chase in a way that it had not yet managed to cling to Eric; that the colors of that fire were attempting to match his skin, his hair, the flush of his cheek. She didn't know what would happen if they finally did reach the same hue, but she could guess.

"Ready?" she asked Margaret softly.

Margaret didn't answer.

Emma grabbed the lip of the porch roof in her hands, held it tight, and lowered herself as far down as she could go. It was awkward; her legs dangled above the concrete steps before she forced her hands to let go. They came, with the addition of a bunch of small splinters, as she fell the last yard.

When her feet hit the ground, she saw the grass ripple as if it were water and she had just broken its surface. Waves of green traveled out from her feet in fading concentric circles, and when they stilled, the green remained, an odd splotch of color against the gray background.

Longland frowned. She saw that much because she had to look to see if Allison—and the baby—were okay. More than that, she didn't take time for, because she could see the dead, stretched out now between Necromancers and fire, and she could see which of them powered the fire that was, even now, destroying Chase.

"Emma—what are you—"

Emma reached out. She reached out while standing still, as she had done with Maria Copis. As she had done the first time, with her father. This time, she felt herself leave her body. It was not a comfortable feeling; it was work. But the last time, she hadn't had the power of five of the dead behind her. She wasn't sure why it made a difference, and didn't have time to ask.

Instead, she ran—across grass that still turned green beneath her nonfeet—toward the Necromancers. Toward Longland, who held Allison. She touched Ally's arm, briefly, brushing it with her fingertips. She whispered two words, *I'm sorry*, and then she let go and turned to face the Necromancer. The woman. Her hair was a pale gold, and it was wrapped in so many fine braids it looked fake.

But she herself looked young, and strong, and utterly wrong. Her eyes were not the luminescence of the dead—but they weren't living eyes, either; they looked as if shadow had pooled permanently where there should have been whites. Emma reached out, not for the Necromancer but for the long, pale form of her dead.

The face of the ghost twisted at an odd angle to look at Emma as she touched him. Him, yes. Beard.

"What's your name?" she whispered.

His eyes widened, and he looked straight at her, as if she were somehow something entirely unlike the Emma Hall she had been in the process of becoming for all of her life.

"Please," she added.

"Morgan." The two syllables were stretched and slow.

"Morgan, come to me." She closed her hand around his arm, and she pulled with all her insubstantial might. She felt the snap of chain, although she couldn't see one, and then he was standing, hand in hers. His hand was cold. She smiled briefly. "Margaret?"

"Here, dear."

"This is Morgan; keep an eye on him?"

The man looked confused, but Emma had no more time. She glanced at Chase and saw, even at this distance, that the fire was going out. She moved, then, to the other Necromancer; the woman was frowning.

"Longland," she said. "I—the power—I think it's gone."

"On *that*?"

Emma moved around Longland's back and reached, again, for the long, thin stretch of a person that was anchoring the fire that lapped against Eric. When they were this elongated, this distorted, it was hard to say much about the dead; she couldn't quite tell if this one was male or female. But it didn't really matter.

She reached out and touched the ghost's arm. "I'm Emma," she said, striving now to be as unthreatening as possible. "And I'm here to free you."

She saw eyes that were six inches long, and very, very narrow, swivel to focus on her. She couldn't really tell if they widened. "What's your name?" she whispered, trying not to flinch.

"Alexander."

"Alexander," she repeated. Her grip tightened, and she pulled. Again, she felt something snap. It was a clean, quick sensation. Alexander appeared by her side, his hand in hers. His hand was also cold, and again, she smiled.

Alexander was younger than Morgan; he was older than Georges or Catherine, but younger, she thought, than Emily; his face hadn't yet hardened into the jaw, nose, and forehead of an older boy. "Emma?"

She nodded. "Emma Hall."

"You're in danger," he told her, shivering. "You shouldn't be here."

"My friends are here," she told him quietly. She looked at Eric. He staggered as the fire guttered, as if he'd been playing tug-of-war with it and it had suddenly let go. He turned and he looked straight at Emma, something neither Longland nor Chase had done.

She saw him nod; it was slight and almost imperceptible.

"Alex," she told the ghost, "you're going to have to wait here for a minute."

She turned to look at herself. At Emma Hall, who was standing, motionless, just before the front steps of a burning house. In the window, she caught a glimpse of Maria Copis' face through the smoke; she didn't, however, appear to be either burning or choking, and her young son, with his wide, luminescent eyes, was staring down at the street.

Emma started to approach herself, which was simultaneously comforting and really, really creepy, when she heard Longland speak.

"I have your friend," he said. "And I advise you both to keep your distance if you want her to remain alive. Leila, take the baby."

She ran the rest of the way to her body, and leaped *into* it. It enclosed her like a womb. For just a moment, she felt it: heavy, solid, inertial, so unpleasantly confining she wanted to leap out again, and be free. But she didn't, because she knew that without a body, she was just another one of the dead.

*No,* Margaret told her. *Not the dead.* But she felt both surprise and approval radiating from this internal voice.

She opened her eyes—her real eyes—and the world was the right color again. The grass was green-brown, the cars were solid, the houses were brick and stone and aluminum siding in various shades. The people wore clothing that didn't suggest that gray was the new black.

The Necromancers were powerless. That's what Emma thought, and that was her first mistake.

The woman drew a gun. She held it to the side of the baby's head, and she told Allison, coldly, to *let go.*

And Allison, who might well have held on had the gun been pressed against her own temple, shuddered and slowly unlocked her arms. Eric and Chase froze, and the other Necromancer—a man whose name was unknown—pulled a second gun, while the woman Longland had called Leila grabbed the baby. Her ability to point a gun while juggling a crying child was poor; she was clearly not a parent. Or not Michael, who, if he could ever bring himself to *touch* a real gun, could have done both.

Longland was still in control, because he had Allison.

From the window above the street, the window from which Maria Copis watched, Emma heard a scream.

It was not, however, Maria's scream. Emma started to turn and something hit her, hard. It wasn't painful, but it was so large, it drove her to her knees fast enough that concrete abraded her skin. Her hands tingled, and her hair rose as if caught in an electrical storm. She felt something leave her, something that she was not entirely in control of— and for better or worse, she let it go.

Leila *screamed.*

Fire erupted around her, and it was not green fire but red and orange, the heart and heat of the flames that had destroyed Rowan Avenue and, with it, so much of Maria's life.

Eric shouted, Allison turned. From her place on the steps, Emma could feel the fire's heat, and Allison was standing right beside it. She shouted and grabbed the baby just before he toppled out of Leila's grip. Longland almost lost her, then, but he managed to hold on.

But the baby wasn't burning.

The other man shouted something, loudly, and then he turned and pointed the gun—not at Eric or at Chase, but at Emma.

Even at this distance, she could see the barrel so clearly it might as well have been a few inches from her forehead.

Longland turned in the direction the gun was pointing, and his eyes widened enough that she could see the whites. "Emma!" he shouted, "you fool! What have you *done?*"

She had time to cover her face or to duck, but she did neither. Instead, almost horrified, she watched Leila burn. Burning was horrible, and although she'd known that, watching it was worse. Any other death, she thought, almost numb. "Andrew!" she shouted. "Andrew, enough! Enough!"

But he didn't hear her, and even if he did, she understood that it wasn't entirely his doing. It couldn't be; he was dead. She understood that what she'd felt was some part of Andrew's power, pushed through her—but it shouldn't have worked that way. And she had no idea how to stop what she'd let go, either.

Paralyzed, she knelt, staring at the barrel of a distant gun.

Wasn't terribly surprised when she heard it fire.

# CHAPTER
## SEVENTEEN

THE BULLET FAILED TO REACH HER.

Confused, she stared as the gun wavered, dipped, and fell. This was because the man who was aiming it staggered and then toppled, part of his face a sudden red blossom.

"Emma, dear," Margaret said urgently, "Call me now. Call me out."

The words made no sense. Emma watched the man topple and watched Longland suddenly curse, spinning, Allison almost forgotten.

Ally kicked him, hard, in the knee, still grabbing the baby tightly. He reached for her with his free hand, and then let go, because he had a knife in his upper arm.

Allison *ran*. She ran, in a straight line, toward Emma, holding Maria Copis' youngest child as if both their lives depended on it. Emma, still on her knees, looked up as Allison reached her, and then she pushed herself off the ground.

Another gunshot.

Merrick Longland cursed, turned, and light flared in the street.

Emma rose and opened her arms and hugged Allison fiercely; they were both shaking. "Ally—"

"Michael's okay. Amy and Skip are okay. Longland left them—" Allison swallowed. "They were okay when we left them."

Emma nodded. "Thank you."

"Emma," Margaret said. "Call me. *Now.*"

"Margaret—"

"Do it, dear. I can't emphasize this enough at the moment."

Another gunshot. Emma looked; Longland was staggering. Without Allison to stand behind, he had to face Chase and Eric, and she knew they would kill him. But death was supposed to happen quickly and, at best, painlessly. Years of watching television had taught her that.

The truth was visceral and ugly, and although she hated everything Longland had done in the brief time she'd been aware of him, she couldn't watch. But she also couldn't look away.

"He would have killed you all without blinking," Margaret said quietly. "And Emma, *call me out now.*"

Emma lifted a hand. She whispered Margaret's name into the noise of fighting: the sullen sound of flesh against flesh, the grunts, the swearing. She knew Margaret had arrived when Allison's eyes widened slightly.

"Thank you, dear. I'm sorry to be so pushy. It's always been a failing of mine."

*No kidding.* Emma, however, was too weary to be unkind. "Could he have—could he have defended himself against them if I hadn't—"

"If you hadn't taken Emily, yes. And more."

Emma was silent for a long moment. "How are Alexander and Morgan?"

"A bit dazed, dear, and a bit confused. They'll be fine, I think."

Emma nodded without looking at Margaret. It seemed important to her to watch, to bear witness, to truly understand the scope of the events she had put into motion. She didn't regret them. She wouldn't change much. Or maybe she would change everything, if she knew how.

Andrew Copis would still be alive. Her father would still be alive.

Nathan would still be alive. People like Chase and Eric would be out of work.

But life didn't work that way, in the end. You lived it, and it happened around you. If you were very lucky—and thinking this, she hugged Allison again—it happened while you still had friends. She had to let go of Allison because the baby was screaming his lungs out, and if Allison bounced him up and down and moved around a bit, he quieted. He didn't sleep, though.

"I think he's hungry," Allison told Emma.

"Which we can't do anything about right now."

When Longland finally fell, Emma looked up to the bedroom window. "Maria," she said quietly, "we'll get ladders and we'll get you both down. I think the baby's hungry, and we've lost the diaper bag."

From high above her head, Emma heard Maria Copis' laugh. It wasn't an entirely steady laugh, but there was a thread of genuine amusement in it, along with relief and a touch of hysteria.

Eric had the decency to clean the blood off his hands before he approached them. Chase? Well, he was Chase. And he looked bad; his face was a mess of blisters, and Emma thought it likely other parts of his body—all thankfully hidden by clothing—looked about the same.

"Your poor hair," she told him softly. "If I were you, I'd do it a favor and just shave it all off."

He reached up and touched his hair, because his hair, unlike his skin, had simply curled and shriveled.

"Allison," Chase said, the word a question.

Allison took a deep breath and nodded. "I'm good. I'm," she added, glancing at Emma, "*fine.*"

"You?" Eric asked Emma. He moved toward her, standing beside Allison and a little closer. It was a bit strange, but Emma had seen so much strange she didn't worry much about it.

"I'll be better once I actually set eyes on the rest of my friends. And the diaper bag," she added, wincing, as she glanced at the baby. "Oh, and the ladders."

He shook his head.

"You knew I was there."

He shoved his hands in his pockets, shrugged. "You got out."

"I did. Maria and Andrew are still up in Maria's room."

"She—"

"It's complicated. Don't ask." Then, taking a breath, she added, "but Andrew is fine, and he's almost out of the fire. Thank you. And Chase?"

"What?"

"I owe you an apology. You were right."

He shrugged and glanced at Eric. "Yeah, well. Eric is still one up on me."

"So, I have a question. If you and Eric were fighting with knives, who shot the other Necromancer?"

Eric and Chase exchanged a glance.

"I did. And now, Eric, and you, young lady with the baby, if you'd care to move out of the way?" An older man, possibly fifty, possibly sixty, was standing about five yards away on the sidewalk. He was dressed in some version of summer casual that had to be decades old, but it suited him, and his clothing was sadly not the most notable thing about him. The gun that he held in his hand was. It was not—yet—pointed at anyone, but Emma stiffened anyway.

She glanced at Eric and saw the expression on his face: this man was the reason he'd moved in so close. Eric was taller than Emma, and broader. "Stay behind me," he told her, and then he slowly turned.

"Is that the person whose phone calls you keep ignoring?" she whispered.

He laughed. "You ask the strangest questions, Emma. But yes, it is."

"I'm not sure I'd dare."

"Eric," the man said, waving his gun. "Please step aside. And you, young lady."

"Ally," Emma whispered, "move."

"I think he wants to shoot you," Allison replied, voice flat.

"Oh, probably. At this point, I wouldn't mind shooting myself." Raising her voice slightly, she said, "Chase, help Allison find a safer place to stand."

Chase nodded and reached for Allison's arm. Allison gave him A Look. Chase ignored it. "I didn't almost get fried alive," he told her through gritted teeth, "so you could be shot by the old man. He'll kill you if he feels he has to," Chase added. When Allison failed to move, Chase swore. "Allison, let Eric handle it. If anyone can handle the old man, it's Eric."

"Allison, *please*," Emma whispered. "You've got the baby."

"Chase can hold the baby."

Silence. "Ally, think about what you just said."

Allison looked at Chase's blood covered hands and grimaced.

"Look, go and get Michael and the others. Tell them that everyone's safe. Well, everyone who wasn't trying to kill us. And get them to bring the ladders."

Allison hesitated for just another minute, and then she nodded, and she let Chase lead her away. Chase didn't return; he went down the street with her, as if he couldn't quite trust her not to turn back. It was surprising sometimes when Chase wasn't stupid.

This left just Eric and Emma, standing in the street in front of the house as if it were one giant tombstone, while above the street, Maria and Andrew waited.

Allison and Chase were halfway down the street when the man fired. Allison turned back instantly, and Chase caught her by one arm, spoke something that no one could hear except Allison, and then dragged her down the street.

Emma flinched, instinctively closing her eyes. Eric, however, didn't move.

The bullet hadn't hit him; it had struck the poor grass and dug a runnel through it. The older man and Eric watched each other in a silence that lasted long enough for Chase and Allison to turn a corner. And then some.

"Eric," the man finally said.

"No."

"You don't realize what the girl *is*."

"I realize, better than you know, who Emma is."

"And you're not enspelled."

"Not more than usual, no."

"Longland was not the threat that this girl—Emma, you called her?—will be."

"She has no training."

The old man looked as if he were about to be sick. He lifted the gun and pointed it at Eric. "She *has no training,* and she burned a Necromancer alive? And you're standing there and telling me not to *shoot*? Eric, what the hell is wrong with you?"

Emma was almost grateful that she couldn't see Eric's face. The stench of charred flesh still wafted on the breeze, such as it was, in the street.

Margaret cleared her throat and stepped forward.

The man's eyes widened. When they narrowed again, his face had lost the look of angry confusion, but the cold fury that replaced it was worse. He would shoot Eric, Emma realized. He would shoot Eric just so he could kill her.

She wanted to be brave enough to step out of Eric's shadow, to stand exposed, to let herself be shot, because if he was going to shoot her anyway, it would at least save Eric's life; she had no doubt at all that he could use the gun—she'd seen him blow off the side of a man's head.

She wanted to be that brave, but she couldn't. The most she could manage was to peer around Eric, in as much safety as she could.

"Ernest," Margaret said, in a tone of voice that had made even her most imperious commands seem friendly and mellow by comparison. "If you shoot either Eric or the girl, I will find some way to haunt you horribly for eternity."

The man's jaw dropped slightly, and his face lost a trace of the look of deadly, implacable fury that had made him seem so terrifying. "Margaret?" Fury, however, was tempered now by suspicion.

"I admit that I wouldn't be so drastic if you put a bullet in your Chase, because that boy has *no manners*, and it would probably do him some good." Margaret folded her arms.

The man—Ernest—looked past Eric to Emma. He was no longer entirely suspicious, but he was a far cry from friendly. "Let her go," he said coldly.

Emma cringed. "I don't know how," she told him. "I'm not sure how I'm even holding her. She kind of does what she wants."

Eric, on the other hand, said, "You know Margaret?"

"He does, dear," Margaret replied. "We were rather close while I was alive, although I admit it was somewhat fraught."

"Margaret—"

"But not without its rewards. Ernest," she said, unfolding her arms, and letting them drop to her sides—Margaret not being a woman who seemed to know how to plead, "Emma does hold us. Emma, dear, do be good and call out the others. Oh, I see that Georges and Catherine are already here. Give Emily a hand."

Ernest's jaw opened very slightly—an old and controlled person's version of shock—as Emma obeyed Margaret. It was, however, true that Georges and Catherine had already come out. "Emma?" Georges asked, Catherine standing slightly behind him and letting him do the dirty work, as usual.

"Now is not a good time, Georges," she told him firmly.

Georges practiced the selective deafness of determined children everywhere. "Can we play with Michael now?"

"Michael's not even here, Georges, and if he were, he'd still be babysitting."

"Yes, he is."

"No, he—oh." She could see them all coming down Rowan Avenue, and in spite of the fact that only Eric stood between her and a madman with a gun, she smiled. "Well," she said carefully, "we have to wait until Ernest decides he's not going to shoot me. Or Eric."

"Andrew would be angry," Georges told her confidently. "I'm sure he'd burn him up, too."

"We *do not want* Andrew to burn anyone else," Emma told Georges quite severely. "But we need to get Andrew and his mother out of that house first. After they come down, you can play with Michael."

"Me too?" Catherine asked.

"You too."

Ernest was staring at the dead in utter confusion.

"You see, Ernest," Margaret said, in a slightly less frosty tone of voice. "Emma is not a Necromancer."

"But she killed—"

Margaret shook her head. "No. She was the conduit, no more, and she was the conduit out of her own ignorance."

"I don't understand."

"Margaret—please." Emma's life goals had never included blaming a killing on a four-year-old boy. "I could have stopped it. I didn't."

"Dear," she said, annoyed at being interrupted, "you didn't even know what it was."

"I knew it was power. I knew it was passing through me. I could have held it in." She paused, and then she lifted both hands where Margaret could see their open palms; she didn't have the ferocious dignity of Margaret and didn't feel that she needed it. "He's four. The Necromancer had a gun pointed at his baby brother. He saw it, and he was upset."

"You have a *four-year-old Necromancer?*" the old man almost shouted. He looked at Eric.

Eric shook his head. "No," he said, and his shoulders relaxed ever so slightly in Emma's view, "the four year old is already dead."

Chase told everyone to stop about thirty yards away. Amy, of course, ignored him entirely. And where Amy went, everyone else followed, tagging along in her wake like intimidated younger siblings. Or like Catherine with Georges.

Ernest paused, the gun hand still steady. "The boy who died in the fire here?"

Eric nodded.

"She bound him?"

"Not exactly."

"Ernest, if you are not going to shoot, put the gun away. You're going to scare the other children." Margaret glanced, significantly, not at Georges and Catherine, but at the rest of Emma's friends.

Ernest, on the other hand, glanced at the three corpses on the lawn.

Margaret grimaced. "Yes, you have a point, there. Will they bring the ladders, Emma?"

"Skip has one of them. He's going to get his head bitten off if he's lost the other one," she added. "Let's get Maria down. If," she added politely, "you're okay with not shooting us until we at least get someone out of a burning building?"

Since the building was clearly not burning, and the world seemed to have slid sideways on the way to upside down, the man slowly holstered his gun. Which, given the heat of the barrel, struck Emma as either brave or stupid.

Not much about the man suggested stupid, though.

While Chase held the ladder, Eric went up it, and he helped Maria Copis navigate her way down the rungs. She was still clinging tightly to Andrew, who in return was clinging tightly to her, and she was forced to climb with one hand and two feet, which was highly awkward.

Eric did not, however, complain.

"Is it over?" Maria asked Emma as she finally put her second foot down on solid ground.

Ernest was staring at Andrew.

"It's mostly over," Emma told her quietly. "I'm sorry about—about the . . ."

Andrew looked at Emma. "She was going to hurt my brother," he said, with special emphasis on the last two syllables. That and not a little anxiety.

"Yes, she was," Emma told him. "You saved your brother's life." She smiled at him. "Andrew—"

Maria shook her head and hugged him tightly.

Ernest, however, said, "I can see the boy."

Allison nodded. "We can all see him, I think."

"It's because Maria is holding him," Emma replied.

"Maria is a Necromancer? Is the entire *city* full of Necromancers?" Ernest said this, with some heat, to Eric.

"Maria's not a Necromancer," Emma replied. "She's just a very, very determined mother." Emma looked at Andrew and at Maria, and knew that she wasn't quite finished here yet.

Maria paused, and then, looking at her red-faced infant, and her slightly worried two year old, she finally set Andrew down. He was less reluctant to go, but he watched her as she took her infant from Allison, sat down on the concrete steps, and began to quietly nurse him.

"He's hungry," Andrew said.

"Yes," Emma told him.

"Emma?"

"Yes, Andrew?"

"Am I dead?"

Maria didn't look up at the question, but she flinched.

Emma sucked in air and then said, "Yes."

"Oh." He turned to look at his mother, his brother, and then his younger sister. "I don't like the fire," he finally said.

Emma said nothing. She said nothing when Andrew's gaze lifted until he was looking up at a point beyond her left shoulder, his eyes widening slightly. While he looked, Emma reached out for Catherine and Georges' hands, and they came, cold to the touch, appearing in front of Michael.

She let them play with Michael, as much as they could, and Michael, understanding that they needed this, obliged, although he was very, very upset at the dead people. Playing with the children did help, though; it was something he knew, understood, and could do well.

But Emma was cold when at last she told the two very disappointed children that it was time for Michael to rest and time for Emma to do something else.

"What?" Georges asked her quietly.

"Open a door, if I can," she replied.

Margaret, who had been conversing with Ernest, who seemed to see her regardless of whether or not Emma was actually touching her, looked up at that. Ernest, his conversation broken, looked as well.

"Dear," Margaret began.

"I have to try," Emma told the older woman. "How long have you been trapped here?"

"Long enough. It's the nature of the world, and the nature of the dead."

"But it wasn't always."

Margaret was notably silent.

"What are you talking about, Emma?" Eric asked. He was still keeping a very watchful eye on Ernest, although Emma had long since relaxed.

Emma turned to him. "Andrew. Sort of." She exhaled. "He's going to be trapped in empty streets for god only knows how long—and it's not supposed to be like that."

"What is it supposed to be like?"

"I don't know. Heaven. Maybe. But something *else*. He's done here. They're all—" she added, extending an arm to take in the dead who now gathered as if it were a company barbecue, "done here. My dad told me there's somewhere else they should be able to go."

Margaret winced and looked away—away from Emma, from Ernest, from Georges and Catherine.

"They can find it from anywhere," Emma continued. "But they can't reach it. It's closed. It's blocked."

"Emma—"

"I want to try to unblock it."

"You can't."

"I might not succeed, but I can try."

Ernest was staring at her. He turned to look at Eric. Neither of the two said anything, but it wasn't their permission she wanted, anyway.

She turned to Maria Copis, who, having finished feeding—and changing—her baby, looked desolately at Andrew. Andrew, who was crouched at her feet looking up.

Allison came to take the baby, who was now both clean and asleep, and Maria reached down to pick Andrew up and draw him into her lap. Then, her chin resting on the top of his head, she looked at Emma.

"He'll be here," Emma said quietly. "He'll be trapped here, like all of the dead are trapped."

"I want more time," Maria whispered.

"We all do," Emma whispered back. They were both silent for what seemed like a long time.

But Maria unfolded, still carrying her son. "I heard what you said to Eric. If you do whatever it is you're going to try, will he—"

"He'll be able to leave."

"But to where?"

"Someplace where there's no pain," Emma replied. "I haven't seen it. I don't know. But my father has. All the dead have. They feel that it's home—no, more like the ideal of home, a place where they're wanted, a place where they belong and where they're loved."

Andrew said, quietly, sitting in the arms of his mother and still looking up, "I want to go there. I'm dead, Mom."

His mother closed her eyes and nodded. "I'm so sorry, Drew. I'm sorry."

But he reached up with one hand and touched her cheek, although he didn't look away from whatever it was that drew his attention. "I can wait for you, there," he told her in a faraway voice.

"Will you?"

He nodded. "I'll wait forever. I'll wait for Stefan and Catherine, too."

Maria swallowed and smiled. She was crying. Emma was not, by sheer force of will. "Yes, Emma," Maria said quietly. "We're ready."

Emma told the others what she wanted to do, but it only made sense to the dead. They stared at her for a moment with something that looked like hunger but was really just a deep and terrible longing, sublimated because it was so pointless.

"Dad?"

"He's not here, dear," Margaret told her.

"But—"

"If you accomplish what you intend, I think he feels he'll have to leave you. The pull is very strong."

"But he said he could find it no matter where he was."

"He hasn't just walked down the street." In a more gentle voice she added, "He's not ready to leave you yet, and he doesn't trust himself to stay. You can't know what we've seen and what we long for. Because you can't know, you don't know how very hard it will be for him. But he does know. And he's not willing or ready to leave you, not yet."

"Is that because I don't want to let him go?"

Margaret's smile was almost gentle. It was also sad. "Partly, dear. I'm sorry."

"How do I—"

But Margaret shook her head. "Only partly. The dead are what they are, and if you will not make decisions for them, respect his. You'll need power for this, dear. And it will be more power than you held when you faced Longland."

Eric sucked in air. "Emma, don't do this."

"Why not?"

"Because she's not telling you the whole truth."

"Then you tell me."

"You can't—you might not—survive the taking of that much power. And even if you do, it might change you."

"You mean, more change than seeing the dead and being able to leech the life out of them?"

He grimaced.

"She has a point," Chase told him. Chase's expression throughout had been very, very odd, and it wasn't an odd that could be attributed to blistered skin and patchy red hair.

"Fuck you," Eric said.

"Why? Eric, she's going to try it anyway. You've known her for long enough to know that. You might be able to interfere—but she won't thank you."

"She can't do it."

"Then she'll fail. What's the big deal?"

Eric turned, then, to Margaret. But whatever he saw in her face gave him no strength and no hope. "I didn't save you from the old man so you could commit suicide."

"No. But that's not what I'm trying to do."

"You'll need the dead, dear."

"I have—"

"More."

Emma deflated. "I have no idea how to bind the dead. I don't even think I want to know."

"No, you don't. But you already know. It's a different binding," Margaret added, "and it's costly, for you, child. You pay for it, and we—the dead—touch a little bit of life again. But what you'll need to do this is far more than we gave you. If we give you everything we have, if we drive ourselves beyond the point of speech or perhaps even thought, we will still not give you enough.

"You need the dead," Margaret added firmly.

She turned to the others. "Will you help me?" she asked them. "Will you help me even if it means you have nothing left?"

As one, transfixed, they nodded.

"I think there are very, very few who would say no," Margaret told her.

Emma nodded. "Then I have to find a way to—to summon the dead. I can gather them, if I find them." She glanced at Maria. And swallowed. *No.*

She frowned. She could hear a voice, and she felt it as if it were a dead person's voice, but none of them had spoken a word.

*You have what you need, Emma Hall. Be what I could not be. Be what she could not be.*

And then she saw the almost translucent image of an ancient, ancient woman, dressed in rags, her flesh like another layer of grimy cloth upon her skeleton. It was the old woman from the graveyard. Emma lifted a hand to cover her mouth, but she managed not to take more than a step back.

Margaret turned toward the old woman, and she bowed and fell silent, moving to allow this most ancient of ghosts to pass her.

"You're not going to kiss me again."

"No."

Emma lowered her hand. Allison was staring at the side of her face, and she reddened. "Who are you talking about? Who couldn't be, and what?"

The old woman shook her head. "If I had survived, I could not do what you will try now. There is only one, in our long history, who could."

"And she?"

The old woman fell silent.

"Emma—"

They both, young and old, living and dead, turned to look at Eric. He also fell silent.

"It is dark, where the dead live. The light they long for has been denied them. But you have other light. Use it."

Emma frowned, and then her eyes widened. She looked at her hands, at the hands that had gripped, for moments, the sides of a lantern in a distant graveyard. As she looked, she saw the sides of it appear, like a layer, against her skin. She saw the writing first, and then the wires, the folds of textured paper. She felt the ice and the cold of it, and it burned her as if it were fire.

But she'd held on to Maria Copis for longer, and that was worse.

Margaret was again utterly silent.

Eric flinched.

Ernest swore under his breath. "You gave her that?"

"I did not give it to her intentionally," the old woman replied, her gaze held by the growing light in Emma's hands. "She took it."

"You *allowed* it."

The old woman did turn, then. "It was meant to be used," she finally said. "It was meant to be used *this* way. She knew *nothing*, and it was the light she reached for." Turning once again to Emma, she continued. "Sometimes they exist shrouded in darkness; they cannot find the way. And then, Emma Hall, we find them, and we lead them home."

When the lantern was solid, Emma lifted it. She shifted position, one hand at a time, until she held it by its top wire; it swung wildly back and forth as if caught in a strong wind.

Georges whispered in a language that Emma didn't understand. She meant to ask him what he saw but fell silent as the lantern began to glow. Its light, which had been so orange and then so blue, became a white that was almost blinding. Almost.

It was brighter than the azure of clear sky; it was brighter than the sunlight. It spread as she watched it, touching the houses that were closest and passing beyond them as if it could blanket the entire city, yard by yard, as it traveled.

Georges came to stand by her side. She thought it was because he was nervous, but when she spared him a glance, she realized that he wasn't; he was standing as close as possible to her because she was the center of that light, and that was where he wanted to be.

And in the distance, as her eyes acclimated to yet another change in color and texture, she saw that he wasn't the only one. From every street she could see, growing larger as they walked—or rode, or ran—the dead came.

# CHAPTER
# EIGHTEEN

THEY CAME IN ONES AND TWOS, to start, but as the time passed, the numbers grew. Eric swore, because Eric could see the dead. Maria didn't swear, but a quick glance at her face told her this was more because she was holding a four-year-old than from any lack of desire.

Emma didn't know the names of the dead, but she thought she should. They looked, or rather, felt, familiar to her. She saw the young, and the old, the strong and the infirm, the men and the women; she saw different shades of skin, heard the traces of different languages. From the language she did understand, she thought that the voices were raised in prayer.

What these dead didn't do, apparently, was see *each other*. They saw her. They saw the lantern that she held in her hand. It was enough to draw them, like moths to flame. And Emma very dearly did not want to be the flame that consumed them.

"This is going to take a while," Eric told Ernest.

"Meaning?"

"You'd better start cleanup detail or Emma and her friends are all going to be on the inside of a jail, which we can't afford."

"Ah. Right."

She asked them their names. She touched them, briefly, as she did. They answered, even the ones who didn't apparently speak English, and she absorbed their names. Not their beings, and not their power, but the simple fact of the syllables that had identified them in life.

She started by telling the first few of the dead what she intended and by asking their permission and their help to do it; she finished merely by taking their quiet, hushed—and heartbreaking—assent. They knew, somehow. They understood.

They gathered in a crowd that made the most exuberant of concerts or political rallies look paltry by comparison. But they gathered almost on top of each other, occupying physical space as if it meant nothing to them. It became hard to look at them and see the mismatch of face and chest and shoulder as they overlapped.

She closed her eyes instead.

With her eyes closed, she could see again, and she knew that, without effort, she had once again slid out of her body. She looked at a world that was gray and at the dead, who were not. She could barely see houses; they were sketched against the horizon as if by an impressionist. The cars and the trees were gone; the plain spread out forever. And above it, on a spiral of stairs that glimmered, she could see it: a door.

"Maria," she said, although she could no longer see Maria Copis.

But she heard, at a great remove, Maria's steady voice.

"Give Andrew to me," she told his mother, as gently as she could.

She didn't know if Maria hugged him or kissed him or spoke to him, although she was certain she had, but after a long moment, she felt the weight of a four-year-old placed, gently, in her arms. The arms that were extended and carrying the lantern. Andrew Copis materialized, and smiled at her.

"Are you ready?" she asked Andrew.

His eyes were shining.

She held the lantern by her fingers and Andrew in the curve of her arms, and she began to climb those stairs as the crowd that gathered all around her took—and held—a collective breath. The dead didn't need to breathe, of course, but maybe they'd forgotten they *were* dead. Her feet were the first to touch the steps.

As she ascended, they followed. They were much more orderly than a concert crowd; they didn't push and didn't shove and didn't swear at each other. But then again, they didn't have to. She thought, for a moment, that they might not need to touch the stairs at all—and wondered if what she was "seeing" was entirely something created for her own benefit.

But it didn't matter. She could climb stairs, and the dead could climb whatever it was they saw in their individual, unconnected worlds. She rose, and they rose, until she was at the top of the steps on a platform that led to a single door.

It wasn't a fancy door; it wasn't pearly gates. It was a simple, thick wood of a kind you didn't see much anymore. It had no handle, no door-knob, no knocker, no bell. It was just there.

She put Andrew down, and then she reached out to touch the door. Her hand stopped an inch away from its surface.

"You're not dead," Andrew told her calmly. He reached out with considerably smaller hands, and his hands did touch the wood. He frowned, though, and looked as if he might cry. "I can't get through."

"Well, no. You have to open it first."

"Open *what*?"

So, she thought, it wasn't just the stairs that were for her benefit. Her father had said he could see light, and Emma demonstrably couldn't. It should have worried her, but she found it oddly comforting. The closed door was like another metaphor, and all she had to do was open it.

Without being able to actually touch it.

She shook her head, and reached for the surface of the door again.

"Emma—"

"Hush, Andrew. I'm not dead—but right now I'm not exactly alive either. I'm here, I'm with you, and with all the others."

He looked up at her for a moment and then nodded. "You brought my mom to me."

"She wanted to come."

He nodded. "She was sad."

"Yes. She's been very, very sad. I think seeing you has made her happier, though. Now, let me try this." This time, when she reached out with her palm for the door's surface, she pushed. The inch between her hand and the flat planks gave way very, very slowly, and even as it did, she felt her hands begin to tingle and ache. It was a familiar sensation, but it grew stronger as she pushed.

She looped the lantern around the crook of her elbow, and she freed up her other hand. She applied that one to the invisible barrier as well, and it continued to give slowly. Sweat started to trickle down her neck, although she felt it at a great remove.

The inch became half an inch, and then a quarter, an eighth, a sixteenth. Every tiny increment required more power, and she took the power that was there, gathering it as if she were breathing it in and exhaling it through her hands.

But when she finally—finally—touched the door, she knew. She felt it, and she felt what lay beyond it, so clearly she could almost *see*. She heard the faint, attenuated cries at her back, and she knew that what she could almost see, they could clearly see. They had given her this, and it had robbed them of the power of their voices, muting them.

She *pushed* hard.

The door gave slowly, fighting her every inch of the way.

But it gave, and when it did, she renewed her efforts because she could see what they saw: the light, the sense of comfort, of home, of belonging. The sense of perfect ease, of place. She felt it like a blow, and she felt herself, somewhere, stagger back at the force of it.

It was like the very best parts of loving Nathan, and it tore at her because she had thought they were gone forever and she wanted them so badly. Badly enough to hold that door against the force that was trying to keep it closed. As she struggled, she felt the dead begin to pass by her. Andrew was the first to go, and this felt right to her, but he was only the first.

The others streamed past as well.

She couldn't count them. She didn't try. She became the struggle, and she knew that all she had to do was keep it open for long enough. How many of the dead would pass through, she didn't know. Not all of them, unless she could somehow wrench the door wide open, and free of all restraint.

But she didn't have to do that. All she had to do was hold it for long enough, and then?

She could go, too.

She could go to the light, and the peace, and the lack of pain and loss, and she could find comfort there, and she could give over all grief, all numbness, all of the horrible gray and guilt and anger that had clouded the last months of her life.

*Emma!*

It would be so easy. It would be so much easier.

The last person slipped through, and her hands now ached with effort, and with cold. She knew she'd run out of power; there was no one left to give it to her. But she could—

Could go. But Nathan, she knew, would not be there. He hadn't been among the dead; she would have known him anywhere. His name, his face, the sound of his voice. Even if she couldn't touch him without the cold. She could pass through this door, and he would be trapped here, and she would spend eternity without him.

And, she thought, she would be dead, and she wouldn't *have to care*.

She swallowed, her fingers slipped, and she moved an inch forward.

And then, clear as a bell, she heard a familiar, quiet voice, uncertainty and fear etched into every word. *Emma, I don't want you to die.* Michael's voice.

She knew that he would be fidgeting, that he would be in that physical state that was one step short of out-and-out panic, and she knew that if she walked through this door, the one short step would be crossed the minute he understood that what he wanted didn't matter.

She didn't love Michael the way she'd loved her father. She didn't love him the way she'd loved Nathan. But she accepted the responsibility of the love she did feel for him, and she let the door go, weeping. Understanding, as she did, that the Maria Copises of this world were doing the same thing.

The door slammed shut with so much force it should have shattered, and while Emma watched it reverberate, it grew eyes.

Shadowed, dark eyes, scintillating with color the way black opals did. They were not—quite—human eyes, although something about them implied that they might have been once, and they were rounded with effort and, Emma thought, fear.

*I will kill you for this.*

She heard the voice and knew that it was the second time she had heard it. The first time had been in Amy's house, when Eric had spoken to an image in the mirror.

She should have been afraid. Later, maybe. Right now she was too caught up in grief, and when she opened her real eyes again, she was weeping. In public. She couldn't even find the strength to tell anyone that she was fine.


Eric drove her home. She left him at the door when Petal emerged, barking in his stupid, loud way. She'd run out of Milk-Bones, and anyway, feeding Petal was not exactly what she needed at the moment.

But need it or not, it was what she had to do, and she walked into the kitchen and found a can of dog food, a can opener, and his dish.

"Emma." She looked up, and she saw Brendan Hall standing in the kitchen, where in any real sense he would never stand again. She'd re-covered just enough that she could turn her face away. She did, but then she turned back to her father, as if she were eight years old. She had nothing to say, and he waited.

"You didn't leave," she whispered, when she could speak at all.

He shook his head. "While the door is closed," he told her, his voice heavy with worry and yet somehow warm with pride, "I'm staying."

"Why?" She had to ask, because she'd come so close to not staying herself, and she, at least, was alive.

"Sprout," he said quietly, and Petal looked up and barked. It wasn't a "strangers-at-the-door-man-the-cannons" bark, which was his usual form of noisemaking; it was tentative and hesitant.

Brendan Hall bent and stroked his dog's head. His hand passed slightly through fur, and he grimaced. "Because," he told his daughter, not looking at her at all, "you're here."

She nodded, and then she reached out blindly for him, and he hugged her. His arms were cold, but she didn't mind.

Her mother was in the living room.

Emma discovered this when she at last let her father fade into what-ever world he occupied when he wasn't with her, and she tried to walk, stiffly, up the stairs. She needed to remove a dozen splinters from her palms, and she needed to change. She probably also needed to burn or dispose of the clothing she was wearing, because it looked as though she'd already tried and had done a truly bad job.

But when her mother called her name, she froze, one hand on the rail. Petal, always hopeful that any spoken word meant food, came out of the kitchen and tried to tangle his blocky body around her legs. She grimaced, looked down at her clothing, and then turned. "Mom?"

Her mother rose. She was pale, and she had that I've-got-a-headache look. Emma realized belatedly that she'd been sitting on the same spot on the couch that Emma often occupied when she was thinking about Nathan. Or thinking, more precisely, about his absence.

The headache look, on the other hand, vanished as Mercy Hall approached her daughter. "Emma!"

Emma started to tell her mother she was fine—because, among other things, it happened to be true—but she stopped. "There was a bit of fire," she said instead.

Her mother's brows rose most of the way up her forehead.

She glanced at the hall mirror. From this angle she could see only a quarter of her body. "It's not as bad as it looks," she added quickly. "But I would like to get changed."

"What *happened*?"

"There was a fire," she repeated. "We were—we tried to help."

"Who is we?"

"Ally, Michael, me. Eric and his cousin, Chase."

"Was anyone hurt?"

How to answer that? "No. No one was hurt." Lie. She should have felt guilty; she didn't. "Let me get changed," she added. "And showered. And maybe you could help me take these splinters out of my hand before—"

"They get infected?"

"Something like that."

Mercy Hall folded her arms across her chest, and her lips thinned. But she drew one sharp breath and nodded. "I swear," she said softly, "It was so much easier when you were two. Then, I *had* to keep my eyes on you all the time. Now? I never know what's going to happen."

Emma, who had walked away from death and its peace, nodded. Her mother would worry—but her mother always did that. What her mother wouldn't have to do, not this time, was stand by a grave and bury her only child. She thought of Maria, then, and she turned and surprised her mother: She wrapped her in a tight, tight hug.

"I *am* fine, Mom," she said, when she at last pulled back.

Her mother's eyes were filmed with unshed tears. "I'm sorry I wasn't here earlier—"

Emma shook her head. "Don't be," she said quietly. Knowing that her mother was thinking about her father. And missing him. Emma wanted to call him out then, to call him back—but she had a strong suspicion that he wouldn't actually listen. He'd always believed he knew what was best for both Emma and her mother.

But he was gone, at least for the moment; Emma and her mother were still here. They had each other. "I'll come back after I've showered. Maybe you can find the tweezers?"

Monday at 8:10, Michael came to the door.

Emma, her bag ready, her hair brushed, and her clothes about as straight as they were going to be for the day, opened the door, waited while he fed Petal a Milk-Bone, and then joined him on the front steps.

The good thing about Michael was that she didn't need to apologize for anything. Whatever had happened, they'd both survived it, and he held nothing against her, not even her near death. He did ask a lot of questions, but she answered them as truthfully as she could, often resorting to "I don't know" because it was true.

They picked Allison up on the way to school. Allison looked surprisingly cheerful, but it was the kind of forced cheer that hid worry.

"I'm fine, Ally," she told her.

"You're always fine," Allison said. "But are you okay?"

Emma nodded. "Mostly," she added, mindful of Michael.

"Maria left you her phone number. She had to get the kids back."

Emma winced. "I'm surprised she'd ever want to speak to me again. She almost died there."

"You almost died there as well."

"Yes, but I can't get away from me."

Allison laughed.

\*    \*    \*

They made it to school, and when they did, Emma saw that Eric and Chase were waiting for them on the wide, flat steps of the school. Although skateboarding was strictly prohibited, people were skateboarding anyway. Business as usual.

But Eric came down the steps to meet them.

"I'm fine," she told him, before he could speak.

"You're always fine," he replied.

She glanced at Allison and surprised herself by laughing. Allison laughed as well.

"Can I talk to you for a minute?" Eric asked her.

"Maybe five. Why?" Allison raised an eyebrow, and Emma nodded in response. She stood still, in front of Eric, while Allison dragged Michael through the doors of the school.

"Are you leaving?" Emma asked him.

"Leaving?"

"School. You aren't really a student here."

He hesitated and then said, "No. If it's all right with you, I'd like to stay."

This surprised her, but she covered it by saying, "Not if it means we have to keep Chase, too."

"I heard that."

Eric chuckled, but he looked pained. "You have to keep Chase, too. He's enrolled."

"But—"

"The old man insisted."

"The old man who was going to shoot me? And probably shoot you as well?"

"That one."

"But—but why?"

"Because he's decided he's not going to shoot you. Or me. Well, not for that at any rate. Emma—"

She looked at him for a long while, and then she smiled.

His turn to look slightly confused. "What? Have I got something on my face?"

"No. But you know, you *did* stand between me and a loaded gun. That's not a bad character trait in a guy." She nodded toward the door. "Unless you want to beat my late-slip collection, we can talk about this later."

She started up the stairs, and Eric fell in beside her; Chase pulled up the rear. "You realize," he said, sounding aggrieved, "that you're forcing me to *go to school* and listen to a bunch of boring teachers talk about crap that has nothing to do with my life?"

"So sue me."

Eric laughed, and Emma smiled again, less hesitantly. It wasn't all despair and loss, this whole living business. Sometimes, it was good. It was important to hold on to that.

On Tuesday night, Emma went to the graveyard. She took Petal, her phone, and Milk-Bones, and she made her long and meandering way through the residential streets, where lights were on in different rooms.

Petal was, of course, offended by the nighttime excursions of the local wildlife, and Emma caught a glimpse of raccoons when she was almost yanked off her feet because she was foolishly holding the lead. She continued to hold it, however.

She looked for ghosts, for patches of strangeness in the architecture, but the dead—at least in this neighborhood—were sleeping. And Eric had said graveyards were peaceful because the dead didn't go there.

Emma, who was not dead, did.

She had thought that, with the realization that Nathan was some-where else, she could give up these nightly excursions, but she'd come to understand that she didn't go for Nathan's sake; she went for her own. For the quiet that Eric himself seemed to prize.

It was a place in which she never felt the need to say *I'm fine.* She didn't feel the need to talk, or be interesting, or be interested; she could breathe here, relax here, and just be herself. Whoever that was.

She found a wreath of flowers standing on a thin tripod, just in front of Nathan's grave, and she swept a few fallen leaves from the base of the headstone before she settled into the slightly dewy grass. It had started here.

Petal butted her with the top of his broad, triangular head, and she made a place for him in her lap, scratching absently behind his ears. The sky was clear, and the stars, insofar as any city with profuse light pollution had stars, were bright and high.

She could pretend, if she wanted, that the entire past week hadn't happened. She couldn't as easily pretend that the last few months hadn't happened, and that hurt more. But . . . maybe she was selfish. Seeing Maria, meeting her, had left her with the sense that she was not entirely alone; that she was not even the only person to suffer the loss she'd suffered.

It helped. She scratched Petal's head, fed him, and looked at the moon for a bit. It was good to be here. It was good, as well, to be home. To be with friends. She rose, picked up Petal's leash, and began to head there.

But as she started toward the path, she stopped, because someone stood in the moonlight. There wasn't a lot of other light here, but it didn't matter. Emma didn't need a flashlight to know who it was.

She walked, slowly, toward him, and when she was a couple of feet away, she stopped.

She hadn't expected to see him. Not here, and not for years. Certainly not in the graveyard where she had come for the silence and privacy that he had given her while they were together.

She wanted to hug him. She was afraid to blink. But his lips turned up in that familiar little half-smile as he waited, as if he knew she couldn't decide what to do. She wanted to say so much, ask so much. But in the end, because he was dead and she knew it, she held out her hand. He took it, and cold blossomed in her palm, spreading up her arm.

She wondered what he felt, if he felt her hand at all.

"Hello, Nathan," she said quietly.

"Hello, Em."

# ABOUT THE AUTHOR

Michelle Sagara lives in Toronto with her husband and her two sons, where she writes a lot, reads far less than she would like, and wonders how it is that everything can pile up around her when she's not paying attention. Raising her older son taught her a lot about ASD, the school system, and the way kids are not as unkind as we, as parents, are always terrified they will be

Having a teenage son—two, in fact—gives her hope for the future and has taught her not to shout, "Get off my lawn" in moments of frustration. She also gets a lot more sleep than she did when they were younger.